Praise for Codename Xenophon:

'Leo Kanaris takes us to post-crash Athens as austerity bites and political corruption spirals... *Codename Xenophon* is compelling and evocative (the sparkling sea and sun)... Kanaris has written a little gem, perfect for the beach.'   Scarlet MccGuire in *Tribune*

'Blessed with all the virtues of a traditional murder mystery, this debut novel has a sharp political edge. Three years in Athens left Leo Kanaris with a loathing for the self-serving parasites and bureaucrats who "had paralysed the country for decades". In *Codename Xenophon*, this insider's view of a paralytic society is seen through the eyes of George Zafiris, a private investigator who does his best to tread the straight and narrow, while those around him are too greedy or plain scared to take responsibility. It is the apparently motiveless killing of an elderly academic that embroils Zafiris in political machinations at the highest level. But, as his dogged perseverance begins to pay off, he comes to realise that even the best intentions can have tragic consequences. With vivid characterisation and a plot that thickens without obscuring the essential threads, Kanaris emerges as a sharp new talent in crime writing.'

Barry Turner in *The Daily Mail*

'The narrative flits from a frenzied Athens to the idyllic islands as politicians, Russian crooks, corrupt (and/or incompetent) policemen thicken the plot, the world-weary Zafiris nimbly negotiating a Byzantine culture in which morality, truth and justice are malleable concepts. The first in a proposed quartet to feature George Zafiris, *Codename Xenophon* is a bleak but blackly comic tale that does full justice to its laconic, Chandleresque heritage.'

Declan Burke in *The Irish Times*

'Anyone picking up this book needs to be cautioned at the outset: it will eat considerably into your time for other things and be extraordinarily difficult to lay aside. In *Codename Xenophon* Leo Kanaris has woven a tight and quirky tale of murder, high-level intrigue and corruption in the timely setting of modern Athens and its island satellite, Aigina.'

John Carr in *The Anglo-Hellenic Review*

'This debut novel is interesting, educational, thoughtful and well worth the time to read. I look forward to more investigations with George Zafiris.' *The Poisoned Pen Review*

'Set in Athens in 2010, Kanaris's impressive debut, the first in a projected quartet, effectively evokes Greece's noble antiquity while portraying its current financial crisis, which his hero, PI George Zafiris, attributes to former prime minister Papandreou, who created the "most bloated, obstructive bureaucracy on the planet." Zafiris, scraping by from case to case, aching from the infidelity of a wife he still loves, and at every step hamstrung by corrupt and arrogant police, investigates the shooting of a Greek scholar and confronts a Gordian knot of governmental corruption, adulterous relationships, and vicious criminals. Struggling to preserve his self-respect, Zafiris prevails – almost. Disgusted by those whose respect for Greece's past leads them to avoid present-day responsibilities, Zafiris worries constantly over his country and its future, but he survives through fitful glimpses of the spirit that gave birth to Western civilization, still strong after 2,500 years.'

Starred review in *Publishers Weekly*

Leo Kanaris

Blood & Gold

Dedalus

ARTS COUNCIL ENGLAND
Supported using public funding by

Published in the UK by Dedalus Limited,
24-26, St Judith's Lane, Sawtry, Cambs, PE28 5XE
email: info@dedalusbooks.com
www.dedalusbooks.com

ISBN printed book 978 1 910213 10 0
ISBN ebook 978 1 910213 57 5

Dedalus is distributed in the USA by SCB Distributors
15608 South New Century Drive, Gardena, CA 90248
email: info@scbdistributors.com   web: www.scbdistributors.com

Dedalus is distributed in Australia by Peribo Pty Ltd
58, Beaumont Road, Mount Kuring-gai, N.S.W. 2080
email: info@peribo.com.au

First published by Dedalus in 2017
Bood & Gold copyright © Leo Kanaris 2017

The right of Leo Kanaris to be identified as the author of this work has been asserted by him in accordance with the Copyright, Designs and Patents Act, 1988.

Printed in Finland by Bookwell
Typeset by Marie Lane

This book is sold subject to the condition that it shall not, by way of trade or otherwise, be lent, resold, hired out or otherwise circulated without the publisher's prior consent in any form of binding or cover other than that in which it is published and without a similar condition including this condition being imposed on the subsequent purchaser.

A C.I.P. listing for this book is available on request.

The Author

Leo Kanaris was a teacher for many years. He now writes full time and lives in southern Greece.

He is the author of two novels featuring the private investigator George Zafiris: *Codename Xenophon* and *Blood & Gold*.

He is currently working on his third George Zafiris novel: *Dangerous Days*.

Characters (in order of appearance)

George Zafiris – private investigator

Colonel Sotiriou – Head of the Violent Crimes Department, Athens Police

Dimitris – proprietor of the Café Agamemnon

Nikolaos Karás – rugby-playing police officer

Mario Filiotis – Mayor of Astypalea

Eleni Filiotis – wife of Mario Filiotis

Andreas Filiotis – brother of Mario

Mrs Kyriakou – secretary to the Mayor of Astypalea

Zoe Zafiris – wife of George Zafiris

Pavlos Marangós – car dealer, Athens

Dr Skouras – Consultant in General Medicine, Red Cross Hospital, Athens

Haris Pezas – owner of an electrical shop, would-be assistant of George Zafiris

Petros Karagounis – businessman, schoolfriend of George Zafiris and Mario Filiotis

Keti Kenteri – violinist

Anna Kenteri – sister of Keti Kenteri

Paris Aliveris – composer, husband of Keti Kenteri

Emmanuel Karyotakis – funeral director

Gavrilis – hotel owner in Edessa

Thanasis and Rena – taverna owners in Pella

Dr Mylona – Inspector of Classical Archaeology, Thessaloniki

Byron Kakridis – Minister of Justice

'O Kokoras' ('the Cockerel') – construction boss and Edessa strong man

Stephanos – school-teacher from Preveza

Father Seraphim – monk on Mount Athos

Nick Zafiris – son of George and Zoe Zafiris

'Stelios' – photographer

Vladimir Merkulov – Russian businessman

Margaritis – butcher in Markopoulo, friend of Haris Pezas

Andreas Marangós – pornographic film director

Part One

The Man on a Bicycle

1 Meeting in Maroussi

Athens, September 2015. George Zafiris, private investigator, was seated at a café in Maroussi, reading a police report. A cup of Greek coffee stood untouched on the table in front of him. The day was cool for the time of year and a breeze ruffled the paper in his hands.

'On Friday 29 August a bearded man, 50 years of age, wearing a grey suit, was riding a bicycle along Spyros Louis Avenue, between the Olympic Stadium and the Golden Hall. A truck loaded with firewood was travelling behind. For unknown reasons the man on the bicycle lost his balance and was hit by the truck. An emergency call was received by police at 11.03 am. Service vehicles arrived at 11.15 am. The driver of blue Magirus Deutz HK 4596, Gavrilis Pagakis, aged 37 from Larissa, was arrested and charged with manslaughter. The victim died from his injuries. He has been identified as Mr Mario Filiotis, Mayor of Astypalea.'

George read the report a second time, folded it, laid it on the table.

Opposite him sat Colonel Sotiriou, Head of the Violent Crimes Unit, watching him closely.

'Well?' said Sotiriou.

'It's written by a moron,' he said.

'I agree it's not a model of report writing,' said Sotiriou. 'But you can't be sure the person who wrote it is a moron.'

'OK,' said George. 'Maybe he's just badly trained. Maybe he's on drugs. Maybe his head is being scrambled by death-rays from outer space. That's not the point.'

'What is the point?'

'Why did Mario Filiotis fall off his bicycle? He wasn't a man to do that.'

'Good question.'

'You must know who wrote this.'

Sotiriou gazed back at him blankly.

'I take that to mean yes?'

Sotiriou did not answer directly. 'He's no fool,' he said.

'What makes you say that?'

'He passed the report to me personally.'

'And what were you supposed to do with it? Apart from the obvious.'

Sotiriou did not reply.

'This was a road accident,' said George, 'not a violent crime.'

'Exactly.'

Sotiriou eyed him attentively.

'OK,' said George. 'So he knows more.'

'That is what I assume.'

'Have you asked him?'

'No.'

'Why not?'

The Colonel ignored the question. 'Give me the report,' he said.

George pushed the sheet of paper across the table. The Colonel held a cigarette lighter to one corner. The report flared and shrivelled in the ashtray.

'What's the officer's name?' asked George.
'Karás,' said the Colonel. 'Lieutenant Nikolaos Karás.'
'Can I talk to him?'
'Only in private.'
'How am I going to do that?'
'He plays rugby.'
'Rugby?'
'That's right.'
George was puzzled.
'It's a kind of football,' said Sotiriou. 'Played with an olive-shaped ball.'
'I know that, for heaven's sake!'
'His team is the Attica Warriors. They train on Tuesday evenings. Olympic complex, B ground. Go there tomorrow, half past eight. Watch the last ten minutes of training. He'll find you.'
'Suppose I'm busy tomorrow?'
'If you want the job, be there.'
'And who's my client?' asked George.
'For the moment I am.'
'You?'
'In strict confidence.'
'Are you paying?'
'Funds will be provided.'
'Public or private?'
'Let me worry about that.'
Sotiriou stood up. They shook hands without warmth and the Colonel slipped away.

George stayed to finish his coffee. He replayed the conversation in his mind, seeing the Colonel's face, his grey-green eyes, the skull-bones thinly covered by tight yellow skin. He was an odd man. Cold, scholarly, hard to fathom. He had insisted on meeting in Maroussi, miles from his office. George had asked yesterday for the police report on Mario's death, expecting to be refused. Sotriou had offered it at once.

He paid the bill and walked down Thiseos Street, past a beggar child mangling out *La Cucuracha* on an accordion, past empty shops with peeling yellow 'To Let' notices, past another beggar – an old man in a worn-out suit kneeling on a folded newspaper – until he came to a bakery on the square. Hot bread smells wafted through the doorway.

He asked for *horiátiko psomí* and handed over two euros. Fifty cents came back with a rustic loaf, still warm in a paper bag. He held it to him like a baby. Outside on the pavement, he dropped the fifty-cent coin into the old man's palm and was thanked politely in return. This was no professional beggar. The voice was educated. He looked like a retired schoolmaster or bank clerk. What torments had this man been through? George did not feel like asking. There were too many cases like that in this endless, tedious crisis.

His friend Mario was dead. He had no space in his heart for anyone else right now.

George walked back up Thiseos Street to his motorbike, unlocked the luggage box and rested the loaf among a jumble of receipts and business cards. He owed the bike to Mario, who had told him to stop driving a car in the city.

'And how the hell am I supposed to get around?' George had asked.

'Ride a bike.'

'A bike in Athens? Think I want to kill myself?'

Mario replied: 'Just living here a bit of you dies every day.'

He swung the Ducati off its stand, kicked the starter, felt the rush of force as he revved the engine. He accelerated quickly into the stream of cars.

On Kifissias Avenue, riding south, he kept thinking of his friend. Above the traffic, the glass towers, the dark haze of exhaust fumes, he glanced up at the blue sky, in which a few monumental nimbus clouds hung suspended. Out there in space he could imagine Mario's soul floating – planing like an eagle, surveying the struggle he had been released from. Athens would seem like a toy village to him, its crazy intrigues as inconsequential as the scurryings of an ant-hill.

He hoped that something survived of that remarkable man. An essence, an indestructible core of energy. It seemed unlikely. Yet also necessary. Otherwise what was the point of anything?

The Olympic Stadium loomed up on his right, its white steel arches like the bones of a bird's wing flung across the sky. On an impulse, he swung off Kifissias onto Spyros Louis. Maybe worth a look, he thought. The scene of the accident.

This road was busy too, a fast-moving horde of cars, trucks and buses. The stadium lay to his right, behind fences, its vast aerial structure a souvenir of the age of extravagance. Where had that all gone? The ambition, the optimism, the belief? All that remained was an enormous bill, the interest payments multiplying, compounding unstoppably, choking the life out of Greece.

He found a place to pull over, where the road widened for a bus stop. He cut the engine and lifted off his helmet, narrowing his eyes at the glare. Around him, a landscape of concrete. Everything on the road moving at seventy to eighty kilometres an hour. A strange place to go cycling. Practically an invitation to some fool talking into his phone to knock you down. But then the whole city was hostile to cyclists. Hostile to pedestrians, dogs, birds, every living thing. George climbed off the bike and picked his way along a narrow strip of pavement. Crushed Coca Cola cans and empty Marlboro packets littered the ground, their colours washed pale by the sun. Weeds thrust pugnacious heads through broken paving stones. The traffic rushed by.

He glanced up, wondering about street cameras. There had to be one along here. All the football matches in the stadium, the wild supporters, the paint-sprayers and seat-burners. That was surely worth a little surveillance? But the lampposts were bare.

Except one, right there opposite the entrance to the stadium. A trio of loose wires dangling off the post like seaweed, just out of reach of his upstretched arm.

He grabbed a quick photo of it on his phone, then straddled his bike and turned for home.

2 Funeral by the Sea

George lived in a 1970s apartment block in Aristotle Street, one of thousands in the centre of Athens. Faced with marble but poorly maintained, it turned a blank and dirty face to the world. Things improved once you got past the grubby entrance hall and up the echoing stairway. An armoured front door, installed a few years ago to discourage unwelcome visitors, led to a five-room apartment, comfortably arranged, with George's books, pictures, music, collections of seashells and old weapons. Sometimes his son Nick was at home, back from his engineering studies abroad. Sometimes too his wife Zoe – when she was not on Andros, leading the artistic life. At the end of summer she would be in Athens more. Andros was cold and damp in winter.

He unlocked the front door, dropped the loaf on the kitchen table and opened the fridge, looking for a beer. There was a bottle of Fix in the door, but his eye went at once to something else: a package on a shelf. The wrapper was from Lourantos, the cheese and salami shop on Andros.

He closed the fridge without taking the beer and went quietly through to the bedroom. Zoe was asleep there, face down, wrapped in a sheet. A bottle of pills stood open on the bedside table.

He inspected the label. 'Fermoxan'. He wondered what that might be.

Back in the kitchen, he opened his laptop.

Fermoxan: used in anxiety disorder, depression, panic disorder, obsessive compulsive disorder and post-traumatic stress disorder. Common side effects: nausea, sexual dysfunction, agitation, blurred vision, constipation, diarrhoea, dizziness, drowsiness, dry mouth, headaches, insomnia, loss of appetite, strange dreams, sweating, tremors, vomiting, weakness, weight gain...

He read this with alarm. Not so much for the grim catalogue of negatives as for what it implied. This was heavy medicine. Prescription only.

George opened the fridge again. This time he took out the bottle of Fix. He levered off the top and sipped the beer, watching the sky, thinking.

Three days ago, he had been in Astypalea. Sprawled in bed in a room he had taken for the night, above the 'Australia' taverna, fretting and turning, unable to sleep. He remembered fumbling for his watch in the half-light, struggling to make out the figures. Twenty past five. It was too early to get up – he had slept at two – but his mind was alert and already at work.

He stood up, moved unsteadily into the bathroom and let rip into the gloom. His mouth was dry, head like a blast furnace.

He pulled the chain; pipes gurgled and clanked all around him. He crossed the room to the open window and stared out at the sky. The town lay below, curved and stepped like the tiers of an ancient theatre. The air was cool and damp. A pair of dogs barked, exchanging warlike salutes across the darkness.

As he watched, still half asleep, the air began to brighten. The sun's first rays struck the fort on the ridge across the bay.

They flared on a flagpole, a line of roofs, the whitewashed cupola of a church. Down in the harbour, still in shadow, a row of fishing caïques lay unmoving at the quay.

He pulled on some clothes and splashed water on his face.

In the kitchen, Olga, the owner of the taverna, was salting an enormous piece of lamb. She paused, wiping her hands on aproned flanks.

'Good morning, Mr Zafiris! Coffee?'

'Please.'

He watched her stir the little copper pot, the gas flames dancing blue and gold.

'Did you know Mario?' he asked.

'We all knew him.'

'What was your opinion of him?'

'A very good man.'

'And as Mayor?'

'He did great things.'

'For example?'

'The airport. New roads. Restoring old buildings. A man of action. Not the usual politician, who is all talk.'

She began scattering potatoes in the roasting tin: each one seemed a token of Mario's achievements. 'Education. Respect for nature. Respect for ourselves. For each other. For the community. We stopped burning rubbish. We cleaned up the beaches, the countryside. We smartened up the town.'

'He built an airport and roads,' said George, 'but respected nature. How did he manage that?'

'What's your problem?'

'It's usually one or the other,' said George.

'Mario held public meetings. Told us that grants from Europe were linked with measures to protect nature. He said,

"You can't have one without the other. You must do it right." Proper accounts, receipts, everything. Have you heard of such a thing? In Greece?'

'Never,' said George.

'When a man like that goes, you ask yourself why didn't God protect him? He always takes the good ones for himself, and leaves us the criminals, the destroyers, the idiots.'

'Who'll take his place?'

'The deputy.'

'What's he like?'

'Nothing special. An opportunist. A follower, not a leader.'

'Will you come to the funeral?'

'Of course!'

She opened the oven door, letting out a blast of hot air, and shoved the tray of lamb and potatoes in.

'Everyone will be there. A man like that comes once in a generation, if you're lucky.'

The coffee bubbled up inside the pot. She poured it into a little white china cup and said, 'Go out and sit on the terrace. It's a lovely day. I'll bring it to you.'

*

At ten o'clock a fishing boat rounded the headland, its mast a white cross against the sea's blue. George waited on the quay. Around him were figures from the taverna last night: police chief, deputy mayor, director of the archaeological museum... None of Mario's school-friends had made it from Athens. One or two had sent apologies. The rest not even that.

The locals were out in force. Old people mostly – bent, wiry, their rough faces hacked out of the same rust-brown rock as the island's farms and roads. The young looked like a different species, fat and pale, crammed into tight black dresses and suits.

Eleni, Mario's widow, stood out, tall and haggard, with her two teenage sons. Their faces were blank as stone. Next to Eleni, a stocky man in his forties, with an angry, restless air: this was Andreas, Mario's brother. George walked over and offered his condolences. Eleni thanked him, her green eyes glittering, electric, and said softly, 'He rests with God.'

The fishing boat touched the quayside. On the foredeck lay the coffin, heaped with white lilies. Six men in dark suits and sunglasses moved forward from the crowd. They climbed on board, hoisted the coffin to their shoulders and stepped awkwardly onto the quay. As they set off towards the town, the crowd formed up behind them.

George walked beside Andreas. It was a tough climb to the church, a steep slope of ribbed concrete, the sun hot on their backs. They trudged heavily, saying nothing. Townsfolk watched from open windows and doorways, crossing themselves as the procession passed.

At last the street curved into the shade and George felt able to think again.

'This is a crime,' said Andreas suddenly.

'What do you mean?'

'They killed him.'

'Who?'

'Everyone. Everything.'

'That's not a crime.'

'To me it's a crime. People abused his generosity.'

'You can't prosecute a whole community.'

'I told him: half the petitioners who come to see you are just trying to cheat their neighbours. The only injustice is what they're planning – with your help. He gave them all a hearing.

Every damned one! Even known liars and tricksters. Why? Why, God damn it?! At the cost of his health? His family?'

'Everyone says he was a good man.'

'I'm sick of hearing that.'

The street cut back into the sun.

'What are you saying?'

'They killed him! These people, his friends and neighbours, all these hypocrites, crossing themselves, looking so holy and miserable!'

The procession faltered as if his accusation had been blasted out on loudspeakers. One of the pall-bearers, an old man, was in difficulties. His strength seemed to drain from him, his feet became tangled. The man behind lost his rhythm under the lurching weight. The syncopation spread. Before they could stop it the coffin was slipping backwards. They could not hold it. It slithered from their shoulders and hit the ground with a loud crash of splintering wood.

'Pah!' snorted Andreas. 'They can't even get this right!'

The pall-bearers stopped, wiped sweat off their faces, glad of the rest.

'You can't blame the public,' said George. 'He should have protected himself.'

'One hundred per cent! They're evil, grasping, cheating bastards. Every damned one!'

'We've all lost a friend,' said George, 'and you've lost a brother. But let's try to be rational. You can't blame these people for something that happened on a bicycle in Athens.'

Andreas gave him a look of pity and disgust. 'You'll see how they did it,' he said. 'Mark my words.'

A murmur began in the crowd, a current of puzzlement. The priest looked about him, his eyes flickering fearfully above the long grey beard. The chief of police stepped forward. Two men started shouting at each other.

Andreas pushed through to the front. 'What's going on?'

George followed. Between the mourners he saw the coffin, one corner smashed open, its blue silk interior visible. People looked away as if in shame, but George's eye was caught by something else, something unexpected. The edge of a clear polythene bag, hanging out of the coffin. He could not see what it contained, but whatever it was it didn't look right. The chief of police told everyone to stand back. He knelt beside the coffin, picked out the bag, unsealed it, and extracted a square, slender box. He raised the lid and found a layer of tissue paper, which he lifted delicately aside. A wreath of tiny golden leaves sparkled in the sun.

*

While the front line of the crowd marvelled, others pushed forward to get a glimpse. The police chief quickly took charge. 'The funeral is cancelled,' he announced. 'Go home. This is now an incident! A matter for the police!'

He organised a cordon around the damaged coffin and repeated the order to go home.

No one budged.

He surveyed the crowd with disgust. 'Shame on you,' he said.

'We want to know what's happened,' said a man.

'You can see what's happened!'

The crowd remained and the police chief with a scornful expression pulled a mobile telephone from his pocket.

'Bring a truck,' he barked. 'Up the main street. Outside the bank. The mayor's funeral has gone *tis poutanas.*'

Andreas shook his head and muttered, 'Listen to him, the

animal! All he knows is *poutanes*.'

The police chief turned to the crowd again. 'I told you to leave,' he shouted. 'Move back! Away from the coffin!'

Soon the rumble of a powerful engine could be heard. The police truck appeared at the bottom of the hill and with much shouting and hooting it ground its way forward through the reluctantly parting crowd.

Two young officers jumped out, dropped the tailgate, and with the help of the pall-bearers loaded the coffin onto the back.

'Where to?' asked the driver as he opened his door. 'The cemetery?'

'Are you mad? Think, man! This is potentially a crime. It needs investigation, a report!'

'Very good, sir. So... where then?'

'The station!'

'Will you come in the truck?'

'No. I need to stay here, speak to the priest, organise this mess. I want you to unload at the station, put the coffin in a cell and lock it. No one goes near it and you answer no questions! I'll be there soon.'

An hour later they were crowded into the police station, family and friends, discussing what to do. Five chairs, ten people, cigarettes burning. Voices talking over each other, competing to make the same few obvious points. The coffin was resting on the bed in one of the cells next door.

'This will have to be officially investigated,' said the chief of police. 'It's a major incident.'

'All I want to know,' said Andreas, 'is where is Mario? Because he sure as hell isn't in any of those plastic bags!'

It was a question no one could answer. They telephoned

the funeral directors in Athens, who said the paperwork was in order. Andreas shouted, 'This is not about paperwork, you morons. It's about a man! My brother!'

He slammed down the phone.

They rang the hospital where Mario had been taken, but the receptionist could not get an answer from the mortuary. There was a strike, she said, try again tomorrow.

'A strike in the mortuary,' said Andreas. 'There you have our country in a nutshell. Death wrapped in death. Public services that serve no one but the public servants themselves!'

'Let's not exaggerate,' said the police chief. 'There are plenty of honest public servants in this country.'

'They should be exhibited in a museum,' said Andreas.

The police chief asked the director of the archaeological service to examine the items in the coffin. She opened half a dozen packages and peered at them with a magnifying glass. She pronounced them to be a mixture of Hellenistic and Roman finds, of excellent workmanship and unusually well preserved. Probably from a tomb, a royal or aristocratic burial. She held one of them up, a necklace of tiny golden bees. For a few moments all were spellbound by their delicate beauty.

The police chief asked her what such objects might be doing in a coffin on Astypalea.

She replaced the necklace carefully in its box.

'Illegal export,' she said. 'That's the most likely explanation. There's never a shortage of buyers, especially abroad. If that's the case, and they have been taken illegally from a dig or a museum vault, burial on a quiet island would be a convenient half-way stage on their journey, allowing them to disappear for a while, until the trail goes cold.'

'But where is Mario?' said Andreas. 'What the hell is the connection between all this gold and my dead brother? He wasn't a smuggler! He wasn't an archaeologist! Where is he?'

'I can't help you with that. All I can do is try to find out where these treasures have come from.'

'Go ahead,' said Andreas. 'It's no bloody use to me.'

Mario's wife asked him to calm down. He snapped back angrily: 'Am I the only one with any feelings?'

'No,' she said. 'You're the only one shouting.'

'Why don't you shout too? He's your husband!'

She stood up abruptly.

'I'm taking the children home. They're upset enough already. You're making things worse, as you always do.'

They left the room with the same stony faces they had shown to the world all morning.

Andreas continued to fulminate. He said he would personally cut off the testicles of whoever was responsible for this crime and throw them bleeding to the sharks.

George looked at his watch. 'I'm really sorry,' he said, 'but I need to get the airport.'

'I'll take you,' said Andreas. 'We're wasting our time here.'

*

George watched the aeroplane float down out of a burning azure sky. It bounced once, settled on its wheels and rolled in, buzzing like a chainsaw. A door opened in its side and steps zigzagged to the ground. A dozen passengers emerged, groping into the fiery light. The two pilots followed, in dazzling white shirts and dark glasses. They stood on the tarmac, taking in the emptiness, the silence.

An announcement crackled out of the loudspeakers. George walked slowly to the aircraft with the other passengers. They bent themselves into the seats in the stuffy interior, the air smelling of hot plastic and upholstery. George felt tired and depressed. He hated leaving the islands – any island, even one he had visited for a funeral. He accepted a boiled sweet from the dark-eyed young stewardess and gazed out at a tumble of rocks beside the runway.

With a roar the plane moved off, accelerating bumpily along the tarmac, lifting quickly into the air. George saw the butterfly-shape of Astypalea laid out below, one of those strange echoes in nature, like clouds that resemble the outlines of countries or lakes that magically form the head of a wolf… Ahead stood Amorgos, a wind-sharpened blade of rock, rising sheer and pale from the water. Beyond it, a hundred miles of sea. Then Athens, the tormented, the addictive, the intolerable… He waved away the offer of a drink and closed his eyes, exhausted.

A change in the engine's note brought him back to consciousness. Sleepily he checked his watch. Thirty-five minutes gone, and they were starting their descent. They sloped down through a ferocious heat haze towards the city, the earth scarcely visible through its mustardy blur of dust and boiling exhaust fumes. Why, he wondered, do I live down there, in all that filth?

3 Conversation with a Fly-Half

Back at home that evening, searching on the internet, George quickly found a rugby club, but it was in Athens, Georgia. In fact he found a complete parallel city to his own, a utopian Athens of functioning public institutions and friendly policemen, with an all-new marble Parthenon gleaming like freshly moulded plastic. He lingered for a few minutes on this improbable place, this mockery of the 'real' Athens rooted in the red soil of Attica, where a pact was made with the Furies to cancel the ancient debt of blood and revenge, building instead a state founded on law, tolerance and mutual respect. That was a pious myth if ever there was one... Smarting at the painful turn of his thoughts, he clicked off the Georgian Athens and returned to his own. He searched on through the results till he found the Athens Warriors Rugby Football Club.

It was one page only. A team photograph showed two rows of muscular young men, wild-haired and grinning. There were no names to the players. Any one of them could have been Police Lieutenant Nikolaos Karás. The team trained on Tuesday and Thursday evenings. Anyone interested could telephone the Secretary.

At the Olympic complex the next evening, in a landscape of empty swimming pools and unused sports fields, he watched a tangle of bodies writhing on the grass. The ball, lost in the knot of limbs, suddenly escaped. A lone figure scooped it up and sprinted furiously for freedom. An opponent raced to intercept him, his arms reaching greedily out. He dodged to the right and ran on. Another appeared, flung himself at his legs, cutting him down. As he fell he flicked the ball to his right. One of his team grabbed it, ran on, passed again, took the return pass and dived over the line. The trainer's whistle shrilled and a shout of triumph went up from his team.

'Bravo ré pousti!'

George was in a cloud of nostalgia. Winter afternoons in London. Mist dripping through bare trees. Wet mud in his clothes and hair. His spirits riding strangely high. Happiness sharpened on a whetstone of cold and discomfort. He tried to explain it to his friends back in Athens, kids who played basketball on balmy evenings and went water-skiing. They couldn't see the point and ignorantly laughed.

The final whistle blew and the players strolled off the field. George waited a while, watching them pull on tracksuits and untie their boots. One of them stood up briskly, waved to the others and jogged across to him.

'Mr Zafiris?'

'That's right. Nikos Karás?'

'The same.' They shook hands.

'Do you have a car?'

'Motor bike,' said George.

'OK, I'll take mine. You can follow me.'

They threaded through the streets south of the stadium to a bar under a quartet of plane trees. They ordered two Fix beers.

'I need to eat something,' said Karás. 'Bring a big plate of *mezé.*'

'It's a high energy game,' said George.
'Seen it before?'
'I used to play.'
'Oh yes? Which team?'
'London University.'

Karás nodded. 'That's the place to learn. The game's too crude here. We like the aggression, but we're not so good on the teamwork.'

'I saw a nice try.'

'That was Thanasis. I gave him the return pass.'

'That's teamwork.'

'I know. And practice. We rehearsed that exact move this evening. But under match conditions we revert to type and it's every man for himself.'

The beer and *mezé* arrived. They filled their glasses and wished each other good health. Karás pushed the plate of food towards George. 'Help yourself.'

George said, 'You eat. I'll just drink for now.'

Karás speared a piece of stewed octopus.

'You've read my report?'

George nodded.

'What did you think?'

'It left a lot of questions unanswered.'

'Of course.'

'You knew it as you wrote it?'

'I did.'

'So why did you file it?'

'I had no choice.'

'Someone put pressure on you.'

'Pressure yes. But it wasn't "someone". More like the whole police command.'

'Why did they do that?'

'I have no idea, but I didn't like it.'
'So you went to Sotiriou.'
'As you see…'
'Why him?'
'He's a relative.'
'A close relative?'
'My mother's first cousin. I've known him since I was a boy. He inspired me to go into the police.'
'I see,' said George.
He wondered whether to say the victim was a friend.
'I'd like to get the story clear,' he said. 'Were you at the scene of the accident?'
'I was.'
'The first one there?'
'I believe so.'
'And what did you see?'
'A long skid. The truck diagonally across the road at the end of it, the bicycle bent and crushed about five metres away, the victim lying on the ground as if he was asleep.'
'What about the truck driver?'
'In his cab. Shaking.'
'Did you talk to him?'
'First I checked the victim.' Karás grimaced. *'Kaput.'*
'Are you sure?'
'No pulse.'
'Was there a medical team?'
'They came in a couple of minutes. They tried to revive him, but nothing.'
'Tell me about the truck driver.'
'I asked him to step out, gave him the usual warnings and assurances. He was like a zombie.'
'What do you mean?'

'Dazed. Frightened.'

'Why frightened?'

'Wouldn't you be?'

'What did he say about the accident?'

Karás hesitated.

'I need to ask you something before I answer that.'

'Go ahead.'

'How do you know Colonel Sotiriou?'

'I've dealt with him over many years.'

'You have a good relationship?'

'Good enough. We've had our differences, but there's respect between us.'

'Why did he approach you?'

'I'm not sure. He knows me. Trusts me, maybe. I'm independent of the police…'

'With respect, Mr Zafiris, there must be several private detectives that he could have gone to.'

'Most of them ex-policemen.'

'Not you?'

'Not me.'

'That could be it.'

'There may be other reasons. Trust is unconscious. An instinct.'

Karás seemed preoccupied by a difficult thought.

'I thought I could trust my colleagues until this happened,' he said.

George said nothing.

'OK,' said Karás at last. 'I'll tell you about the truck driver. Just before the accident he saw something odd. A car was travelling in front of the cyclist. A hand came out of the window on the passenger's side and threw something out. A handful of… what? He couldn't see, maybe tacks or ball bearings or broken glass. They flashed in the sun. They made the cyclist swerve suddenly and fall into the path of the truck.'

'When did he tell you this?'

'Right at the end.'

'He volunteered it?'

'Yes. I asked him if he remembered anything else. That's often the question that tells.'

'Why isn't it in the report?'

'It wasn't in the official statement.'

'Did you record it?'

'No. The machine was off by now.'

'You were still in the police station?'

Karás nodded.

'So why didn't you switch the machine on again and record it?'

'He asked me not to.'

'You could have insisted.'

'I know. Maybe I should have done.'

'Did you go back and check the road?'

'I planned to, but something else came up.'

'What do you mean?'

'My superior needed a job doing urgently.'

'He knew you were going back to check the road?'

'Yes.'

'And he stopped you?'

'Not exactly. He said he would take care of it, and gave me that other job.'

'So he stopped you?'

'I suppose so.'

'Did *he* check the road?'

'Not personally. He sent another officer.'

'And?'

'Nothing suspicious was reported.'

'You told him about the car in front and the stuff thrown out of the window?'

'I did.'

'How did he react?'

'No reaction. Just said he would send someone.'

George fixed him with a grim look. 'You messed up every single step of the way.'

'I can see that now.'

'How about the bike?'

'It was a total wreck.'

'Maybe there was glass in the tyres? A nail or two?'

'I haven't looked.'

'For heaven's sake! That's the first thing to do!'

'You're right. I should have done it. I'll check it tomorrow.'

'So the driver made his statement, signed it, you asked if he wanted to add anything else, he gave you some crucial evidence and you ignored it?'

'No. I then asked him to change his statement and he refused.'

'Why?'

'He said he couldn't be sure.'

'Could he remember the number plate of the car in front? The colour? The make?'

'No. The moment I got interested he shut down.'

'Where is he now?'

'Released.'

'I thought he was arrested?'

'Only briefly. We let him go.'

'You have his address?'

'In Larissa.'

'We may need to talk to him.'

Karás looked embarrassed. He gulped some beer.
'You can talk to him. I won't be allowed to.'
'Why not?'
'I'm off the case.'
'Who's on it now?'
'No one. It's closed.'
'Closed? That's insane!'
'I know.'
'You objected, I hope?'
'Strongly. I was told to forget about it. There are times, said my boss, when keenness kills.'
'What the hell is that supposed to mean?'
'I don't know.'
'So what's his plan? Let the killer come forward and apologise of his own goodwill?'
'Maybe some kind of long game.'
George took a slow sip of beer.
'Are you willing to help?'
'I'll do what I can,' said Karás. 'But I won't be much use if I lose my job.'
'Understood. Give me a safe number to call you on.'
The lieutenant scribbled a number on a card. 'That's my mother's flat. She lives downstairs.'
'You visit her often?'
'Twice a day.'
'OK,' said George, handing over a card of his own. 'Let me know the driver's name and address. And find a way to examine the bicycle.'
'I will.'

4 The Answering Machine

Zoe was up when he got home, watching a film on TV. He asked her gently how she was.

'I don't want to talk,' she said.

'When you do, I'm here.'

'Someone called,' she said indifferently.

'Who?'

'I don't know. There's a message on the machine.'

He listened to the recording. It was Andreas, Mario's brother, his voice sullen and dark. 'Come back to the island, George. Soon. Go through Mario's papers. Get there before someone else does.' He left no number, just a few seconds of silence, then: 'That's all.'

George checked his diary. The next few days were free. Only Zoe was unwell. He couldn't leave her alone.

The telephone rang. He picked it up. A different male voice asked for George Zafiris.

'That's me.'

'My name is Haris Pezas. Hector's brother.'

George was too surprised to speak. He sounded exactly like Hector, his old colleague now lying in a cemetery near Corinth with five bullets in his chest.

'How are you, Mr Zafiris?' asked Haris brightly.

'I'm fine.'

'We met at Hector's funeral.'

'I remember. It's good to hear from you, Haris. How can I help?'

'I need some advice.'

'Of course. About what?'

'I prefer to speak face to face.'

'I'm in Athens. I can't leave the city at present.'

'No problem, I'll come into town. Tomorrow morning? Eleven o'clock?'

'Café Agamemnon, 45 Aristotle Street.'

'Which part of town is that?'

'In the centre. Between Kolonaki and Exarchia.'

He put down the telephone and wondered what this was about. He feared some kind of claim for compensation. Hector had died while working on a job with him, but he had gone against George's orders. The family knew that and they did not seem the types to go chasing opportunities in that way, but people were getting desperate for cash these days. There was no telling what extreme need might push them to.

He sat down next to Zoe on the sofa. She was watching a chat show, celebrities talking about celebrities. It made no sense to him. Not much to her either, judging by her blank face.

He offered her a beer.

'No,' she said. 'It doesn't go with the pills.'

He put his arm around her shoulder. 'Does that go with the pills?'

'That's OK,' she said, smiling a little sadly.

*

Haris Pezas was a slightly shorter version of Hector, with the same muscular build, eagle's beak nose and sharp blue eyes. He wore a loud check shirt in pink and yellow. His brawny legs were stuffed into skin-tight blue trousers, ending in a pair of emerald-green suede shoes. Even Hector with his technicolor tastes would have struggled to wear those. They were clearly expensive, but they did not suit him. It was hard to imagine them suiting anyone.

'I want you to know right away I don't blame you for Hector's death,' said Haris.

'That's good of you,' said George.

'He was impulsive sometimes.'

'I just wish I'd been there to stop him physically,' said George. 'All I could do was shout down the phone.'

'It's such a waste...'

'You must miss him?'

'Horribly.'

'We all do,' said George.

Haris unpocketed a string of worry beads and swung them to and fro, staring across the street.

Dimitri brought coffee, took in Haris at a single doubtful glance, and returned to his newspaper in the corner.

'How's business?' asked Haris.

'Not bad.'

'Affected by the crisis?'

'Of course. The great days have gone.'

'Haven't they just!' He gave George a sympathetic look. 'If only we had a decent leader! A Venizelos, a Karamanlís. Even...' He peered suspiciously over his shoulder: 'Even a Metaxás!'

'That would be interesting. Our last military dictators didn't do too well.'

'We need someone with a big broom to clean out this pigsty of a state.'

George recognised Hector's right-wing style, which used to drive him crazy. He wondered when Haris would get to the point.

'Have you come to talk politics?' he asked.

'No way! I'm here for a good reason.'

'Tell me,' said George.

'I have an electrical shop in Corinth. It's done well over the years, but lately business has dropped badly. I blame the big retail chains, Media Markt, Kotsovolos… Huge warehouses filled with washing machines and fridges. No one buys from the small shops any more. Just plugs, fuses and lightbulbs. Rabbit droppings. There's no living in that.'

'I know it's like that in Athens.'

'In the provinces it's worse. People will drive for two hours to save thirty euros on a washing machine. The petrol wipes out the saving. In fact they lose money but they don't see it. And it's killing us. So I'm thinking about diversifying.'

'Into what?'

'That's where I want your help. I'm thinking about security and surveillance.'

'Surveillance equipment? You'll be up against MediaMarkt again. And suppliers on the internet. They'll undercut you every time.'

'No. Not surveillance *equipment*.' He stopped, looked George in the eye. 'Just plain surveillance.'

'You want advice?'

'If that's the best you can do.'

'What else can I do?'

'Maybe offer me work?'

'Now?' This was a surprise.

'Now or later.'

'Do you know anything about it?'

'I used to help Hector.'

'With what?'

'Photography. Watching buildings, watching people…'

'You didn't get bored?'

'Of course I did!'

'What did you do when you got bored?'

'I told myself how lucky I was to have work.'

'Fair enough. You can keep accounts?'

'Of course. Like a Swiss banker! But that's not what I'm thinking of.'

'What are you thinking of?'

'Proper work. Helping you. Like Hector did.'

'Hector was a professional.'

'He taught me a lot.'

'How come?'

'I was interested. We even thought of forming a partnership. Pezas Brothers, Private Investigators. Sounds good, doesn't it?'

'It takes more than sounding good.'

'I know!'

'What stopped you?'

'Someone had to look after the shop.'

'Do you have a wife?'

'I do. Twenty-two years married. Three kids.'

'What does she think of this idea?'

'She supports it – as long as I don't take any risks.'

'Then forget it.'

'I've said I'll be careful. And I will. But she doesn't want me carrying a gun.'

'She's got a point there. Do you know how to use one?'

'I do.'

'How come?'

'Military training.'

George waved this away. 'I did national service too. Learnt to drive a truck and clean toilets. The weapons training was not serious.'

'I was lucky,' said Haris. 'Had two years in a first class unit.'

'You must have volunteered.'

'Of course.'

'Where did you serve?'

'Navy. Special forces.'

'You don't seem the type,' said George.

'There isn't a type,' said Haris.

'I mean, you seem like a gentle sort. Comfortable.' He thought of the green suede shoes. 'A little artistic.'

'That's exactly what I am. But if you want to see my medals…'

'That won't be necessary. You may be more useful than I thought.'

'What have you got in mind?'

'Nothing… Are you a gadget freak like Hector?'

'Totally!'

'Well that's positive. Everything else you've said rings alarm bells in my head.'

'If they're electrical I'll fix them.'

George laughed. Haris had Hector's absurd over-confidence as well as his looks.

'I would help if I could,' said George. 'Anything for Hector. But money's tight, work's thin, I barely have enough for myself.'

'I can well believe it,' said Haris. 'Which is why I'm

prepared to work for nothing for three months.'

'Doing what?'

'I don't care! The boring stuff. Emptying waste bins. Cleaning telephones.'

'That's the interesting bit.'

'OK give me the really boring stuff then, whatever that is.'

'There really isn't anything now.'

Haris stood up, shook hands and said with a bright smile, 'Well, what the hell. It's kind of you to see me, and I hope you'll give me a call if you change your mind.'

'A pleasure, Haris.'

He watched the suede loafers go flashing verdantly down Aristotle Street. 'If I take him on,' he thought, 'those shoes will have to go.'

5 Information Underload

Nikos Karás called him that afternoon from his mother's house.

'The news is all bad.'
'What do you mean?'
'The bicycle has been disposed of. Also the truck driver's file.'
'Disposed of? In what way?'
'I don't know. Probably taken out to the rubbish tip at Keratea.'
'That's totally illegal.'
'I know.'
'Can you find out any more? Who gave the order? Who carried it out?'
'It's going to arouse suspicion.'
'Are you sure about Keratea?'
'That's where the city rubbish goes.'
'And the police rubbish? Is that just dumped in the street?'
'No. A contractor collects it for secure disposal.'
'What's the contractor's name?'
'I don't know.'
'Can you find that out? Now?'
'OK.'

George hung up. This was getting tricky. Avenues being

closed down. He remembered the phone message from Andreas Filiotis: 'Come back to the island, George. Soon. Go through Mario's papers. Get there before someone else does.'

He found Zoe reading in the bedroom.

'I need to go to Astypalea,' he said. 'But I don't want to leave you here alone.'

'I'll be OK,' she said, looking anything but.

'Why don't you come with me?'

'And do what?'

'Relax. Swim. We'll get a nice hotel.'

'What are you going to do?'

'I have to go through Mario's papers.'

'How long will that take?'

'A day or two.'

'Do I have to see his crazy wife?'

'Only if you want to.'

'I certainly don't!'

'No problem. Just stay out of sight.'

'What if she sees me?'

'Where?'

'On the island?'

'Tell her you didn't want to disturb her at this time of loss.'

She thought for a moment or two. 'You know what? I can't be bothered.'

'Please come, Zoe!'

'Don't force me.'

'I'm buying you a ticket.'

'You're wasting your money.'

'I'm doing what I have to do. Please pack an overnight bag.'

'Certainly not.'

She returned to her book.

*

Before leaving for the airport he found Dimitri in the Café Agamemnon and explained the situation.

'I'll keep an eye on her,' said Dimitri.

'Can you make sure she eats?'

'Don't worry. She'll be fat and healthy like a little partridge when you come back.'

'I wish,' said George.

At the airport he got a phone call from Karás, who had spoken to the refuse contractor. All police paperwork was immediately shredded. There was no chance of tracing a file once it left the station.

'OK,' said George, 'what about your notes from interviewing the driver? Do you still have them?'

'I do.'

'We can trace him through his number plate.'

'I guess so.'

'That's something at least… What about the bicycle? They can't shred that.'

'Disposed of. He would not say where.'

George thanked him, and asked him to find the truck driver's address.

His flight was called as Karás rang off.

Despite his frustrations, George enjoyed the flight to Astypalea, the ATR 400's propellers whirring through a haze of afternoon sun that lay wide and golden over the Aegean Sea. As they came in to land, the island's rocky hillsides were tinted with the rose light of early evening.

A taxi took him to a hotel on the edge of town.

At once he noticed the silence – deep and luxurious, with a distant occasional music of waves, birdsong or wind through the trees. Sitting on the hotel terrace, sipping wine, he felt the stillness of the island around him, time slowed to the gentlest pace, and his mind felt free. The city, with its dirt and smells, its ceaseless grinding roar, seemed a nightmare, a place of torture. How could anyone think clearly there? Or feel he belonged on earth?

*

The Filiotis house stood in its own walled garden on the edge of town, an imposing white 19th-century mansion with dark green shutters. Mario had inherited it from his parents, modernised it, brought up his family there. They also had a flat in Athens, which Mario used for his business trips. George had not been to the island house for ten years. He could not think why, only that meeting in Athens was easier.

He knocked at the front door. Eleni opened it, offering a pale cheek to his kiss. Her white-blonde hair was pulled tight around her head, her face severe, her eyes bleak and exhausted, with no hint of welcome.

She led him through the hall to the *saloni,* the official reception room, where family photographs, seldom-used furniture and heavy amber worry beads sat meticulously arranged like exhibits in a museum. The house was not as he remembered it from his last visit, when the children were young and toys and books were flung about in carefree disorder.

Eleni placed herself stiffly on the edge of a white sofa. He asked her how she was coping.

'I get by,' she said.

'How about the kids?'
'They left soon after the funeral.'
'Are you on your own?'
'I am.'
'It's not good to be alone too much.'
'I know. I see people.'
'I'm pleased to hear that… Tell me, do we know any more about that material in the coffin?'

'Yes. The director of the archaeological museum has been very efficient. She took photographs and sent copies by email to her colleagues around Greece. One of these, the Inspector of Antiquities in Thessaloniki, recognised them. They come from a site near Pella, an ancient goldsmith's workshop, excavated three years ago. They were not recorded as missing. The Inspector is coming to the island next week to meet the Chief of Police.'

'That's good work. Any news about Mario?'

She looked nonplussed. 'What kind of news can there be?'

'I meant about his body.'

'We've been talking to the funeral directors.'

'And?'

'They're not helpful. They seem to be scared of admitting their mistake. Especially to the authorities.'

'Their mistake has stopped those ancient treasures being exported,' said George.

'The police won't see it that way.'

'We don't know that.'

'The funeral directors could go out of business over this.'

'Deservedly!'

'Come on,' she said. 'It's a mix-up.'

'It's more than that,' said George.

He asked if there was anything he could do.

'Well... If *you* could find a way of talking to them, you might get a result.'

'Who?'

'The funeral people.'

George was surprised.

'Andreas has been trying to frighten them,' she explained. 'He's failed. They only retreat into secrecy. You at least can talk to them without threatening.'

'Don't be too sure,' he said.

'Why don't you try?'

George agreed, but remained sceptical.

They sat in silence for a while, she avoiding his eyes.

'Eleni, I need your help,' he said at last, as gently as he could.

'With what?'

'I'm curious to know if he died accidentally or not.'

'Does it matter now?'

'Of course it matters! I'm surprised you ask.'

'He's with God. We hope close to God. In a place of peace. But only his conscience and God's mercy will decide.'

'That is beyond dispute,' he said. 'But I have more practical things in mind.'

'Tell me.'

'With your permission I would like to look around his study, which might take a few hours. Second, I want to speak to someone totally trusted in the Town Hall, someone who understands the meaning of confidentiality. Third, and most important, I want to talk to you.'

'About...?'

'What he was doing, people he was seeing, where his life was going.'

'I'm not really happy about this.'

'Why?'
'I don't want to discuss it.'
'I see.'
George observed her. Although she sat still, a terrible restlessness seemed to agitate her soul.

'Can we just start,' he said gently, 'and see how we get on?'
'All right,' she said unhappily, 'but where?'
'How about his study?'
She stood up. 'This way.'
He followed her along a gloomy corridor smelling strongly of floor polish. At the far end she opened a door into a large book-lined study with a heavy mahogany desk at its centre. The desk was empty of papers.

'Surely he didn't leave it like this?' said George.
'I've cleared it up.'
'So quickly?' Mario had been dead less than a week.
'I felt I had to.'
'Where did everything go?'
'The Town Hall.'
'Why there?'
'Everything he did in here was work, which he brought home every evening and slaved over after dinner. The room was a horrible mess.'
'There must have been personal papers too.'
'He kept those separate.'
'Another study?'
'More of a cupboard.'
'May I see?'
'No.'
'There could be crucial evidence there.'
'You'll never find anything. It's chaos. And private.'
'Of course. If you'd rather not…'

'There's nothing there for you.'

'I can look very fast.'

'No.'

George tried to disguise his disappointment. 'OK,' he said. 'I'll respect your wishes.'

'Thank you.'

'So this is the only room to look at?'

'Yes.'

'May I?'

'Go ahead.'

He sat at the mahogany desk and began opening drawers. Every one of them was empty apart from a few pens and sheets of notepaper from a hotel in London. He glanced at the waste bin. That too was empty. Around the walls, the bookshelves were filled with rows and rows of legal volumes, all in heavy brown bindings with gold lettering.

'This is a waste of time,' he said.

She returned his gaze blankly.

'I need to see his private papers.'

'You can't.'

'Eleni, this is important! He could have been murdered.'

'The private papers won't help you.'

'You don't know that.'

'Don't ask again!'

'In that case I'm going to have to go to the Town Hall and see whatever you've removed from here.'

'OK,' she said.

'Can you give me a contact name there? Someone who can be trusted.'

She seemed surprised. 'Trusted? In the Town Hall?'

'You must know people.'

'All too well.'

'None of them are your friends?'

'Some call themselves friends,' she said. 'People who took advantage of him, and would not hesitate to betray him if it suited them. I have a different notion of friendship.'

'So do I. And I'm sure Mario did.'

'He found it impossible to distinguish between the true and the false. Anyone who smiled at him was trusted. That is not how a wise man behaves.'

'I'm sure he wasn't so naive.'

'He was very insecure.'

'I don't agree.'

'Then you didn't really know him.'

George found her accusing tone offensive.

'Perhaps he gave people the benefit of the doubt? Perhaps that's how he got results?'

'What results?' She spoke with disdain.

'You only need to look at the town. It's in great shape, in spite of the crisis.'

'Whatever he achieved was through his own hard work,' she said. 'Work at the cost of everything else that a man should value.'

'You mean the family?'

'You know what I mean!' She almost shrieked this at him.

George did not reply. He was trying to think of a way around this woman's resistance. She was ferocious in her resentment. In the absence of words he became aware of a fly buzzing at the window, banging against the glass in an effort to escape.

Eleni walked over, weariness in every step, and let it out. The silence returned. She stared vaguely out as if waiting for someone to appear along the road.

'I'm sorry to stir up such bitter memories,' said George.

She said nothing.

'We'll never know what happened to Mario unless people are prepared to talk about him.'

She flared up. 'What have we been doing since you arrived? You're trying to pump me for evidence! As if I killed him!'

'You've told me nothing,' said George coldly. 'All I can gather is that there was some strain or disagreement between you which was not resolved when he died.'

'You could say that of any marriage on earth.'

'Of some more than others.'

'So?'

'I'm not judging you,' he said.

'Of course you are! Judge and be damned! Have the courage to admit it!'

'How could I sit in judgement on you?' said George. 'If I died tomorrow, my wife would say exactly what you're saying about Mario. This isn't a status competition.'

'You could have fooled me.'

'Listen,' said George. 'You're taking this the wrong way. All I want is to find out why Mario died.'

'Have I asked you to do that?'

'No.'

'Has anyone?'

'Yes.'

'Who?'

This was a difficult one. He could not not mention Sotiriou and the police.

'Andreas asked me. And one or two of his friends.'

'Are they paying you?'

'Expenses only. I'm doing this out of friendship. Out of love for an exceptional man.'

'If you're doing this for love, you're wasting your time.'

'Sometimes one must act on principle, not for gain.'

'You can forget both in this case.'
'I thought I might be helping you too.'
'I've told you what I think.'
'Tell me again, Eleni.'

She groaned. 'His life was lost long before he died. His true killers are the environmentalists. Greenpeace, WWF, every idiotic group on the planet that filled his head with their impossible ideals, while our family died of neglect!'

'Your family seemed happy to me.'

'Then you're an idiot too. Look at me! Do I look like a happy woman?'

'If you did I would be worried,' said George.

'My unhappiness started long before he died!'

'You blame that on him?'

Her eyes blazed. 'Who else? I had one husband. One life. Which I gave to a man who had no idea what to do with it.'

'I'm sorry,' said George. 'I didn't know.'

'Well,' said Eleni, 'now you do.'

George now understood the lifeless feeling in the house. It suddenly seemed no accident that he had not visited for ten years. An impulse of pity for his old friend surged up in him. Was this what he came home to every evening? This accusing stare? This crippling fire of self-righteousness?

He felt desolate. 'There's nothing more I can do here,' he said.

She did not reply.

'I just wonder what you would have liked Mario to do,' he said.

'Really? You wonder that?'

'I do.'

'How about making some money? Wouldn't that be a start?'

'You look pretty comfortable,' said George.

'I'm not talking about comfort!'

'Then what? What more could you reasonably ask?'

She waved the question contemptuously away. 'You're as bad as he is.'

George stood up. 'Clearly there's something I'm not getting,' he said.

She said nothing.

'I can see myself out,' said George.

She turned and walked to the front door.

As he left her he said, 'I'm at the Aegean Hotel until five. If there's anything else you feel you can tell me, just leave a message there.'

She nodded and closed the door.

6 Town Hall

George walked into town, the hot September sun drilling into his back. This was turning into an utterly futile trip. He felt he must do something to redeem it.

He went over the possibilities. Eleni was hopeless. She might change her mind at some point in the future when her pain and resentment had faded, but for now – short of breaking into the house to search through Mario's private papers – he could see no possible progress. The only other chance was his friends and colleagues on the island. There must be people in this town who could tell him what company Mario had been keeping, what risks he was running, perhaps even why he had died. The difficulty was to find them, and, having found them, question them.

At a quiet corner in the shade he stopped and called Colonel Sotiriou.

The reception was hostile. 'I told you not to telephone me.'

'You did not.'

'I'm telling you now.'

'It's urgent,' said George.

'What's happened?'

'The package has disappeared.'

'Where have you looked?'

'I went to the sports ground and talked to the caretaker. The rooms are bare. They've been emptied.'

'Where else?'

'The family home. Also empty. Now I'm going to ask at the Town Hall.'

'Don't step on any toes.'

'I shan't.'

'When will you be back in Athens?'

'Tonight.'

'I'll call you.'

The Colonel hung up.

*

By the time he reached the Town Hall, George had developed a plan of attack.

At the reception desk he asked for the Deputy Mayor, who was not available. This was as George expected. He asked for a series of other officials, all unavailable, until the receptionist, taking pity on him, asked what it was about.

George said he was a friend of the late Mayor, with a particular interest in forming a cyclists' campaign group in central Athens.

'Who can I talk to?' he asked. 'I was going to meet Mr Filiotis, but obviously that's impossible now.'

The girl's eyes filled with tears. 'I'm sorry,' she said. 'Such a good man!'

'He was the kind of character this country needs,' said George. 'We all admired him. But the best way to honour his memory is to carry on with his work.'

'Of course.'

'He must have had a good team here.'

'He did.'

'Are they going to carry on?'

'As much as they can. But things are difficult.'

'Is there someone in charge?'

'Not really. Not yet... Let me think who might be here today that can help you...'

She consulted a list. 'His secretary, Mrs Kyriakou, perhaps?'

'She knows all his contacts, understands the issues?'

'I would say so. Let me call her. Your name please?'

A minute later a middle-aged woman emerged from a door in the corridor. She approached him with a friendly smile.

'Mr Zafiris? I think I saw you at the funeral.'

'I was there,' said George.

She led him into her office, which was remarkably clear of papers. George deduced that either nothing was done there or this woman was well organised.

She offered him a chair. 'Cup of coffee?' she suggested.

'Why not? Greek if you can manage it.'

'We can. How do you take it?'

'Métrio.'

She picked up the phone and ordered two medium sweet coffees. Then she turned to George and said brightly, 'How can we help?'

This was so thoroughly the opposite of what he had come to expect from civil servants that it took George a moment or two to recover. Rudeness, arrogance, laziness, obstructionism... Any of those would have been normal. But courtesy? Helpfulness? And coffee? It was unheard of.

Feeling slightly ashamed of the necessary lie, George gave his cover story. Mrs Kyriakou did not ask too many questions, but quickly and efficiently looked up the names of other cycling organisations in Athens and around the country, with the names of people to speak to. George conscientiously took notes, wondering all the time how he could push the conversation on to what he really wanted to discuss. The coffee was brought in. He reached for his wallet but she had the money ready.

'Allow me,' said George.

'Don't you dare!'

He accepted with thanks.

'Mr Filiotis was a hospitable man,' she said. 'We maintain the tradition.'

This was his opening.

He asked her if the new Mayor planned to continue Mario's work. She replied, with only a slight hesitation, 'He intends to.'

'He was ambitious wasn't he?'

'He was.' She spoke proudly of the projects and initiatives that Mario had cultivated, his contacts all over the world, from Argentina to Canada, Senegal to Japan. 'He had hundreds of friends,' she said.

'He didn't make enemies?'

'A lot of people ask that. You'd be amazed. Very few. He had such a clear vision, such conviction. Everything he said made sense. We can't go on burning up the earth's resources, destroying the atmosphere, heating up the planet. We're killing ourselves! We'll be flooded, we won't have air left to breathe. And what for? To keep the oil companies happy!'

'It's those vested interests that I'm worried about,' said George.

'They know the truth. And the genius of Mario – sorry, I mean Mr Filiotis – was that he helped them to see it. He wanted partnership, not antagonism.'

'In Athens people are saying he was killed deliberately.'

'It wouldn't surprise me.'
'What do you mean?'
'Athens is the world capital of conspiracy theory.'
'I thought you meant something else.'
'What?'
'That he really *was* killed deliberately.'

She stopped and looked at him more closely. George began to feel distinctly uncomfortable.

When she spoke again she chose her words with care.

'I don't want to speculate on the death of Mr Filiotis. As far as we know it was an accident.'

'That's the official story.'

'And you don't believe it?'

'I'm not saying that,' said George. 'But given the possible impact of Mario's policies on vested interests, it wouldn't surprise me.'

'Are you sure you want to start a campaign group?'

George mistrusted the question. 'Why do you ask?' he said.

'I thought you might be afraid of getting killed yourself.'

'No,' said George. 'I'm not afraid.'

'Good,' she said. 'The more people take up the cause, the more power we have.'

'Of course,' said George. 'But I still don't know what you really think.'

'What I really think is nobody else's business,' she said. 'Have I answered your questions?'

'Yes. I just…'

'What?'

'I'm curious to know what else Mario was up to. This is nothing to do with my campaign group. Just as a friend.'

Mrs Kyriakou looked puzzled. 'What exactly do you mean?'

'I mean apart from cycling and the environment, what other projects did he have?'

'I don't see the relevance of this.'

'None at all,' said George. 'It's just curiosity about my friend.'

'Have you seen his website?'

'No.'

'Take a look.'

'What's the address?'

'Mariofiliotis.gr'

'I hadn't thought of looking on the internet.'

'He used it a lot.'

George stood up. 'You've been very kind,' he said.

She shrugged off the compliment. 'I would do anything for Mario,' she said.

7 Threads in a Web

Back at his hotel, George settled down to explore Mario's website.

The range of ideas and interests was immense. Transport systems, alternative technology, recycling, water treatment, footpaths, folk music, organic farming, public health, urban regeneration, eco-house building, marine propulsion, wildlife conservation, ethical investments, legal and institutional reform, renewable energy, education, sports facilities, fair trade, the media – there was scarcely a branch of human activity that he did not touch on somewhere. He called his website a 'worldwide hub for sustainability'. It glittered with photographs, buzzed with discussions. All very impressive, but George felt mired in possibilities, swamped with information. He was no further on. Somewhere in that mass of detail there might well be a clue to Mario's death. But where? And how would he know when he found it? Almost any of those initiatives, if it crossed the wrong people, could have cost him his life.

He thought about Mario pedalling through Athens. If he had been knocked down deliberately, the people who did it must have followed him. They would have known where he started his journey. They may even have started alongside him. Had they just met him? Could it be as simple as that?

He needed Mario's diary or phone. Both would have been with him when he died. So now they would be in police hands. Therefore unreachable.

Then he thought about Mrs Kyriakou. Perhaps she might have a record of Mario's schedule?

He telephoned her office.

She was surprised to hear from him so soon.

'I forgot something important,' he said. 'Mario promised to introduce me to someone useful for my campaign. We were going to meet on the day he died. I couldn't make it, but he promised to tell me about it afterwards. He must have been on his way from that meeting when he was killed.'

'You want to know who he was meeting?'

'That would be useful.'

'Let me check the diary.'

She was quiet for a few moments. Then: 'Mr Zafiris?'

'Yes?'

'There are three letters and an address: EAP, Leoforos Kymis 136.'

'Who is EAP?'

'I don't know. I've never seen them in his diary before.'

'No matter, I'll find out. Thank you very much.'

'He had two more meetings that day. Do you want those names too?'

'Why not?'

'Petros Karagounis, and Dr Milton Skouras.'

'Any addresses for those?'

'Karagounis no address. Dr Skouras at the Red Cross Hospital.'

George scribbled down the details as she spoke. With a twinge of conscience for deceiving such a helpful woman he thanked her and laid down the phone.

He was quickly back on his laptop searching for Skouras and EAP. He had no need to look up Petros Karagounis, who was an old friend. Still, he wondered what the business connection between them might be.

EAP was obscure. It could stand for Employee Assistance Programmes, English for Academic Purposes, Europe Athlétisme Promotion, and the European Association for Psychotherapy... But there was no connection there with any of Mario's interests, wide as they were, and no company or organisation with that name registered at Leoforos Kymis 136. He would have to go and visit in person.

Dr Skouras was easier to find, although just as hard to explain. A physician with a career that included spells in the US and Britain, he was a visiting professor at universities in Thessaloniki and London. Mario might have been to see him for private or public reasons. Skouras did not sound like the kind of character who would take out a contract on another man's life. But even that could not be taken for granted. People are unpredictable.

*

Back in Athens that evening, he bought Zoe a bunch of flowers on his way home. She was half asleep in front of the television and smiled wanly when she saw them. There was a depressing atmosphere in the apartment. It was stuffy, hot and dark.

George kissed Zoe on the forehead and said, 'I'll put the flowers in water.'

In the kitchen he found the fridge empty. 'Did Dimitri not feed you?' he asked.

'He tried.'

'How hard did he try?'

'Very hard. I had to kick him out. But it's not his fault. I don't like being told what to do.'

'You have to eat!'

'I know,' she said wearily.

'I'm going to get some food. I'm hungry. I want you to eat too.'

'I'll try.'

He ordered a roast chicken from the local takeaway, with pitta, salad, tzatziki and beer. They said they would deliver in half an hour. The light on the telephone flashed as he spoke, indicating a message on the answering machine.

He pressed the 'play' button and listened: Haris Pezas pressing for another meeting, then an unknown woman called Anna Kenteri.

He decided both could wait until tomorrow, and went through to the kitchen to lay the table.

8 Among Doctors

Next morning, as they lay in bed together, Zoe asked George to bring her a cup of coffee. 'I have something to tell you,' she said.

In the kitchen, George opened a fresh bag of *mousto* biscuits, sweetened with grape juice and cinnamon, to go with the coffee. Still in a sleepy haze, he carried the tray into the bedroom.

'Something's wrong with me,' said Zoe solemnly.

'Tell me.'

She began a tangled tale. Feeling unwell a month ago, she had been to Pierris, their old family doctor in Andros. He had listened, examined her, asked questions, and sent her home with a prescription for mild tranquillisers, to be taken if she became anxious.

This visit did not reassure her, so she went to a private specialist in Athens.

This doctor ordered tests.

She also went to a second doctor in Athens. A rival specialist who ordered different tests.

The test results were 'not good'. She did not say which ones – first, second, or both. She was now afraid and depressed. One of the specialists prescribed stronger anti-depressants:

fermoxan. He also recommended surgery.

The other specialist said surgery was risky, would not cure the problem, and could quite possibly make it worse.

So what was the problem? She did not say what it was, or where, but gestured towards her abdomen.

It was, she said, 'inside' her.

When George asked why she had not told him about it before, she said she didn't want to worry him.

'You've worried me now,' he said.

'I can't avoid it any longer.' A panicky light flashed in her eyes. 'I'm being possessed by something, I think of it as the death force.'

'There is no such thing as the death force,' he said decisively.

'It's everywhere!'

'It's not a force. It's just the way things go when they lose energy.'

'How come I feel it inside me, like a presence?'

'It's your imagination.'

'I feel it very strongly.'

George hated this kind of talk. 'I don't believe this force exists. It's a fantasy.'

'You don't believe it? You're so used to death.'

'I see it often, but it still tears me apart.'

'That's exactly what it's doing to me. From inside my own body. I'm being eaten alive by my own cells.'

'That's a horrible image.'

'It's a horrible feeling.'

'I'm sorry,' he said. 'Is this cancer, or something else? Something mental?'

'We're not sure yet. But it could well be cancer.'

'Where?'

'My stomach.'

'Do all the doctors agree?'
'No. Dr Pierris still thinks it's something else.'
'What?'
'Something psychosomatic... But he's not a specialist. And he's old-fashioned.'
'He's also not charging monstrous fees.'
'That's not the point.'
'You're right.'
'Can you talk to them? I'm so confused. All these opinions!'
George stroked her hair and told her he would take care of it.

Later that morning, he left messages with the secretaries of Zoe's three doctors. Every one of them was busy with patients or 'in a meeting', and he had no doubt they would fail to call him back. Only the old-fashioned Pierris might manage it – if he remembered. With the others it would take five or six attempts. They would have patients queueing up to see them, crisis or no crisis.

He emailed his son Nick to tell him Zoe was unwell. Then he called Haris Pezas and asked if he was ready to work. Haris said he was.

'This is a straightforward job,' said George. 'I want you to find out all you can about a person, or maybe it's a company or an association, with the initials EAP. The address is Leoforos Kymis 136. I've tried the internet, so don't waste your time with that. You'll need to go there in person and sniff around, maybe watch from across the street, or a café nearby, see who goes in and comes out, learn what you can. But – this is the important bit – don't let them know you're doing it.'

'What am I looking for?'
'General information.'
'When do you want this?'

'Soon as possible.'
'I'm on my way.'

One more call: the girl on the answering machine, Anna Kenteri. He listened again to the recorded voice. It was edgy, nervous, self-pitying, and it sounded like trouble. But trouble meant money. He punched the numbers aggressively, wanting this out of the way. Her voice irritated him. She was probably the kind of person who wants work done for free.

She picked up at once.

'You called me back!' she said.

'It's normal.'

'I can't tell you how important that is to me.'

'What's the problem?'

She explained. Her sister, a violinist, had vanished five days ago. Leaving no note, no message, no clue.

'Has she ever done anything like this before?' asked George.

'Never.'

'Is she mentally stable?'

'Totally.'

'Could she have fallen in love?'

'She's married.'

'That's not necessarily an impediment.'

'Love isn't the problem, Mr Zafiris! Something bad has happened. I know it.'

'How can you be sure?'

'She calls me every day. Only now she hasn't for five days.'

George found her unsettling in a way he could not define. Her insistent manner. Her familiarity. He wanted to end the conversation.

'The cost of an investigation is five hundred euros per day,' he said.

'OK,' she replied.

'Paid in advance.'

This had the desired effect. 'I need to think about that,' she said.

'Fine,' said George. 'Expenses are on top. You have my number. Think as long as you like.'

A few minutes later Nick called, concerned about his mother. George told him not to worry but asked him to talk to her, say reassuring things. Nick said 'of course' and George took the phone through to the bedroom.

9 Dinner with Petros

That night he had dinner with Petros Karagounis. They sat in a vine-shaded courtyard with barrels stacked high along one side. Such places were vanishing from the centre of Athens. One day soon the owners would retire to their village in the Peloponnese. The taverna would turn into an overpriced coffee bar with sofas and American music. Bossa Nova if they were lucky. Techno or rap if not.

Spyros came to tell them what was on offer tonight. They ordered grilled fish, tomato salad, fried potatoes, a half-litre of retsina.

Petros had once been a company executive. He had built a factory on the edge of the city for Universal Ceramics, managed it profitably for twelve years, done the same again in the Far East with lower labour costs, and made three times the money. Ten years later, back in Greece, he was told by the bosses in Illinois to run the Athens factory down. Citing the globalisation of business and the need to trim costs, he was forced to dismantle his own creation, firing the people he had brought in and educated in the ways of the company, asking them "never to give less than two hundred per cent". He felt like a traitor. It robbed him of sleep. One morning he reported for duty to find there was only one person left to sack. With a hollow feeling in his stomach he opened the letter from head office. 'Dear Mr Karagounis, Regretfully I have to tell you…' A week later, as he jogged in the park to lose weight, all the tension and bitterness of those working years exploded inside him. A doctor walking his dog nearby diagnosed a heart attack, kept him going till the ambulance arrived. That was two years ago. He had been putting his life back together since then.

His new mission statement was 'avoid stress', but that is a tall order in Greece.

'What are you up to?' asked George.

'I'm working on solar power.'

'OK,' said George. 'Is there money to be made?'

'Theoretically, yes. Every country in Europe has to generate a fifth of its electricity from renewable sources by 2020. The government issues licences to private investors, with the promise to buy from them at a certain rate for a fixed number of years.'

'There must be a catch,' said George.

Petros nodded, took a gulp of wine. 'Of course. Dealing with the government is no joke. They're disorganised, inefficient, devious and arrogant. And they keep changing the rules. They give a deadline for applications, you run around like a lunatic to do everything in time, then a week before the deadline they announce new rules. So you have to scrap everything and start again.'

'That's happened to you?'

'Twice already.'

'Why go on?'

'I've invested time and money. If I stop that's all wasted.'

'So they've got you.'

'They always have!'

'I'd go mad in your position.'

'That seems to be the intention.'

'So get out.'

'No. I want to beat them. Anyway, I'm used to the Third World, so I know what to expect.'

'As bad as that?'

'Worse! Much worse! We are supposedly a developed nation. So we have two standards. The official and the unofficial.'

'That's an old story.'

'Ever since the European Union started pumping money into our economy we've been pretending we're a modern state. In fact the old ways have simply continued, hidden under fat layers of bureaucracy and waste.' Petros wiped a hand across his eyes. 'To be honest I'm getting too old for this kind of crap.'

'How do you stand it?'

'I don't know.'

'You could employ someone?'

Petros nodded wearily. 'I probably should. But when you've had to fire as many workers as I have – friends, colleagues, good people – you think twice about offering someone a job.'

With a sudden pang of guilt, George thought of Haris. He should have contacted him. He had heard nothing since this morning.

'You've just reminded me,' he said. 'I took someone on today. I need to give him a quick call.'

'Go ahead,' said Petros.

He called Haris's number. There was no reply. He left a brief message and turned back to Petros.

'I wanted to tell you about Mario's funeral.'

Petros winced. 'I feel bad for missing it,' he said, 'but I had an appointment at the Ministry.'

George told him to put it out of his mind. 'There were plenty of people there. His wife was too wrecked by grief to notice who turned up.'

'I can't believe he's gone,' said Petros.

'None of us can.'

'He was too young!'

'Wasn't he just!'

'At least he died happy.'

'How the hell do you know that?' said George.

'Lovely family, good career, mayor of his island, popular man. And all cleanly done. A man of principle. He achieved things.' Petros gave him a wistful look, filled with pain and nostalgia. 'Why should Mario be taken, and not one of the thousands of cockroaches who run this country?'

'That,' said George, 'is what we all want to know.'

They ate for a while in silence.

'Did you speak to Mario about solar energy?' asked George.

'I started to.'

'Was he interested?'

Petros nodded. 'Of course. The island's very wild. Unspoilt. Lots of space. I thought of buying a piece of land.'

'Did he like the idea?'

'Let's say he was cautiously open to it.'

'Why cautiously?'

'If it was wind farms he'd have said no.'

'Really?'

'He hated them. "Ugly white propellers," he called them. Solar is different. Less visible.'

'So you have mountains covered with photovoltaic panels instead of propellers?'

'You hide them away. Remote spots in the countryside. Valleys, not peaks.'

'Those were exactly the places Mario wanted to protect.'

Petros shrugged his shoulders. 'He wanted to protect everything. Nature, old buildings, trees. Even views for heaven's sake! He was a conservation fanatic.'

'So how would he have helped?'

'I told you, I'm making green electricity. We're on the same side.'

'He would have blocked every planning application you made.'

'Maybe not.'

'How come?'

Petros frowned. 'It's complicated.'

'You'd make him a partner?'

'That kind of thing.'

'I'm trying to find out what his other business interests might have been,' said George.

'Why?'

George was on the point of explaining. He must not say too much.

'Mario was a more complex figure than we thought.'

Petros seemed mystified. 'Really? Give me an example.'

'His family life for a start.'

'In what way?'

'His marriage wasn't exactly happy.'

'How do you know that?'

'Eleni told me.'

'At the funeral?'

'No. I spoke to her yesterday.'

'So you're in touch?'

'I felt I should be.'

'She's crazy of course. You know that?'

'I wasn't aware of it.'

'A religious fanatic. She made Mario extremely nervous.'

Petros said no more for a while. He turned the wine in his glass thoughtfully.

'I have a feeling,' he said, 'that Mario got in too deep with some of his projects.'

'Why do you say that?'

'You get a sense with certain people that they're spinning too many plates. One of them has to crash. Then one by one they all go. That's how it was starting to be with Mario. I suspect he couldn't cope.'

'So what were these spinning plates?'

Petros counted them off on his fingers. 'Running the island, expanding the airport, setting up a faculty of the Aegean University, organic fish farming, alternative technology... Every week a new project. He talked about sustainability, but his own programme was the most unsustainable thing on the planet.'

George was thinking about this when his phone rang.

The number for Haris Pezas came up on the screen but the voice was wrong.

'Come and get your friend.'

'Who are you?'

'Never mind. You just get over here quickly.'

'Where is he?'

'You know where he is.'

The phone went dead.

George stood up. 'I have to go,' he said. He put some banknotes on the table. 'Can you deal with this?'

'What's happened? You look terrible.'

'Something bad.'

He searched for a number on his phone and scribbled it on the tablecloth. 'If you don't hear from me by midnight, call this number. Speak to Colonel Sotiriou. No one else. Tell him to come to this address: Leoforos Kymis 136. With back-up.'

10 EAP

George ran home to pick up his Beretta, ankle holster and a tin of ammunition. Glancing in the bedroom, he found Zoe asleep. That saved explanations. He left her a note with Sotiriou's number and hurried down the stairs.

In the street he grabbed a passing taxi and gave the address on Kymis.

The driver keyed it in to his GPS. 'It's a used car place?'

'Could be,' said George. 'Just take me there.'

'That's what it says here. It will be closed at this time of night.'

'I expect so. This is a private meeting.'

'As you wish.'

He drove on in silence, the radio quietly burbling bouzouki music. George watched the buildings of Leoforos Alexandras speed by – the police headquarters, the central criminal courts, the bullet-scarred workers' housing blocks. His mind racing, he tried to work out what might have happened, and how to stop even worse things from happening.

The taxi pulled up outside a car showroom. A dark building with plate-glass windows and a floodlit forecourt, closed off with chains. Inside, under spotlights, a selection of gleaming black limousines and high-end sports cars: Ferrari,

Lamborghini, Maserati.

'This is it,' said the driver. 'Shall I wait?'

George glanced along the avenue, still busy with traffic.

'No,' he said. 'I'll be fine.'

He paid the fare and got out. Along the right side of the forecourt he could see a tall fence marking the boundary with the next property, a yard selling firewood. On the left a concrete track led to an alley. He took this, walking as casually as he could, feeling the weight of the holstered Beretta above his left ankle.

The alley was a dark block of shadow. As he entered, a security light snapped on. A man in black combat trousers and T-shirt stood in front of him. A slab of a man, armed with a pistol and a long wooden truncheon.

'Where are you going?'

George said, as calmly as he could through his accelerated heartbeat, 'I've come for my friend.'

'Name?'

'Zafiris.'

The man pointed to the door. 'In there.'

George entered a narrow corridor with unpainted concrete walls. He walked slowly along, smelling stale coffee and cigarette smoke, towards a left turn at the end. With an unpleasant feeling he heard the man follow him in and lock the door.

Around the corner stood another guard, blocking his way.

George stopped. He could hear the first guard's footsteps approaching from behind.

The guard in front put out his hand, as if asking for payment.

'What do you want?' asked George.

'Empty your pockets.'

George pulled out a few banknotes and coins from his trousers.

'Jacket?'

He emptied the side and front pockets. Phone, business cards, notebook, folding knife, pen. The tin of ammunition was on the inside. He hoped it didn't show.

The guard said, 'Spread your arms and legs.'

They were going to search him. Quickly, to avoid trouble, George said, 'And this.' He handed over the ammunition tin.

The front guard took it without reacting.

'Where's the gun?' he said, his cold eyes hardening.

George pointed to his ankle. He felt strong hands grip his left leg from behind and run down to the holster, then quickly flip up his trouser and pull out the gun. The rest of his body was swiftly searched. The guarded stepped aside. 'Go ahead,' he said.

The corridor opened into a big, comfortable office – sleek desk, leather armchairs, chrome-framed posters of Formula One cars, signed portraits of their drivers. At the desk sat a heavily built, bearded man in his forties, cream shirt and dark blazer, heavy gold wristband. Everything spoke of luxury and high spending. The man glanced up at him, a pained expression on his face.

George's possessions were placed on the desk. The tall man fingered them with distaste.

'So,' he said. 'You carry a knife and a Beretta?'

George said, 'It's a normal precaution.'

The man looked displeased.

'I don't like armed visitors. What are you doing here?'

'My job,' said George.

'And what's that?'

'Private investigator.'

The man seemed even more displeased.

'What are you investigating?'

'I've come to pick up my friend, Mr... '
'I know his name!'
The man glared at him.
'What's your interest in EAP?'
'I had a friend, Mario Filiotis. He had a meeting here shortly before he was killed, the Friday before last.'
The man's expression did not change.
'And?'
'I wondered what he was doing here.'
'What does anybody do here? We sell cars.'
'He wasn't a car enthusiast.'
'So you sent your little man to snoop around.'
George shrugged his shoulders. 'It seems to have caused some offence.'
'It has,' said the man quietly.
'I hope I've explained,' said George.
'No.'
The man picked up the Beretta and aimed it casually at George's head.
'Does this work?' he asked.
'It does,' said George. 'And I'd rather you didn't point it.'
'Really?' The man seemed amused, but the gun stayed on him.
'Just in case this goes off – which it could easily do – you'd better tell me, right now, who's hired you and what you're after.'
'I was hired by the family,' said George.
'What family?'
'The Filiotis family.'
'And what are you after?'
George said, 'I don't know yet. Maybe you can tell me.'
The man slipped off the safety catch. 'You'll have to do

better than that.'

George disliked the man's tone, but he disliked that little black hole in the Beretta even more. 'I'm looking into the circumstances of his death.'

'I heard it was an accident.'

'Maybe not.'

'Why do you say that?'

'I have reasons. And I'm puzzled why he would come here, since he wasn't interested in cars.'

The man's index finger began to move. George ducked as the muzzle flashed. The room seemed to explode with the detonation, which quivered in his ears, deafening him. The bullet smashed into a picture behind him, shattering the glass.

George slowly straightened. He met the man's eyes, trying not to show fear.

The man said, 'We have high net worth customers here. Security is a priority. Our clients don't like assholes like your little hired pimp asking questions around them. Do you understand that?'

'Of course.'

'No, not "of course", smart-ass! If it was "of course" you'd have got it first time round.'

'I suppose so. But I knew nothing.'

'And now you know!' The hand moved again. George flinched, but the gun did not fire. The man watched him with amusement.

'Mr Filiotis came here looking for finance. That's your story for the family.'

George thought about this, watching the man's hands, on a razor's edge of tension.

'Finance,' said George. 'Is that part of your business?'

'Of course it is. These are expensive cars.'

George risked another question. 'I don't understand. Was he trying to buy a car?'

'No,' said the big man wearily. 'He was here to meet a client, a particular client of ours who *might* have been interested in financing one of his schemes. Unfortunately, the stupid prick turned up on a bicycle. Not a good idea. People in finance have a more elevated idea of transport.'

George tried hard to stay calm. 'What scheme?'

The man shook his head. 'You've asked enough. Now get out before this thing goes off again.'

'What about my friend?'

'You'll find him in the alley.'

George said, 'Can I have my things?'

The man flicked the safety catch, unclipped the magazine and emptied the bullets onto his desk. He swept them into a drawer with the ammunition box and pushed the gun over. 'I don't want to see you again,' he said. 'Or your pimp.' He leaned back in his chair and lit a cigarette.

'Get out,' he said through a mouthful of smoke.

George collected his possessions in silence.

One of the guards led him back along the corridor and unlocked the door.

'Where's my friend?' asked George.

The man pointed into the dark beyond the security light.

'Where?'

'You'll see him.'

The man stepped back into the corridor and pulled the door shut. The key turned in the lock.

11 Boxed

George stepped out of the pyramid of light. Beyond it the dark seemed to fizz in the spill-over glare from Kymis Avenue, silvered in the dampness of the night. He stood still, letting his eyes adapt, trying to push back the guilty thoughts jostling in his mind: why had he sent Haris on a risky mission like this? The man was a beginner. An apprentice. Did he want two dead men on his conscience? Brothers?

The outlines of the alley began to appear. Two high black walls, with a faint grey track running straight ahead in between. At the far end, thirty metres away, a parking lot, jammed with cars. He walked towards it, tense, alert, aware only of the present moment and its dangers. The rushing of cars on the avenue seemed to sweep away every trace of the past.

As he reached the end of the right-hand wall he made out a dark, square shape, a cube of blackness about a metre high, partly blocking the alley. He stretched out his hand to feel it. A cardboard box. He took his phone from his pocket and switched on its flashlight. The top of the box was taped down. The sides bulged a little. Someone had scrawled "Return to Sender" in thick red marker pen on the top.

George peeled away the parcel tape and lifted the flaps of the box. Inside was a black rubbish sack, its neck slightly open, a sweet-sour stench of urine leaking from the hole. He had to step away to grab a breath. Returning he glimpsed a few strands of light brown hair at the opening of the sack. His heart began to thump. The hair belonged to a head. The head, he could now see, as he pulled down the sack and turned his flashlight on the blotchy and battered face, belonged to Haris Pezas.

He fumbled at the sack, rolled it down over the shoulders, and carefully pulled away the bands of parcel tape that forced Haris's mouth open. A slow wheezing breath hissed over his hand, like air escaping from a punctured tyre.

'Haris?' he queried gently.

There was no response. George tried again, feeling the neck for a pulse. It was warm. That was something.

'Haris, it's George. You're OK now.'

A slow, rasping breath. The eyes flickered open, took in nothing, closed. Another breath. The eyes opened again, weary and afraid.

'You're safe now,' said George.

Another wheezing breath. A cough. A dribbling attempt to spit.

'Where are they?' whispered Haris.

'Inside the building. We're alone out here. I'll take you home.'

'Get me out of this bag.'

'Of course,' said George.

He rolled the sack down and found more tape around Haris's hands and feet. Unfolding his knife, he sliced through it. Haris groaned and swore loudly, flexing his fingers and rolling his shoulders. George helped him stand but he staggered like a newborn foal.

'How long have you been in there?'

'No idea,' he muttered. 'Hours. Just let me kill those bastards!'

'Not now,' said George. 'Put your arm over my shoulder. Let's go.'

They hobbled over to Kymis Avenue, where they found a taxi.

'Where to?' asked the driver.

'Corinth,' said George.

'No!' said Haris. 'My wife mustn't see me like this. She'll kill me. Nor my sister. I need a hotel.'

'Change of plan,' said George. 'Forget Corinth. Take us to Aristotle Street, number 43.' He turned to Haris. 'You'll stay with me tonight.'

'There's no need,' said Haris.

'You're going to do what I say.'

Haris grunted. 'That's done me no good at all today.'

'I'm sorry about that,' said George. 'I had no idea they would be so unpleasant.'

'I'll bet you had a damn good idea. Isn't that why you sent me?'

'Not at all!' said George, shocked. 'I wanted to give you a chance.'

'A chance at what? Dying?' He took a handkerchief and spat into it. 'That bloody tape, it's disgusting.'

'You're not meant to eat it.'

'I had no choice.'

'How are you feeling?'

'Homicidal.'

'Can we talk?'

'Go ahead.'

'What did you find out?'

Haris turned a comically bulging pair of eyes in his direction.

'What did I find out?' He shook his head with incredulity.

'You spent at least six hours on the job.'

'Two things. Two extremely obvious things. They sell cars. And they're gangsters.'

'That's all? I picked that up in the first five minutes.'

'So did I.'

'How did you spend the rest of the time?'

'Watching the place, asking around in the neighbourhood...'

'Where did you watch from?'

'The coffee bar opposite.'

George glanced down at Haris's feet. 'In those shoes?'

'I didn't bring spares.'

'There's your mistake. Don't wear anything that stands out from the crowd, certainly not a pair of emerald green loafers straight off a Milan catwalk. Someone sees those, they'll never forget them.'

'You should have told me.'

'I was intending to. Now you know.'

'Damn right I do. Any other advice while we're on the subject?'

'Be invisible. Be ordinary. The moment people know you're an investigator, you're finished. The guilty ones clam up and the innocent ones want to discuss Montalbano and Poirot.'

'What's that?'

'Forget it. So what did you find out as you watched them?'

'Nothing.'

'Did anyone come or go?'

'No.'

'No one stopped to look at a car?'

'No.'

'That's possibly significant.'

'Why?'

'It suggests they do very little business. Did you ask anyone about that?'

'I asked in the café.'

'What exactly did you say?'

'I said the car dealer didn't look busy.'

'Any response?'

'The girl behind the bar was eastern European. Cold white blonde. Tight jeans with false diamonds, pink trainers.'

'What did she say?'

'She said "normal business". Very bloody interesting.'

'Did you ask her what kind of business? What kind of customers?'

'No I did not.'

'Why not?'

'Because those two security guards came in. That's when my trouble started.'

'Tell me about that. How did it start?'

'They didn't even order any drinks. Just walked up to me and said, "Come with us." I asked where, and they said, "Over the road. The boss wants to see you." '

'The big man with a beard? In the fancy office?'

'That's the one. He asked why I was snooping about in the neighbourhood, gave me a spiel about his VIP clients and their security, and when I told him the truth he turned his two cretins on me.'

'What exactly did you tell him?'

Haris flared up. 'The truth! I've already told you that!'

'I want to know what words you used.'

'Does it matter, for heaven's sake?'

'I wouldn't ask if it didn't!'

'I said I was hired by you to find out about his company.'

'Did you tell him why?'

'How the hell could I do that? I don't know why! But whatever I said the bastard didn't believe me. Listen, George, I could have been killed in there! And I'm just starting to wonder if Hector died because you sent him on one of your suicide missions...'

George reacted angrily. 'Hector went off on a lunatic mission of his own. I begged him to get out, I knew it was a death-trap, but he wouldn't listen. He took a crazy risk to protect a woman, and they both died. It was his choice, not mine.'

Haris pulled a face. 'He was working for you.'

'He was working *with* me, on his own contract.'

Haris threw up his hands. 'You're splitting hairs.'

'Absolutely not. He was his own boss.'

'He was a brave man, not a fool.'

'You're right he was brave. But on that occasion he acted like a fool. And he paid for it. Much too heavily...' George felt himself crumbling. 'Dear God, how I miss him!'

'You can't miss him as much as I do.'

'What is this, a competition?'

Haris did not reply. He had his face in his hands.

The taxi turned off Kymis and onto Spyros Louis Avenue. They were following the route Mario must have taken on his last journey. As the Olympic Stadium loomed up on their left like a floodlit skeleton, George put his hand on Haris's arm and said, 'Look, I'm really sorry. About everything.'

'Leave it,' said Haris. 'He's gone and it's over.'

George wanted to ask more about the interrogation, but decided to leave it for now.

It was well past midnight when they reached Aristotle Street. The apartment was quiet and dark, lit only by the street lamps.

George led Haris softly into the kitchen and closed the door before switching on the light. In the harsh white glare he could now see properly what the 'cretins' had done.

Haris's face reminded him of a rugby player's after a particularly brutal game. The skin was discoloured, purple in places, the flesh swollen and misshapen. One of his lips was split, and a blur of dried blood covered half his chin.

'You're right not to go home,' said George. 'Go and clean up in the bathroom. I'll bring you some fresh clothes, fix you a drink.'

He took a whisky bottle and two glasses from the cupboard.

'I don't drink,' said Haris.

'Tonight you should.'

'Why?'

'To numb the pain.'

Haris shrugged his shoulders and made for the bathroom.

12 Unboxed

As he waited in the kitchen, his phone rang. It was Colonel Sotiriou.

George swore to himself. In a flash he remembered that he was supposed to ring Petros, who must have called Sotiriou.

'What's the problem?' asked the policeman.

George described the evening's events, stressing the violence.

'Was I woken up to be told about this?'

'It was a mistake. I meant to call a friend to give him the all clear.'

'And you gave him my number?'

'In case of emergency.'

'That's 112.'

'This was special. We might have needed your help.'

'Might have? Don't you dare do that again.'

'It's OK. My friend doesn't know who you are.'

'I'll tell you what's OK!'

'Very well,' said George.

He expected the call to end there, but the Colonel stayed on the line, silent and irritated.

George could hear the sound of a match being struck, the first drag on a cigarette.

'Where does this take us?' the Colonel drawled.
'I have only suppositions,' said George.
'Let's start with them.'
'EAP may be legitimate and blameless. But they overreacted. They behave as if they have something to hide.'
'They have a motive for that.'
'Which is?'
'High-end clients.'
'That's bullshit.'
'How do you know?' asked the Colonel.
George back-pedalled. 'OK, I don't *know* it's bullshit. But my experience of high-end operations is the opposite of that. They don't create an atmosphere of fear.'
'What kind of atmosphere do they create?'
'Pleasant. Smooth. Everyone obeys the rules. Everyone is polite.'
'Until someone breaks the rules, or poses a threat. Then all hell breaks loose.'
'Haris Pezas is no threat to anyone.'
'They don't know that.'
'They should. He wears bright green suede shoes for heaven's sake! Who is going to be a threat looking like that?'
Sotiriou inhaled again. 'It's the man that carries the threat, Zafiris, not the shoes.'
'He's a shopkeeper! And he looks like one! You'd have to be pumped up on steroids and paranoia to think that man could be up to anything.'
Sotiriou insisted. 'This man of yours was going around asking awkward questions.'
'I wish they had been awkward! In fact he didn't even ask questions. He said things like "not much business at EAP" to a girl serving in the coffee bar. Where's the menace in that?'

Sotiriou did not reply for a few moments. When he did he sounded weary. 'Listen, Zafiris, I've never met any of these characters, and I certainly don't intend to. But let's suppose for a moment that you're right. Where do we go next?'

'I managed to get some information. They told me Mario was there for a financial meeting. An introduction to a rich client. That needs following up.'

'How do you propose to do that?'

'Ideally I'd like a full police check on EAP: tax returns, accounts, background, plus surveillance.'

'That's not going to happen. And you know very well why. This is a very delicate operation.'

'I appreciate that.'

'Just do the job properly. And keep me out of it. I must be at arm's length, or we're all finished.'

George laid down the phone and poured two glasses of whisky. He was watching the ice cubes crackle and dissolve as Haris reappeared.

'Nice shower gel,' said Haris, 'but it stings like hell if you get it you know where.'

'Don't put it there.'

'I'll know next time.'

'You look a lot better,' said George.

They clinked glasses.

'Who were you talking to?' asked Haris.

'Someone you don't need to know about.'

Haris looked offended. George tried to reassure him.

'This whole operation is undercover. I'd like to tell you more, but I can't. The less you know the better.'

Haris seemed unimpressed. 'I've always believed that if you ask a man to do something, it helps if he understands it.'

'In general yes. In this case absolutely not!'

'OK,' said Haris sceptically. 'I shall stop asking myself questions. Only this – is there any work for me tomorrow?'

George responded nervously. 'I hadn't thought of that,' he said. 'But if you mean it –'

'Of course I mean it!'

'I still need to know more about EAP.'

Haris put his head in his hands.

'You mustn't go back there,' said George.

'Don't worry! I'm not.'

'Do you have any friends in the used car business?'

'Not in Athens.'

'Corinth?'

Haris thought for a moment. 'In Corinth yes.'

'Someone you can trust?'

'As long as you're not buying a car.'

George laughed. 'OK… Ask this person about EAP. But maintain total discretion. You can start whenever you like. Take your time.'

They sipped their scotch quietly, until Haris yawned and said, 'Well, it's been a hell of a day. I'd like to sleep now…' He emptied his glass and was about to put it down on the table when a thought occurred to him. 'By the way there was one thing I didn't tell you about.'

George said, 'Really?'

'I didn't just go to the café,' said Haris. 'I visited the other businesses in the neighbourhood. There was a paint shop, a petrol station, a sign-maker, a woodyard, a print shop…'

'I remember the woodyard,' said George. 'It was just next to the showroom, on the right-hand side.'

'That's it.'

'There's a big fence between them.'

'No. It looks like that, but in fact it's a cage.'
'Is that important?'
'No. I just wanted to point out it isn't a fence.'
'Whatever,' said George.
'And in fact the building with the car showroom runs right across the two lots. They're connected.'
'Really?'
'In more ways than one. All the other businesses talked about EAP as if they couldn't give a damn. They had no contact with them. It was different at the woodyard. The girl in there, dark-haired, nicely dressed, hell of a figure, she spoke well of them. "First class people, the best cars in Athens." All 24-carat bullshit of course, but interesting to note. It was right after talking to them that I went to the café and the two gorillas came and got me.'

George was now listening carefully. The truck that knocked down Mario had been full of firewood.

'Now at last we might possibly be getting somewhere,' he said.

Haris frowned. 'If I knew where we were heading I might share your happiness.'

'I'm sorry,' said George. 'I can't tell you.'

'That's all right,' said Haris. 'Just don't give me another day like today. I wasn't born to be a parcel.'

13 A Body in the Bushes

George was sitting in the Café Agamemnon the next morning, waiting for Dimitri to bring a cup of coffee, when he heard his phone ring.

'Mr Zafiris? Anna Kenteri. I have bad news. The police have found my sister's body.'

'I'm sorry.'

'I knew she was dead. I knew it!'

'Where did they find her?'

'In an old quarry between Galatsi and Filothei. A place called Tourkovounia.'

He knew the spot. It was used by dog-walkers and mountain bikers during the day, by drug dealers at night. A strange place. It should have been lovely, with views to the mountains around Athens, south to the sea, even the distant Peloponnese. Yet there was something disturbing about it. The suburbs were ugly. Loners and no-hopers hung about there. The atmosphere was sinister. He remembered a fez-shaped rock that blocked a stretch of the horizon. That too was called 'Tourkouvouni', the Turkish mountain, after the old Ottoman barracks at its base, a reminder of the foreign occupation that had stunted the Greek nation for four hundred years, conditioned its thinking and carried the blame for its failures ever since.

'Are they sure it's her?' he asked.
'Quite sure.'
'What happened?'
'She fell off a cliff twenty metres high. She was lying in the bushes with a broken neck.'
'Who found her?'
'A man walking his dog.'
She tried to go on, but her voice disintegrated into sobs.
George waited before asking, 'Would it help to meet?'
'Not now. I'm in a terrible state.'
'Of course. Take your time.'
'What do you do, Mr Zafiris, when someone dies? Someone you love more than yourself?'
'I don't know. It's very difficult.'
'I believe she was murdered.'
'Really? You have reason to say that?'
'I do.'
'Talk to the police. That's all you can do. Tell them everything you know.'
'Can you help us?'
'I don't see how. Let the police start their investigation. They'll talk to the family. Let's see how they get on.'
'Can you keep an eye on them?'
'Who?'
'The police.'
'That's hard to do.'
'Please try. You must have contacts.'
'I'll do what I can.'
'Thank you, Mr Zafiris. I'm relying on you.'
She hung up and left George feeling empty, nauseous. When his coffee arrived he found it impossible to drink.

He walked down the hill towards Panepistimiou Street, hoping to settle his troubled thoughts. He passed the familiar shops, struggling after six years of crisis to do any business at all: the upholsterer and curtain-maker, who had once laid out luxurious Italian fabrics in his window and now displayed a single dowdy chair with a yellowing card saying *'all work undertaken';* the model aeroplane shop, dusty with unsold boxes; the music store, no longer frequented by hopeful young guitarists and drummers; the bookshop, the shoe-shop, the printer, all empty of customers. Only Evantheia the florist struck a positive note. Between the shops and along the apartment blocks every piece of spare wall had been sprayed with graffiti. *Property is theft. Banking is terrorism. Merkel is Hitler. Pay up or we'll quit the euro...* Simplistic slogans and hideous cartoon graphics. Hooded figures of death, swastikas and dollar signs. Did anyone believe this nonsense?

He turned right on Panepistimiou. Once a river of honking traffic, shimmering in its own exhaust fumes, it was relatively deserted now. Just a few lonely cars and buses rumbling along the spacious boulevard, the shop-fronts shuttered. He walked a block towards Omonia Square, thought better of entering its atmosphere of despair, and turned right again up the hill.

It was a hot day, silent and still. He pushed on, quickening his stride. He was thinking about his life now. After a quiet summer, things were getting complicated again. Zoe was ill, Mario dead, his wife Eleni a bitter wreck... And that poor violinist, dropped in the bushes of the Tourkovounia like a piece of rubbish. She was not strictly his business yet – but if the police did their usual job she soon would be.

Back at home Zoe was out of bed and in the kitchen, peeling fruit.

He asked how she was feeling.

'The same,' she said glumly. For some reason the fruit seemed to him a good sign.

He decided to try Dr Pierris again. Two days had passed and he had not called back.

To his surprise he was put straight through.

'I had a cancelled appointment,' he said. 'What can I do for you?'

George said he had spoken to Zoe, knew about the tests and the conflicting plans for treatment, and asked for advice. Pierris was guarded in his reply.

'There are diagnostic techniques that are far more advanced and complex than anything I know. Those two Athens specialists are well spoken of. I can't tell you which is right.'

'What would you do?'

Pierris did not reply for a few moments. 'That's difficult,' he said. 'If money was no problem I would say go to a generalist, someone with experience but not out of date like me. Don't mention the other diagnoses, just present the symptoms. See what the reaction is.'

'In other words a fourth opinion?'

'It sounds terrible, I know.'

'You know what all this costs?'

'Of course. It's not cheap.'

'What do you do if you're poor?'

Pierris sighed. 'I'm just making a suggestion.'

'Can you recommend someone?'

'You could try Arapaglou or Skouras…'

'Skouras?'

'He's at the Red Cross. He's very good. But let him make his own assessment. Don't load the dice.'

George thanked him and hung up. Skouras was one of the

people Mario had seen on his last day. He had already tried ringing him once. Perhaps he might have better luck today.

The Secretary at the Red Cross Hospital was polite. She apologised for not ringing back, saying that Dr Skouras had been called away on urgent business.

'You are on his list,' she said, 'and on his conscience.' George was glad to hear it. 'Dr Skouras will be back tonight,' she added. 'I'm sure that he will return your call tomorrow.'

George said he could do without the call; he simply wanted an appointment. Somewhat surprised, she offered him a time on Friday morning – two days from now. He agreed. He was not sure how he would combine the two parts of his visit, the personal and professional, but he would manage.

14 Three Brothers

Haris phoned him at the end of the day to tell him that Christos, the car dealer, had been able to give him some useful information about EAP. But he had been nervous about handing it over. He wanted to know who was asking and why. Haris had assured him that anything he said would be treated in confidence.

'And I hope that's right,' Haris added, 'because if this gets back to him in any form – any form at all – it will poison our family for the next five generations.'

'Why your family?'

'He's my cousin.'

George gave a solemn promise.

'OK!' said Haris. 'Get a piece of paper and a pen. These are the facts:

1. EAP is a genuine car sales operation, with a showroom in Athens and another in Thessaloniki. But even at their high prices no one believes they run at a profit.

2. They have further sources of income. One is vehicle and personal finance, which they offer to customers with very few questions asked. The rates of interest are high.

3. They also offer a security service, specially tailored to celebrities and wealthy individuals, which sits well with the

Blood & Gold

luxury car business. The security staff are mainly Russian and provide useful back-up in the case of non-paying loans.

4. The owners are three brothers: Efthimios, Andonis and Pavlos Marangós. Hence the name EAP.

5. Efthimios is known as the clever one (*exypnos*), Andonis the ugly one (*aschimos*), and Pavlos the queer one (*poustis*). This is the unofficial version of 'EAP'.

6. The family, originally from Edessa, has apartment blocks in Athens and interests in banking, art and media.

7. They are disliked by other dealers, who generally avoid doing business with them.'

George said, 'Your cousin seems well informed.'

'He should be. He's president of the Car Dealers Association.'

'Does he know which of the brothers it was our privilege to meet?'

'Pavlos.'

'Why?'

'Efthimios is short and wiry, Andonis is fat, Pavlos is tall and fit.'

'And a psychopath?'

'He didn't mention that.'

'OK. I need to think about the implications of all this,' said George. 'Leave it with me overnight.'

'As long as you like,' said Haris.

George re-read the list of facts under the light of the reading lamp. Considered objectively, the story Pavlos Marangós had told him was plausible enough. Mario had been looking for finance, and people go to strange places for money, usually when the more obvious places won't supply it. When they're in trouble for example. Or have already borrowed too much.

Blood & Gold

But why EAP? There was something unexplained there.

He called Eleni, and asked bluntly if her husband had been in debt.

She said he had not.

Her voice was hesitant, however. Defensive, just like before, but now more vulnerable and circumspect. He commented on this.

'I'm so used to bad news about him that I expect more every day,' she said.

'You've had the worst,' said George. 'Nothing worse can come.'

'Don't say that! Each day brings horrible surprises.'

Not wanting to get into a therapy session, he returned to the subject of debt. Had she followed Mario's finances? Did he have credit cards or loans? Did he have any major projects that needed the help of a bank?

She answered in the same vague, non-committal way each time. She had left all financial matters to him.

Had she opened his post since he died?

'No,' she replied. 'I haven't been able to face it.'

'Open all his letters,' he said. 'And call me at once if any of them are about money.'

'Why are you interested?' she asked suddenly. 'Did he owe you?'

'No.'

'Then why?'

George explained briefly about EAP.

She had never heard of them, nor of Marangós. Nor, when he asked her about him, of Dr Skouras. He was surprised how little she knew of her husband's life.

George went to fetch a beer from the fridge. Catching sight of a packet of ham on the shelf, he realised he was hungry. He made a sandwich with some feta and sweet red peppers in oil, spread out the daily newspaper on the kitchen table, and began to read as he ate. The sandwich was good but the news was bad. The Prime Minister, Mr Tsipras, had called new elections. Experts were trying to predict who would win. George found it hard to concentrate. National politics gave him a deadly sense of *déjà vu*. One gang of parasites succeeding another, sucking the life out of the nation, giving nothing back but empty promises. How much did the people of Greece have left to give?

The other news was worse. The islands of the eastern Aegean were under assault from refugees, desperate families from Syria, Iraq and Afghanistan who crossed the sea from Turkey in inflatable boats. This had been going on since the spring. Some drowned – the paper showed a photo of a dead child in the arms of a policeman – but hundreds of thousands made it and travelled on up to Macedonia, Serbia, Hungary, heading for the prosperous lands of northern Europe, which were not particularly keen to have them.

At this rate, one way or another, Greece would soon be destitute. He pushed the paper aside, too depressed to continue reading. He finished his sandwich and swallowed the rest of the beer. He watched the second hand circling the kitchen clock.

He returned to his desk and read again the seven points on Haris's list. Something else niggled him. He dialled Haris's number.

'I meant to ask you,' he said.
'What?'

'You served in the special forces, correct?'
'Correct.'
'I'm surprised you didn't react more violently to your treatment at EAP.'
'That would not have been a good idea.'
'They gave you enough provocation.'
'Sure.'
'So?' said George.
'They also had superior force.'

George thought of the two massively-built security guards, their air of ruthless menace.

'Could you,' he asked, 'have taken out those two big men, if you'd wanted to?'

Haris gave a contemptuous snort.

'Does that mean yes or no?'
'I'm not going to answer that.'
'Why not?'
'It's a stupid question.'
'It seems reasonable to me!'
'Think about it, Mr Zafiris! I go in unarmed, unprepared, and meet those guys. They're big, they're strong, they look like psychos, quite possibly on steroids or cocaine. And they have guns. Would you try to "take them out" as you put it?'

'Of course not. But I'm not trained.'

'Trained or untrained,' said Haris, 'there's a choice – either control the situation or get out. You didn't send me in there to "take them out". Remember that. You said, "Go and find out what you can." That's what I did. After that it was a matter of survival.'

'I'm sorry,' said George. 'I had no idea what we were getting into.'

'Next time, buddy, make sure you *do* know. It's not so

bloody difficult. It's just three words. "Know your target." A little homework goes a long way.'

'Haris,' said George, 'I respect what you're saying.'

'Pleased to hear it,' said Haris. 'If you want to plan an operation against EAP let me know, and we'll do it properly.'

'Of course.'

'Good night,' said Haris. 'Sleep well.'

15 Dr Skouras

Next morning George drove Zoe to the Red Cross Hospital for her appointment with Dr Skouras. His clinic was a surprise. Freshly painted, clean, with comfortable black leather chairs, a water machine, well-tended indoor plants, it might have been imported whole, vacuum-packed, from Switzerland. Zoe gave her name to the receptionist and they sat down. George held his wife's hand, which was limp and nerveless.

She was not happy about coming here. It had been a struggle to persuade her. The last thing she wanted was more opinions.

George explained again. 'Skouras has a good reputation. Let's hear what he has to say.'

'He's just another specialist waiting for his fee.'

'That's exactly what he's not.'

'Let's see.'

After a short wait they were called in. Skouras was tall, bearded, precise in his dress, with a silk tie and an ironed shirt under his clean white coat. His blue eyes observed Zoe attentively as she described her symptoms.

He asked her to lie down on a couch and drew a curtain. George heard him telling her to indicate where the pain started, what kind of pain it was, whether constant or intermittent, static or dynamic. Then he asked, 'Here?... And here?' At one point she yelped. 'Yes! There!'

He spoke softly to her after that and drew the curtain open. Then he addressed them both.

'You've consulted another physician?' he said.

Zoe glanced at George, uncertain how to reply.

'We have,' said George, 'but...'

'Who referred you to me?'

'My doctor in Andros,' said Zoe. 'Dr Pierris.'

'I don't know him,' said Skouras.

'Does that matter?'

'Not at all. Have you had any tests?'

Again Zoe looked doubtful.

'If you have, I might as well see the results.'

George said, 'We prefer it if you start with your own diagnosis.'

'That's fine. But I'm sure you've had tests, and if you have the results, from a reputable hospital, you may as well let me see them, and then we can save time.'

'Are we short of time?' asked Zoe anxiously.

'We could be,' said Skouras with a slight raising of his eyebrows.

'We've been given quite the runaround,' said George. 'Contradictory opinions, rival treatments costing thousands of euros. If you don't mind, we'd like you to make your diagnosis without influence from others.'

'I understand that,' said Skouras. 'It's not quite how this works. With these symptoms we have three possible diagnoses, not fifty-three. This could be a tumour, a chronic infection, or a cyst. One of these would justify immediate intervention of a costly and possibly damaging kind. The second requires antibiotics, and quickly. The third is best treated by leaving it alone. The test results would confirm which it is. It's your choice. Do you want to order new tests, or give me the results you already have?'

Zoe said, 'Give him the results, George! For heaven's sake, let's finish this!'

George opened his briefcase and handed over a large white envelope. Skouras examined the contents. At a certain point he showed surprise, shaking his head, apparently in distress.

'Thank you,' he said, handing the papers back. 'That's very interesting.'

'What's the problem?' asked Zoe.

'In my opinion this is a cyst,' said Skouras.

'What does that mean?'

'It poses no danger.'

'Oh God,' she cried, 'are you sure?'

'Yes.'

'I'm so frightened! I feel sure I have cancer.'

Skouras said, 'You do not have cancer. You can have the cyst removed surgically, but it's not urgent. And I would like you to let me know in a day or two if the pain stops following this diagnosis.'

'Of course.'

Zoe reached for her handbag and extracted a sealed white envelope.

Skouras glanced at it and raised his hand.

'That's not necessary.'

'I know, but everybody does it, and I wanted –'

'Forget it. What is more urgent is to make a complaint about the two specialists who recommended emergency treatment. That is pure gangster medicine.'

'Does it involve the police?'

'No. You can write to the general medical council. If you want to make a contribution, do that. Denounce them.'

'I don't want anything to do with public offices.'

'I don't blame you.' A weariness swept over his features. 'But you'll do us all a service.'

Zoe smiled. 'I'd rather give you the envelope.'

'It's easier, isn't it? But the answer is no. Some time this disgusting system has to stop.'

George stood up. 'You must have many more patients to see,' he said.

Skouras stood up too.

'I wanted to ask you about something else,' said George, 'but perhaps another time?'

Skouras said, 'Why not now?'

'It's a personal matter. About Mario Filiotis…'

'Oh.' Skouras immediately changed expression. Gone was the relaxed professional. His eyes became troubled, uncertain. 'What do you want to know?'

'I know he saw you just a few hours before he died,' said George.

'I'd like you to tell me what this is about,' said Skouras.

George explained. 'Mario was a friend from school, and we've been close ever since. I'm an investigator by trade. I'm not convinced that he died by accident.'

'Do you have any evidence?'

'Circumstantial. But strong.'

'I see. Well, that's news to me,' said Skouras.

'Can you tell me what business you had with him, doctor?'

'Business?'

'Did he come as a patient, a friend…?'

Skouras thought for a moment. 'I'm not comfortable discussing this. All I know is that you're the husband of a patient. Possibly not even that.'

'What can I say to reassure you?'

'I would prefer to have this conversation another time.'
'Of course. Let's make a date.'
'Give me your card and I'll call you.'
George handed over his business card.
'If you want testimonials,' he said, 'I have plenty.'
'No doubt,' said Skouras. He offered his hand, in what felt to George like a very final way.

As they walked away down the hospital corridor, Zoe said, 'What a wonderful man.'

'Let's see,' said George.

*

Zoe spent the evening on the telephone to relatives and friends, announcing that she was out of danger. She was suddenly youthful and energetic again, with the light of hope rekindled in her eyes. She seemed euphoric, almost drunk with new optimism. George was concerned but made no comment. He sent a text message to Nick: 'Your mother is in the clear.'

Shortly afterwards his phone rang. He expected it to be Nick, but was surprised to hear the voice of Dr Skouras.

'I hope nothing has changed in your diagnosis,' he said.

'Nothing at all,' said Skouras. 'I am not calling about that. It's the other matter.'

'Yes?'

'I've gone to some trouble to check your credentials'

'Fine,' said George. 'Perfectly understandable.'

Skouras went on. 'Mario and I were in discussion for several years about a project.'

'What kind of project?'

'I can't give you any details.'

'Why not?'

'It's confidential.'
'Why is it confidential?'
'It was part of our agreement.'
'But now he's dead?'
'It remains an agreement.'
'And will the project continue without him?'
'I don't know. It may. But he will be a hard man to replace.'
'Why did he come to see you that day?' asked George.
'It was just an update.'
'Was he worried? Preoccupied?'
'He was always worried.'

George said, 'In my experience Mario was a calm, clear-thinking man, always positive, a problem-solver.'

'He was certainly that, but he also had another side,' said the doctor. 'This was a big project. Not an easy, everyday thing. He invested a lot of time and energy in it. We both did.'

'I wish to God you would tell me what it was.'
'No doubt.'

George tried another approach. 'What was the last thing he said to you?'

Skouras pondered for a moment. His voice softened. 'I believe he said, "This time we're going to make it." '

'So you had difficulties? Frustrations?'
'Of course.'
'The usual?'
'What do you mean?'
'Bureaucracy, official documents, delays…'
'Of course.'
'Anything else?'

Skouras began to sound irritated. 'You won't get any more out of me, Mr Zafiris.'

'Let me ask one more question. Do you know where Mario

went after he left you?'

'No.'

'A used car dealer called EAP.'

Skouras was silent.

'Does that mean anything to you?'

When the doctor spoke again, his voice had changed. 'I wish you hadn't said that name. That is the worst possible news you could have given me.'

'Why?'

'I'm not even going to say the word.'

'What word?'

'Put an end to this investigation, Mr Zafiris. That is my recommendation.'

'What word?'

'Let Mario rest in peace.'

'What word, doctor?'

'Otherwise watch your back. And put your affairs in order.'

'I'm asking you, what word?'

'There is no word,' said Skouras wearily. 'Not from me anyway.'

'You could be in danger yourself.'

But the line was already dead.

Part Two

North and South

16 *Memento Mori*

Of all the green spaces in Athens, George had a special liking for the First Cemetery. An island of tranquility in an ocean of angry metal, its alleys of tombs and statues were shaded with cypresses and scented with lemon blossom. Birds chattered in the branches and swooped through the dappled light. Gravediggers, priests, mourners with bouquets of flowers, gardeners with barrows and rakes, delivery men from the florists – these were its human population in the daylight hours. At night who knew what spirits hovered there? Palamas, Trikoupis, Venizelos, flitting restlessly over their troubled land?

The First Cemetery was the end of the road, the burial ground of all hopes and dreams, yet it was a comforting place. A city of the dead, life pulsed there, flickering and glittering more brightly than in the crazed cementopolis around it. Life in death, more hopeful than death in life. Friends and relations of George's lay there in the cool gardens, their faces still vivid, their voices still audible to his inner ear. He enjoyed walking and sitting among them, remembering.

In the anteroom to the chapel, the family of Keti Kenteri sat stiffly on benches around the walls. Her violin lay on her coffin in the centre of the room, a white lily crossed over the strings. The air was heavy with incense and the perfume of flowers. Friends stood in line to shake hands with Anna and her parents, whose ravaged, tear-furrowed faces seemed hacked into unconnected lumps by the butcher's knife of grief. Beyond them stood Keti's husband, Paris, his features rigid and blank, a mask of pale withdrawal. George joined the line, moving slowly forward to murmur a few words of condolence. He took his place among the friends. Such youthful faces, such lively eyes, all solemn, subdued, shattered.

A priest swept in – a commanding figure in gold-embroidered robes. He began to chant the liturgy. He went fast, for they ran burials end to end here, a production line stretching to the Day of Judgement. 'May the servant of God Katerina find a place of rest among the saints, her eternal soul now parted from the flesh. Have mercy, O Lord, and forgive her sins, both voluntary and involuntary...' As he chanted, the censer swung on its silver chains, giving off puffs of scented smoke. The mourners crossed themselves and stared into the clouded space. George's mind wandered from the dead girl's violin to the inconceivable vastness of a place where all dead souls are gathered.

Suddenly the service was over, with an odd silence in which no one seemed to know what to do. The priest stood still, letting the silence settle. Then the spell was broken, the pall-bearers stepped forward and raised the coffin to their shoulders. The doors were opened, letting in a brilliant cascade of light. The party straggled out into the white marble glare of the courtyard. They turned along the main avenue, past flower-strewn graves, moving like ghosts in the heat.

At the Kenteri family plot red earth was piled along the edge of a gaping trench. Down went the coffin on long webbing straps. The first handfuls of soil. Then shovelfuls, rattling and grating, until the coffin, and the violin and lilies resting on it, were engulfed. Paris dropped in a red rose and bowed his head.

George observed the family. Some weeping, some drained of tears. Anna's mother was barely capable of holding herself upright. Her husband steadied her. Paris stood a little apart, maintaining a severe and formidable composure, as if his soul had followed his wife's into the next world, leaving his body on earth, an empty husk.

Back along the sun-dappled alley the mourners made their way. At the main courtyard a man in a grey suit stood by a doorway, directing them into a hall where tables were set out with vases of flowers and neat little rows of coffee in cups, glasses of brandy and slabs of yellow cake on white china plates. George took a glass of brandy and a piece of cake. He saw Paris at the end of the table, alone.

George attempted a few words. Paris placed a hand on his arm and said gently, 'I'm sorry, I don't know your name, and it's kind of you to make the effort, but forgive me. I can't talk.'

George left him to his sorrow. He took a sip of brandy, savoured its burning descent, and asked himself what he was doing here.

He wandered about the room for a while, nodded to Anna, who was deep in earnest conversation with a red-headed girl. He felt more out of place every minute.

It was a short walk to Averoff Street. H.M.Karyotakis & Sons, Funeral Office, said the sign. A clean, prosperous, businesslike place. Mirror-polished marble floor, walls hung with sample headstones and an oil painting of the founder, Haralambos M. Karyotakis (1910–1996), sleek and universally obliging in a well-cut suit.

A girl at the reception desk smiled as George came in. George did not smile back. 'My uncle has just died,' he said. 'I need to fly his body to Stockholm for burial. Can you handle that?'

'Of course,' said the girl.

'Cost?'

She picked up the telephone.

'Mr Karyotakis? There's a gentleman here with a question about Stockholm.'

The receptionist put down the phone and said, 'Come with me.'

She led him into a spacious office where a plump, innocent-faced man sat behind a large and improbably tidy desk. He stood up and shook hands.

'Manolis Karyotakis. How can I help?'

George introduced his special problem. It was complicated, he said. His uncle's widow, being Swedish, did not believe a Greek company would be capable of organising the transportation safely. She wanted to hire a funeral director from her own country.

Karyotakis appeared to swallow the bait. 'Your aunt's concerns are understandable,' he said, 'but unfounded, I promise you.'

'Stockholm is a long way,' said George.

'It might as well be next door. Tell us where to pick up the deceased and we'll take care of everything, all the way through.'

'Sorry,' said George. 'Through what?'

'Embalming, dressing, providing a coffin, customs clearance, fees, special cargo licence, refrigeration, everything. Where is your uncle at present? In a hospital?'

George shook his head. 'He died at home.'

'My condolences to the family.'

'I'm afraid my aunt will need more than that. Do you have any evidence of your international experience?'

'Evidence?'

'Yes.'

Karyotakis looked puzzled. 'What do you want? Customs documents? Waybills?'

'Something that shows you do this on a regular basis.'

'I've never been asked for such a thing before,' said Karyotakis.

'So?'

'Just think about it. Athens is a cosmopolitan city, full of tourists, expatriates and business visitors. Several of them die each year and we have to send them home.'

'I just want proof.'

'It's logical! People don't like to think about death, but it's all around us. We think of it as the great enemy, but in fact...'

'Spare me the sermon, Mr Karyotakis. I just want a bit of documentary evidence.'

The funeral director's neck muscles tensed. He was clearly furious.

'I am not in the habit of showing company documents to people who walk in off the street.'

'OK,' said George, standing up. 'I'll try somewhere else.'

Karyotakis gestured for him to sit down. He picked up the phone. 'Roula, bring in the client register.'

There was a knock on the door and the receptionist came in with a bulky blue ledger under her arm.

'Give it to the gentleman please.'

George took the ledger and flipped it open. Entries began in January 2008.

'Last week,' said Karyotakis, 'you'll see there was a delivery to Moscow. About ten days ago we had one to Sydney, Australia. Before that if I recall correctly we had deliveries to New York, Buenos Aires, Chicago, Milan... I promise you, every one of them arrived safely!'

George checked for entries around August 30th. His eye fell on the letters NY, USA. The body of Philip Medouris, delivered to Bartley & Corrubbio Funeral Home, Brooklyn.

'Thank you,' he said, laying the ledger on the desk. 'What are your fees?'

Karyotakis said smoothly, 'First we like to know what the family wants, then we deliver it. At an excellent price.'

'Please be more specific.'

'We start at two thousand five hundred euros, excluding air transport and contingencies such as refrigeration in case of delays.'

'What guarantees do you offer?'

'All transportation is fully insured.'

'Does that cover everything?'

'What do you mean *everything*?'

'I've heard horror stories,' said George. 'Lost ashes, even lost bodies.'

'There's nothing to worry about,' said the undertaker. 'We use the best carriers in the business.'

'I have witnessed a case of a lost body,' said George. 'Quite recently in fact.'

'That has never happened to us.'

George marvelled at the man's mendacity. 'Really?' he said. 'What would you do if a body got lost?'

'We would make every effort to trace it. No stone left unturned. We would work day and night! Not to speak of compensation and insurance.'

'Let's get this clear. You swear to me that this has never happened to you?'

Karyotakis hesitated. 'I have heard of cases, of course…'

'Let me name one.'

'Wait a moment, what is this?'

'Filiotis. Mayor of Astypalea. His coffin came to the island last week, only he wasn't in it. It turned out to be full of archaeological loot.'

'Ah, now that does remind me...'

'It should! Your firm was in charge.'

Karyotakis was suddenly agitated. 'What do you want?'

'I want an explanation.'

'So this uncle story is just bullshit?'

'Never mind the uncle. Filiotis was a friend. His family are devastated. All they got from you was a brush-off. After cancelling a funeral!'

Karyotakis stayed cool. 'Let me have a look.' He picked up the ledger and turned slowly to the relevant page. He ran his index finger down the column, checking names, then picked up the phone again.

'Roula, bring me the file for Mr Filiotis please. This year, August 30th.'

He turned back to George. 'We'll get to the bottom of this,' he said mildly. 'I'm sorry if you feel let down.'

'It's not me, for God's sake! It's the family.'

'Of course...'

Roula reappeared, placing a grey file on the desk. Karyotakis opened the file and began flicking through papers.

'Certificate of death, notes of telephone conversations, order for coffin, headstone, transport arrangements, funeral flowers, pall-bearers... It's all here.'

'Only the corpse was missing! Did you not collect it?'

'I'll check... It says here that we delivered the coffin to the hospital, where... Now that is slightly unusual, I have to admit. Normally we pick up and... OK, Let me talk to our technicians.'

George listened carefully as Karyotakis made the call. He asked plenty of questions. Where did you go? Which hospital? Was it the mortuary or a separate room? Did you see the body? Who handed it over? Was the coffin closed? Was the lid screwed down? You made two visits? One to deliver the coffin, the other…? OK, one visit. The coffin was delivered separately, by the carpenter, and later you collected it, already loaded. It was screwed shut when you collected it? You didn't open it? Why didn't you? We have rules! Did the weight feel right? Was there anything else…? All right, everything seemed normal, but it wasn't! How the hell could you know who it was? Or what it was…? Never mind what was in there, I'm telling you it was not the person it was supposed to be! You've made a mistake and I have some very upset relatives on my hands! The procedures are there for a reason! Go to hell!'

He banged down the phone. 'There you are,' he said. 'They never checked!'

'Why not?'

'He took the order from a senior doctor. Didn't like to question him.'

'And who was this senior doctor?'

'He doesn't know.'

'Do you mind if I look at the file?'

'It's confidential.'

'It's either me or the police.'

Karyotakis pushed it wearily across the desk.

George scanned quickly through the papers. He found and noted down the collection address: the Hermes private clinic in Halandri. An illegible doctor's name was scrawled at the bottom of the consignment note, another on the death certificate. He took photographs of both with his phone.

'You're not supposed to do that,' said Karyotakis hopelessly.

'And you're not supposed to lose bodies,' said George, handing back the file.

'If I can help in any other way...' said Karyotakis.

'I'll be in touch,' said George.

He took a taxi up to Maroussi, thinking all the way about Mario. It looked as if his body had gone to New York by mistake, in place of a coffin full of ancient gold. So who was Philip Medouris? Just a name presumably. And the people in New York? Dealers in illegal antiquities, no doubt expert and sophisticated, but crooks nonetheless. How would they react? That would depend on who they were, what they had paid, how they operated. Could be violent or not. Would certainly be annoyed. He had known such a dealer once, a clever man from London, educated, slippery, eloquent, who spent half his life touring the Mediterranean in search of ancient treasures, the other half in meetings with collectors. According to him archaeology was simply 'tomb-raiding by professors' and would barely exist without contraband to fund it. 'A hundred and fifty years ago archaeology wasn't even a word, never mind a discipline.' George thought him too clever by half, a thoroughly unscrupulous person.

Unless it was not a straight switch. A three or four way manoeuvre, and not necessarily international. That was also possible! He checked the photos on his phone. The firm had dealt with five burials that day. Any of those could have been involved in the mix-up, deliberately or not. Perhaps Mario's body was still in Greece? This would not be easy to untangle.

He got out of the taxi at the Town Hall in Maroussi and walked up to the square. Colonel Sotiriou was sitting at the same café table where they had met three weeks ago. Now there was a scattering of autumn leaves on the ground, and a ragged old man in a filthy anorak wandering about, babbling nonsense to an imaginary audience.

Sotiriou looked healthier today. His eyes brighter, his skin less slack and pale. George asked where he had been.

'Amsterdam.'

'On holiday?'

'Police conference.'

'It's done you good,' said George.

'No doubt! And I'll tell you why. I have colleagues from countries where the police have a chance of actually doing their work. I like to hear their optimism, their talk of teamwork and co-operation. Even if I have nothing to offer in return. Only procedures, politics and paperwork. Nineteenth century practices for a twenty-first century world!'

George was surprised at the man's chatter. He was normally a minimalist: taciturn, circumspect, cunning. For fear of discouraging him George made no further comment. He ordered a coffee and asked how the weather had been.

'Cold,' said Sotiriou. 'Autumn has already begun up in the north. They're wearing gloves and scarves. That at least makes me feel good to be a Greek! Now tell me why you wanted to meet.'

George gave him an update on Mario's case. He watched the Colonel closely as he described the visits to Eleni, the undertaker and EAP, curious to see if there was any reaction. But Sotiriou showed no surprise. He listened, gravely and impassively. At the end he asked if George thought the violence at EAP was anything more than 'a bit of theatre to give you a fright'.

'They gave someone else a fright,' said George, and thought this a good moment to quote Dr Skouras: ' "Try to end this investigation, Mr Zafiris. That is my recommendation." '

Sotiriou merely remarked, 'That is an obvious thing to say.'

'It may be obvious but the fact is those guys are dangerous. Would you consider watching EAP?'

'Out of the question.'

'Why?'

'I don't have enough men for official business, never mind off the record stuff like this. If EAP are involved I can't make a move until they're in the bag.'

'What do you mean, "in the bag"?'

'When I have rock-solid evidence.'

'That doesn't make sense.'

'It makes extremely good sense. Just think about it.'

'Without your help what powers do I have?'

'A citizen's powers.'

'Against people strong enough to cancel a police investigation! I don't fancy my chances.'

Sotiriou pushed a cigarette into an amber holder. He lit it and said calmly, 'You, Mr Zafiris, can move silently and discreetly. Unlike me. Whatever I do is public and highly visible. I have very little freedom. But you have both freedom and my support.'

'I'd love to know what that support is, because I'm not seeing anything.'

'I'm with you. You know that.'

'You might at least tell me what you know.'

'I've told you. If Filiotis was murdered, his killer has protection at a high level.'

'Could it be EAP?'

'You tell me.'

'You're impossible,' said George.

'You're asking for things I cannot give,' replied Sotiriou.

'I'll need some money.'
'How much?'
'Seven thousand five hundred.'
'You'll get it. How many days' work is that?'
'Fifteen.'
'You can't have done so many.'
'With my assistant I've done eight. We'll need at least another seven.'
'Go up to fifteen. After that you'll need further clearance.'
'From whom?'
'From higher up.'

George nodded. This was typical of Sotiriou. He hoarded information like a miser, gathering it greedily to him. Never gave any away.

'What do you know about Keti Kenteri?' asked George, changing the subject.
'Why do you ask?'
'I've just been to her funeral.'
'Are you a friend of the family?'
'No. They've asked me to look into her death.'
'I see… Tough case. No witnesses, no weapon, no motive.'
'You're familiar with it?'
'Only from the weekly reports.'
'Are you getting anywhere?'

Sotiriou waved his hand, directing smoke into the sky.

'Why is that?' queried George.
'It will take time.'
'Can I see the notes?'
'Of course not!'
'Can you tell me who your men have interviewed?'

Sotiriou smiled bitterly. 'I'm sure you can tell me quicker than I can tell you.'

'You make me feel I'm wasting my time,' said George.

'Not at all! You've been most informative. Let me know when you have any more to tell me.'

17 The Musicians

A few days later, Sunday, George and Zoe took a walk along the pedestrian boulevard that skirts the base of the Acropolis. Past the new Acropolis Museum and the Odeon of Herodes Atticus, down the hill towards the Theseion and the Keramikos. On their right lay a substantial piece of ancient landscape, miraculously undisturbed, the autumn sunshine glowing in the olive trees. This was a blessed zone of beauty that cast a mysterious spell on the city, charging it with hope, lucidity, confidence and strength.

Yet out past the houses of Plaka, the concrete battalions were massing, choking the plain as far as the mountains – Parnis, Penteli, Hymettus – scrambling up their rocky slopes like the waves of a dirty sea. This was the grim side of Athens. Where Greeks struggled to make neighbourhoods out of pitiless channels of asphalt, glass and fume-blackened cement.

In the gardens by the Theseion, a handful of poorly dressed traders sat behind tables crammed with superannuated objects: old wristwatches with discoloured dials, inkwells, cheap vases, chipped wine glasses, cutlery, books, battered trays. No one was buying, no one even looking. The vendors themselves were a sad and dispirited lot, men with straggly grey hair, women with exhausted eyes, waiting to light the next cigarette.

Zoe said, 'Why would you buy?'

George did not answer. Someone was waving to him from a café table on Adrianou. He screwed up his eyes to see better. It was a woman in a black dress, with wild hair.

'Who's that?' exclaimed Zoe.

'I think it's Anna Kenteri. The sister of the violinist.'

'You must talk to her,' said Zoe.

Anna greeted them. 'What are you doing?'

'Enjoying the city,' said Zoe.

'It's such a beautiful day. Have a coffee with me?'

'I'm sorry for your loss,' said Zoe.

Anna's eyes filled with tears.

'How are you?' asked George.

'I was going to call you,' said Anna. 'I've had a very disturbing conversation – with one of Keti's friends.'

George glanced at Zoe. 'Go ahead and talk,' said Zoe. 'It's fine.'

'Tell me,' said George.

'A few days before she disappeared, Keti told this friend that she was frightened.'

'Of what?'

'Her husband, Paris. And his jealousy. His *insane* jealousy.'

'OK. Do we know any more about this?'

'He used to question her about where she went every day, who she saw, who she rehearsed with, where they went for a drink. Endless details.'

'Did he have any reason to be jealous?'

'She led a busy life.'

'That's not an answer to my question.'

'I'm thinking about it… I doubt it very much.'

'Did she say anything about this to you?'

'No. She kept her marriage private.'

'Was she happy with him?'

'I always thought so. But how happy can you be with someone who interrogates you like that?'

'You used the word *insane*. Was that Keti's word?'

'It was her friend's word.'

'What exactly was insane about it?'

'It was getting out of control. He was following her, calling her friends and colleagues. Turning up at rehearsals, apparently to give her a message but in fact to check that she was really there...'

'Anything else?'

'She had an uncomfortable feeling. That he had become a stranger. That he meant to punish her.'

'Even though she did nothing wrong?'

Anna nodded.

'Have you checked this friend's story?'

'In what sense?'

'Have you spoken to Keti's colleagues? Have they witnessed any of this jealousy?'

Anna dismissed the idea. 'This girl wouldn't lie about such a thing. She's totally straight.'

'Don't be too sure. She may have some grudge against Paris.'

'I know her. She's not like that.'

'We have to be cautious. Unsupported accusations can be as bad as the crime itself.'

'Maybe. But how can I possibly check? Many of Keti's friends are also *his* friends.'

George considered the matter. Anna took a packet of cigarettes from her bag. She lit one.

'What do you want me to do?' asked George.

'Talk to Paris.'

'He'll deny it.'

'Of course. But still you might learn something.'

'He's not an easy man to talk to.'

'I know that…' She flashed a sudden smile at him. An electrifying smile. 'But you on the other hand are very easy to talk to…'

'I'll do what I can,' said George. 'Can you give me his details?'

'Stephanou Delta 44, Filothei. The number is 376 9852.'

'Is that home or office?'

'Both.'

'One more thing,' said George. 'Is he a musician too?'

'He's a composer and piano teacher.'

'Successful?'

Anna frowned. 'So-so.'

'Was he jealous in that way too?'

'I believe so.'

'I'll go and see him,' said George.

Late that afternoon George took the bus to Filothei. It was an uncomfortable journey. After jolting about through leafy backstreets and squares, the bus sighed to a halt outside a shack selling lottery tickets and ice creams – an odd relic among the enormous white villas and elegant apartment blocks. George walked down the hill, past lush gardens and security gates, past Jeeps and Range Rovers gleaming in the October sun, wondering how many of their owners ever paid any tax.

Delta Street lay to his right, a gently undulating road with houses along one side and a park densely planted with pine trees on the other. Number 44 was a simple but substantial old house with cream stucco and the palest of grey shutters. It stood out from its neighbours for its quiet good taste.

He pressed the bell and waited for a reply. A private security patrol car drove by, slow and watchful. A minute later he pressed the bell again. Still no reply. He looked up at the house. An upstairs window was open. The sound of piano practice could be heard, repeatedly attacking a difficult passage of Beethoven. Whoever was inside must be deaf or very determined. He pressed the bell again, keeping his finger on the button until it hurt.

Paris came to the window, dishevelled and unshaven.

'What do you want?' he asked angrily.

George said, 'I need to talk to you.'

'Who are you?'

George explained.

'I'm giving a lesson!'

'Then I'll wait.'

Paris said brusquely, 'I'll come down.'

George waited. Ten minutes later Paris appeared, looking fresher and tidier. A fleck of blood on his throat betrayed a recent shave.

'Excuse the delay,' he said, 'I was not presentable.'

'How about your pupil?'

'She's fine.' He waved a shapely hand. 'How can I help?'

'Are we going to stay out in the street?'

'I'm afraid I can't invite you in.'

'Why not?'

'The house is in a terrible state.'

'I don't mind.'

'No, but I do.'

'I see. Well, this is not a suitable conversation for a public place, but it's your choice. I want you to tell me what you know about Keti's death.'

Paris recoiled in surprise. 'Just like that?'

'Why not?'

'What business is it of yours?'

George did not say he had been hired by Anna. Merely that he had been 'retained'.

'I've already told the police the whole story,' said Paris.

'What you've told them is becoming harder and harder to believe.'

'Why do you say that?' The young man's eyes were calm.

'Keti's colleagues have started to talk.'

'They've always talked. They're artists. Friends. They gossip.'

'This isn't just gossip. Bad stories are coming out.'

'Really?'

'Stories of jealous behaviour.'

Paris shuddered fastidiously.

'Excuse me, but I call that gossip! They don't realise what harm they're doing.'

'This is serious stuff. Potential evidence.'

Paris sighed. 'I don't know what you expect me to do about this. People talk maliciously about my wonderful Keti, and I have to live with it. Not just the pain of losing her – a pain which will never leave me – but also the sorrow of hearing these rumours being spread by her so-called friends!'

'You're not listening, Paris. These stories aren't about Keti. They're about you. And they're extremely damaging.'

'It's their word against mine! How can I defend myself?'

'Forget defence. That's up to your lawyer. Your decision is a moral one. Do you lie or tell the truth?'

A flash of anger lit the musician's face. 'You've clearly made up your mind!'

'Not at all. But I take these stories seriously, and the police will too.'

'The stories are false. Utterly false. And that too is a moral matter!'

'You're very good at deflecting the argument.'

'Am I?' Paris suddenly blazed with fury. 'Do you know what happened to Keti?'

'I do.'

'Tell me!'

'Why?'

'Just tell me!'

'She fell, or was pushed, over a cliff.'

'Where?'

'The Tourkovounia.'

'You know that? Good! Because I knew nothing for six days! Six days of indescribable agony!'

'I can imagine.'

'I don't believe you can. This is beyond imagining. Torture of the soul! A freezing emptiness that grows and grows into the immensity of space! How can you imagine that? Are you a poet? Have you lost someone in precisely that way?'

'No,' said George.

'And then they find her. The most terrible day of my life. How could anyone harm that lovely creature?'

George saw the torment in the man's eyes, the appeal for sympathy. He was determined to resist it.

Taking a card from his pocket he said with cold formality, 'This is my number. I'm giving you an hour.'

'For what?'

'Your decision.'

'There's no decision to be made. I've told the truth.'

'One hour. Then I'm calling the police.'

Paris looked appalled. 'I don't know why you're threatening me, what you hope to gain. No doubt someone in Keti's family is behind all this. They're the world's most poisonous people, with the sweetest of coatings. If you've given them your trust, watch out! You never know where the sting will come from, but it will come, be sure of that! And you can tell them from me – officially – that I regard this visit of yours as an act of harassment. If I ever hear from you again I shall go to the police.' He held up George's card, his eyes gleaming defiantly. 'Thank you for this. I shall keep it so I know where to find you.'

George eyeballed him. 'Don't fool yourself, Paris. This is only going to get worse for you.'

'It cannot possibly get worse!'

'Oh yes it can.'

Paris returned his stare. There was a furious strength in his eyes, an authority, that made George doubt for a moment his whole line of approach.

Then Paris said, 'You think I killed Keti, and you're wrong. And while you harass me, the guilty man is free to strike again.'

'Let's hope he knows when to stop,' said George. He turned and walked off down the road, hearing the gate click shut behind him.

18 Missing

At his desk again, George switched on his computer and searched for the Bartley & Corrubbio Funeral Home. There it was: 145 Henry Street, Brooklyn. 'A proud sixty-year history of cremation and funeral services to the community.' The website was rich in lilies, purple-draped family portraits, tributes from grateful customers.

A sleepy voice answered the phone. George apologised for calling so early – it must be seven in the morning in New York – and explained his problem. The voice quickly became more alert. 'Let me just bring up the name on our system,' it said. Then, after a few seconds, 'OK, I have it here. Philip Medouris. Arrived September 3rd. Delivered Brooklyn crematorium on the 4th. Funeral and cremation September 5th.'

'So he's a pile of ash now.'

'He has been cremated.'

George swore.

'I'm sorry, sir?'

He asked if he might be put in touch with the family of Mr Medouris.

'That's not possible, sir, but if you write care of us we will gladly pass on your letter.'

'Is there a family?' he found himself asking.

'Sir?'

'There was something odd...' he began, then thought better of it. 'I suppose you didn't open the casket?'

'We would not normally do that.'

'Did the family open it?'

'I really don't know. We handed over the casket to the crematorium as stated in the contract.'

'But you stored it overnight, between the 3rd and 4th of September.'

'That's correct.'

'I need to know if anybody from the family spent time with the coffin, enough time to open it and look inside.'

'I can't tell you that, sir.'

'Did you see any of the family?'

'Not personally.'

'I have reason to believe the casket contained the wrong body.'

'That would not be our responsibility.'

'No. I understand that. But maybe the family would have checked.'

'I doubt that.'

George explained. 'The Medouris family are Greek, and the tradition in Greece is an open coffin up to the time of burial.'

'This is the United States of America.'

'Don't people want to see their loved ones in America? Take a last look?'

'It depends on the people, sir. I don't know why you're asking these things, but –'

'Did *anyone* there, from your company, from the Medouris family, or anybody else at all, check inside the coffin?'

'I can't tell you that.'

'It's the one thing I very much need to know.'

'That's private family business. We don't discuss these matters with third parties.'

George was frustrated. 'I'm going to leave you my number,' he said. 'If you can find out any more for me, anything at all, I'll be very grateful, and so will the family here in Greece. They found an empty coffin at the funeral and they're very upset.'

'That's understandable.'

'I'm not asking for any big secrets, just that one thing... Which crematorium did you say?'

'Lavender Lawn. Brooklyn Heights.'

'Thank you,' said George. 'I look forward to your call.'

He hung up. Then found Lavender Lawn Crematorium and telephoned the number given on the website. A well-trained lady with a brassy voice confirmed that Mr Medouris had been cremated on September 5th. She would not discuss the ceremony, or how many mourners attended. George said he was a friend of the family and wanted to send a tribute. The lady said he could send it to the crematorium and it would be passed on to the family.

George replaced the phone. Everything was in order. At the same time everything was wrong. Mario Filiotis had been burned to dust in a far-off city, while his family grieved over a vacant coffin. And someone in Brooklyn, with the real or assumed name of Medouris, had been expecting a consignment of ancient gold, but found a corpse in its place. Of the two, only Mario was likely to rest in peace.

He telephoned Eleni and gave her the news.

'Are you sure of that?' she asked.

'We'll never be sure,' he replied. 'All that's left is ash.'

For a time she was silent.

'The people in New York were expecting gold,' she said.

'Instead they got a body. They didn't make any queries? They just went ahead and burnt it?'

'That seems to be what happened.'

'They would have reacted.'

'Privately, yes. But officially they could only do what they were pretending to do in the first place.'

'There's more to this,' she said.

'Quite probably. But short of sending someone to New York…'

'Would you go?'

'I would, but it might be better to hire someone over there.'

'Of course.'

She thanked him for his efforts. George said goodbye, knowing this would not be the end of it.

At five-thirty, he rang Sotiriou about Paris Aliveris. The Colonel listened patiently and, without dismissing George's suspicions, gave him to understand that they would be put on a shelf and, until someone in his overstretched, under-funded and demoralised department found time to deal with them, ignored. George warned that a man who could push his wife off a cliff and lie so convincingly was not a man to be left at liberty, but Sotiriou reminded him that supposition, even on the part of a respected investigator, did not amount to grounds for arrest.

'You should at least send in the forensic team,' said George.

'Forensic team? What do you expect them to find?'

'Traces of soil on his shoes, in his clothes. Or his car.'

'Very good! And then he will say it's his right to go walking in the Tourkovounia!'

'And kill people?'

'That is your assumption.'

'Any story he tells will have to be backed up. If there's anything there to link him to that death you've got a chance. Without that you've got nothing.'

Sotiriou did not speak for a few moments.

'Well?' said George impatiently. 'How about it?'

'You really are the most tiresome informant.'

'Give me a break, Colonel! I'm doing you a service.'

'We'll see.'

'So you'll send a forensic team.'

'Let me think about it.'

'Not too long! He'll –'

'I have another call, Mr Zafiris. No doubt we'll talk again soon.'

The phone went dead.

What George had been prevented from saying by the Colonel's interruption was 'he'll try to escape'. He thought of calling back just to say those words, but anger and frustration stopped him. Instead he went home to have a quiet evening with Zoe. He cooked *penne all'arrabbiata*. They drank a bottle of red Naoussa and watched an old black and white comedy on television, deliberately forgetting all serious things.

Next morning at ten Sotiriou telephoned him. Something had happened overnight. Having considered the matter carefully, he had decided to send a forensic team to Keti Kenteri's house in Delta Street. They had visited at six-thirty this morning. The owner was not there. His resident housekeeper, a Filipina, said he had gone on holiday. The team had nevertheless begun its work. Meanwhile enquiries at the airport revealed that Paris had left for Bucharest the night before.

'Why Bucharest?' asked George.

'I hoped you would be able to tell me.'

'I can't,' said George. 'But what difference does it make? He's gone.'

'So it would seem,' said the Colonel. 'We must hope he doesn't stay away too long.'

George at once telephoned Anna Kenteri. Did Paris have any connections with Romania? She could think of none, except that the country was known for its musicians; he quite possibly had friends and colleagues there. Was he a gregarious type, he wondered? Did he form alliances and friendships easily, or was he a loner? How much did she know about him generally? Anna replied decisively: he was a good communicator, had many friends, used to be a lot of fun. George picked her up on this at once. Why 'used to be'? She replied that a change had come over him in the last few years.

'Coinciding with Keti's success as a performer?' asked George.

'I need to think about that.'

'Tell me about the change.'

She hesitated. 'Hard to describe. The humour seemed to fade. The lightness. He used to cook wonderful meals, held evenings at the house with improvised sessions, using any instruments that happened to be there, playing jazz, folk songs, Middle Eastern melodies. But gradually all that stopped. Was it the crisis? I don't know…'

George asked about his origins. He came from Edessa, she said, in Northern Greece. A landowning family with a big old village house a few miles from the town. He had an older brother and sister. The brother was an executive in a bank, the sister a university professor in Boston.

'Are the parents still alive?'

'I believe so.'

'Did they get on well with Keti?'
'She loved them!'
'And they loved her?'
'Just as much.'

It sounded almost improbably happy. He decided he he had better talk to them. She gave him their address.

As he wrote the word 'Edessa' he was reminded of something, but he could not remember what. He knew he had heard the town mentioned recently, but by whom? In what context? It was just out of reach. He checked back through the notebook where he wrote down the significant points of each day's work, names, addresses, phone numbers, connections, ideas, occasional mind maps. There were some notes he had made about the Hellenic Navy and the frogman special unit, his conversation with Dr Skouras, and further back the seven points Haris had given him about EAP... And there it was. One of the places where the family had property... If Paris's parents lived in Edessa, they might have some useful information. It gave him two reasons to go and visit them. Plus the fact that Edessa was near Pella, where those golden wreaths had been discovered. That was three reasons.

What to do about Zoe, however?

He told her his plan and asked if she felt like coming along. She said there was no need. She was feeling much better. In fact she was planning to call Dr Skouras and tell him, since he had asked.

George said, 'Please don't tell him I've gone to Edessa.'
'Why?' she asked, surprised.
'Just don't. It's a personal matter.'
'I don't like it when you don't explain,' she said.
George said, 'He might spoil things for me.'

'Intentionally?'

'No. I don't think so. Or maybe yes. I can't tell. Just don't mention it, OK?'

19 Edessa

George kept his car, a red Alfa Romeo Spider, in a garage on Ippokratous Street. In financial terms it made no sense, but there had to be more to life than the figures on a balance sheet. Reducing everything to numbers is an obsession of mankind; it generates wealth but ignores emotion, assigns false meanings and risks destroying life itself. This was why he had quit his job at the National Bank, and never missed its suffocating arithmetical atmosphere of complacency. How can you measure, in monetary terms, the summer air swirling around your head, the engine roaring in your ears? What numbers could possibly represent the open road? What units of currency? Five hundred dollars a minute? Ten million?

He knew what the car cost to run. He knew its price on the market. But he had never attempted to assess its importance to him. As well as a joy to drive, it was a relic of his youth. Just by sitting in it and turning on the ignition he felt connected to his younger self, as if the flowing petrol and flickering electric sparks were running through him and the engine were part of his soul.

With the country's economic crisis and the drop in his income, he would soon have to think again. You can only ignore money if you have enough of it. He was running short now. The Alfa was a luxury and he knew it. It might have to go, and with it all the pleasure it brought him.

It was also, as his friends pointed out, a bit conspicuous for a private detective's car.

The road north out of Athens was a gift from the European Union. A big modern highway, six lanes wide, it flew from Piraeus to Thessaloniki, ignoring the labyrinthine suburbs and pot-holed country lanes. It took an annoying S-shaped detour around the northern end of Evvia, past Lamia and Volos, before resuming its flight towards the north, but that was a small price to pay. The scenery was huge, majestic, a grand tour of Greek history and myth. Thebes, Thermopylae, Mount Olympus... He drove along shores mirrored in level sea, around mountains that dissolved in their own slate-blue shadows. He stopped to eat grilled squid in a waterside taverna at Arkitsa, drove on into the golden afternoon.

As he turned inland for Edessa he found himself among fertile hills, rich in vineyards and orchards. The town stood on a great cliff that reared abruptly from the lush valley floor, a rush of water spilling from its lip like an overflowing rain spout. He had a sudden immobilising sense of *déjà-vu,* a pang of memory from childhood that was fierce yet imprecise. When had he been here before?

Pulling the Alfa over to the side of the road, he closed his eyes and tried to let the memories return. At last a distant visit to an uncle and aunt presented itself to his mind, playing in a courtyard with a cousin, a boy in blue shorts and white shirt with slicked down hair. They had not known what to make of each other. His younger sister too, curly and blonde, more fun, more congenial. He could smell again the box hedges in the garden, taste the *krema* sprinkled with cinnamon which they served the children every afternoon after their siesta. He saw the town's river come shooting over the precipice, a wild white fall of water that he had wondered at as a boy, transfixed by its terrifying energy as it hurled itself into space.

He reached into the back for his overnight bag. Inside was his address book. Perhaps his cousins were still there?

He found the number and tried it. A recorded message told him the line was no longer in use. Perhaps not surprising after so many years. But he had an address too. He would try that.

On the way into town he was unpleasantly surprised to see election posters for the former Socialist Minister of Home Affairs, Byron Kakridis, now a convert to Syriza. Not a man that he wished to be reminded of, a crook and a bully who still owed him a few thousand euros and the country several million.The putridly handsome face grinned out with bogus benevolence from lampposts, walls and railings, promising a bright future despite the bankruptcy that he had done so much to create. Next to him were the posters for other candidates – New Democracy, Pasok, KKE, Golden Dawn. Kakridis had somehow beaten them all, been elected again, despite his lamentable record. George wondered how that had been achieved.

The Hotel Pindos, a converted private house, had just five guest rooms. It was in the old part of town, in a row of buildings along the cliff-top, with immense views fading into the haze across the plain.

The owner, a young man called Gavrilis, opened the shutters onto the balcony and said, 'You feel as if you're flying.'

George asked if the business felt that way too.

'No,' said Gavrilis decisively. 'We're struggling. No more weekenders from Thessaloniki, no one from Athens. A few travelling business people like yourself and the occasional foreigner who gets lost on a quest for Alexander the Great. Come downstairs and I'll make you coffee,' he said.

George followed him down to a big kitchen where rows of jars full of jam were set out on the table with a pile of labels in one corner.

'Fig jam,' said Gavrilis. 'For guests, friends, family – and for sale.'

'I'll buy one,' said George.

'More than one I hope,' said Gavrilis. 'Greek coffee or espresso?'

'Greek.'

'I'm glad you said that. It's since we learnt to drink Italian coffee that things have been ruined here.'

'You can't blame the coffee!'

'I don't. We're to blame. Importing everything. Now we even import debt!'

George said nothing. He was sick of talking politics.

Gavrilis stirred the coffee in the pot, waited for it to boil, then poured it into little white cups. He placed a small piece of *loukoumi* dusted with icing sugar on each saucer.

George asked him if he happened to know his cousins Aliki and Philippos Zafiris.

'Of course,' said Gavrilis. 'They had a beautiful house. One of the best in Edessa.'

'Are they still there?'

'No, they sold it and moved away.'

'Why?'

Gavrilis looked vague. 'They were trying to convert it into a hotel. But things went wrong.'

'What sort of things?'

'They handled it badly. Tried to go it alone, trod on people's toes, and the timing was wrong. Bang in the middle of the crisis.'

'Where are they now?'

'I don't know. France, I think. Or Canada.'

'Whose toes did they tread on?'

'Many people.' Gavrilis seemed uncomfortable. 'It was a great shame.'

'And the house?'

'Destroyed by fire.'

George nodded. 'A great shame indeed.'

After coffee, George walked into town to look for the Aliveris house.

It was not quite as he imagined it. In fact it was not a house at all, but an apartment in an expensive block. Underground garage, wide verandahs overflowing with plants, well-dressed couples entering and departing. He pressed the bell at the gate and a light came on. A video camera explored his face.

'Who's there?' asked an aged voice.

'George Zafiris, private investigator.'

'I don't know you.'

George began to explain but the light went out.

Annoyed, he rang again.

As soon as the light came on he was talking. 'Your son is in danger,' he said, 'I need to contact him urgently.'

'Our son is not here.'

'I know that, but I need to speak to him.'

'He has a telephone.'

'He doesn't answer when I call.'

'Then he doesn't want to hear from you.'

The light went out again.

George pressed the bell a third time. 'The police in Athens are looking for him.'

'So?'

'He seems to have left the city.'
'We don't know you.'
'Call Anna Kenteri. She'll tell you about me.' He repeated his name in case they had forgotten it.

The light went off again. George waited by the gate, thinking it must be a family tradition to keep people hanging about in the street. A humiliating business. It made him feel foolish, standing on a pavement talking into entry phones. At times like this he regretted giving up smoking. So much of Greek life is waiting. Cigarettes are its perfect partner. A way of turning the nation's vast reserves of energy into ash.

The light came on again. 'Are you there, Mr Zafiris?'
'I'm here.'
'We've spoken to Anna. She says you are investigating Keti's death.'
'Exactly.'
'So why do you want to speak to Paris?'
'I have a very good reason, but I'm not going to stand here talking into a machine.'
'We don't let strangers into the house.'
'Then meet me in a café in half an hour. The one in the public gardens, by the waterfall.'
'Very well. How will we recognise you?'
'I'll be at a table, alone, with a can of soda. I'm wearing a blue shirt.'
'Yes. I can see you at the gate. The shirt looks grey-blue rather than plain blue.'
'That's right. See you in half an hour.'

On the way to the gardens, walking through the streets in the shade of orange trees and cypresses, with doves burbling in the branches, George was disturbed by a call from Colonel Sotiriou.

The head of the Violent Crimes Squad was nonplussed to find him five hundred kilometres away and unable to meet. He had things to say. George encouraged him to say them. Sotiriou replied testily that some of what he had to say was not suitable for the telephone, but he could tell him that Keti Kenteri's phone had been found in the bushes on the Tourkovounia. This was a potential breakthrough. Technical experts were working on it, extracting and analysing the data. One thing stood out at once, however: a recorded conversation between Keti and her husband, in which he spoke angrily. It was not entirely clear when the recording was made but it might even have been immediately prior to her death.

'It looks as if you were right, Mr Zafiris,' the Colonel concluded. 'This is our evidence!'

George asked him what his next move would be.

'We are in touch with the Romanian police. They are already searching for him.'

His mind buzzing from Sotiriou's news, George took a seat in the public gardens and ordered a soda. As he watched the river flow through its concrete gully, hurrying towards the precipice, he asked himself how he could possibly put this matter to Paris's mother and father. Their son was a killer. There was little they could do to help, except persuade Paris to turn himself in, co-operate with the police, and hope to get a verdict of a crime of passion or – with medical help – a plea of insanity. It was not much of a prospect, but better than a life sentence for murder.

He had almost finished the soda when an old gentleman in a baggy brown suit approached his table. George stood up and shook hands.

The old man ordered lemonade – 'Loux if you have it, with

two ice cubes in the glass' – smiled kindly at George and asked how he could help.

George fumbled his way into the conversation. He tried to keep things general at first: Paris's character, his hopes and ambitions. The old man talked freely. He was a retired professor of music, mild in his manners, amusing, articulate, sensitive. 'For a nation that loves music, we are quite exceptionally cruel to our musicians,' he said. 'Very few can make a living. They must either teach, go commercial, or emigrate.' His description of his son, even allowing for a father's subjective view, was hard to square with the angry man he had met in Filothei, someone guilty of jealousy and murder. All his life until this tragedy, he had been admired and liked. Hard-working, helpful, magnanimous – 'animated by a profound Christian belief tempered by studies in Buddhism. He is very interested in the monastic tradition and its links with the east, through meditation and prayer...' George listened, neither believing nor disbelieving, finding here two different people. But he had seen photographs of Keti and met her sister. There flowed in those girls an electric charge of sexuality that could destroy a man's peace of mind and divide him from his better self, no matter how much he prayed and meditated.

He could not bring himself to tell the old man the truth. His pride, his happiness, his whole existence would be shattered.

George said, 'If Paris phones, you must ask him to contact me.' He handed over a card. 'He may be unwilling, but you should tell him it's for his own good.'

The old man suddenly stiffened. 'You have not said so explicitly, but is Paris a suspect?'

George replied carefully. 'As you know, the police always go first to the family. Then to friends. Very few people murder strangers. In any case running away is not a good plan. It's invariably taken as a sign of guilt.'

'He could be away on business.'

'Quite so,' said George. 'But in any case he should call me. The worst thing he can do is hide.'

'I will pass on the message,' said his father, a little sadly. 'If he calls.'

20 Alexander's Gold

The next morning, as he enjoyed a pot of black coffee and Gavrilis's fig jam on fresh bread, he studied the map of the region. If he set out soon he could get to both Vergina and Pella in one day. These were places he had long wanted to visit, but had never found the time. At Vergina a series of Macedonian tombs had been found in the 1970s. They included the probable tomb of King Philip II, father of Alexander the Great. Nearby at Pella stood the capital city of Alexander's empire. It was from a workshop near there that those exquisite gold wreaths had come. Whoever tried to export them to America in a coffin must have had access to those finds.

It occurred to him that he could approach the problem from the top or the bottom of the hierarchy. Usually the higher the functionary the more forked the tongue. With knowledge and position came suspicion and a taste for intrigue. Whereas from the workers and assistants you got something closer to the truth – if they knew it.

Gavrilis was interested in his plans and advised him to visit his Uncle Thanasi, who ran a taverna in Pella. 'He knows everyone.'

George set off, full of hope. The Alfa was running well, the day was warm, and he drove with the hood down. He reached Vergina after an hour, parked in the empty car park, and walked over to the archaeological site.

The tombs lay under a low hill. In a dark, theatrical atmosphere the treasures were exhibited in isolated pools of light. Bronze weapons, chariots, drinking bowls, tripods, lamps and figurines. In one cabinet were the grave goods of Philip: a golden chest for his bones, with a sixteen pointed star on its lid. An iron breastplate banded with gold. An ivory head, with that bearded warrior face, one-eyed, crafty, forceful, weary. Beside it a golden wreath bristling with oak leaves and acorns, delicate as new blossom. A miracle of craftsmanship. According to the catalogue this wreath, the heaviest and most elaborate ever found from the ancient world, had slight scorch marks, with acorns and leaves missing. 'It was evidently on the head of the king as the flames began to lick around his bier, hastily snatched off by the priest before it could be destroyed, to be buried with the ashes of his bones washed with wine and wrapped in a rich purple cloth, exactly following the rituals of burial described in Homer's *Iliad*.'

Intrigued by the place, George bought a book by its excavator, Manolis Andronicos. A legendary figure now, who twenty years ago had joined the unseen world that he spent his life investigating. His photo on the inner cover – goatee beard, heavy black glasses, pensive gaze – seemed to defy death, or look beyond it.

As he bought the book George tried to engage the museum guardian in conversation. The man was polite but said little. George learned that visitor numbers were down this year, and that pay for museum staff had been cut by sixty per cent in the past seven years, all thanks to 'the never-ending crisis'. His attitude, however, was calm and resigned: 'We got ourselves into this fix and we have to get ourselves out of it. A solution will be found. We can't let ten million people starve.'

Returning to his car, George noticed a black Skoda on the far side of the car park. Two men sat inside, their windows rolled down, smoking and chatting. They had not come into the archaeological site and George wondered what they were doing there. Perhaps waiting for someone? It was an odd place to wait. But they showed no interest in him, and he drove off.

At Pella he found another site, as deserted and extraordinary as Vergina. Here was a recently built museum, spacious, elegant, with arrays of objects from everyday life: furniture, tools, pottery, mosaics, laid out as if in a private home. The guardians were a pair of young mothers, deeply absorbed in a conversation about their problems. 'Something's wrong,' said one, a big girl with a mass of black hair, heavy eye make-up and pale skin. 'We work, cook, clean the house, do the shopping, take care of the children, deal with our crazy mothers-in-law, then we have to look great on Saturday night and be ready for sex. Any time, day or night, no matter how we feel – tired, worried or depressed – and enjoy it! Be inventive! But where did the liberated woman go? What happened to her? Are we liberated or just worse enslaved?'

The other one, blonde and petite, with sharp dark eyes, maintained quietly and insistently that at least with a university degree and a job she felt able to stand up for herself. 'In the old days we had no such rights.'

George interrupted to ask about the people in charge of finds.

'Thessaloniki,' said the blonde one. 'The Inspectorate. It's all controlled from there.'

He bought a few postcards, asked for directions to Thanasi's taverna and drove to the nearby village. The taverna was on the square, its owner was expecting him.

Over lunch he was treated to the local gossip. Thanasi enjoyed telling stories. The news about the missing gold was well known here, even though it was supposed to be restricted information. No one could say who was responsible or how the gold had been smuggled out, but a new Inspector of Antiquities had been appointed in Thessaloniki and had promised to get to the bottom of it. In Thanasi's view this was unlikely to happen, as the Inspector was a political appointment 'with no idea of anything except the Party and the socialist paradise it was supposed to be creating'. Unfortunately, he added, the Greek people had been stupid enough to give these charlatans their vote and so they were now setting about the destruction of the country. 'The socialist paradise,' he added, 'is nothing but jobs for the Party members and a general obliteration of the economy.'

'Do these people come and eat here?' asked George.

'Who?'

'Inspectors of Antiquities, Party officials?'

'Of course! Everyone comes here.'

George considered this.

'When I think about that gold,' he said, 'the way it was stacked in the coffin, probably for export...'

'Definitely for export!'

'...it seems to me that an archaeologist in Pella, or a storeman with a key, or whoever it was on the spot, cannot possibly have organised all this in isolation. There must be an art dealer, a high-class smuggler, a middleman of some kind with international contacts who knows where to sell these things. Which can't be easy, because we're talking about stolen goods.'

'That's true,' said Thanasi. 'There's always a middleman.'

'Any idea who that might be?'
Thanasi frowned. 'Local? Or national?'
'Do you have anyone in mind?'
'I don't mix with people like that.'
'You said everybody comes here. I thought this would be an ideal place – out of the way, plenty of good material…'

Thanasi was distracted. Two men had come in and sat down at the far side of the taverna.

'Hold on. I have customers.'

Thanasi went over to take their order, which was briskly given, without any conversational preamble. They obviously knew each other, but there was no friendliness. Thanasi hurried through to the kitchen looking preoccupied. The two men lit cigarettes.

George observed them quietly. They looked like provincial businessmen, cynical and complacent. They were not talking. He glanced away down the street and was surprised to see the black Skoda, parked right behind his Alfa.

'What were we saying?'
Thanasi was back.
'The middleman.'
He smirked. 'You could start with those two.'
'Really? Who are they?'
'They work for a big local boss.'
'Name?'
'He's known as *O Kokoras*.'
'The Cock? What's that about?'
'I don't know. Status I expect.'
'Real name?'
'Not spoken aloud.'
'But you know it?'

'If I do I won't say.'

'Is he independent or part of a network?'

'Who knows?'

'What about these two? What do they do?'

'Business.' He spoke the word contemptuously.

'Is there any chance they're following me?'

'Why do you ask?'

'I saw them at Vergina, in the car park. It seems a strange coincidence.'

'How would they know about you?'

'That's it…'

'It depends what your business is. What is it, by the way?'

'Not really business,' said George. 'My friend Mario Filiotis was Mayor of Astypalea. It was his coffin that was found to be filled with gold from Pella. His family want to know where his body went.'

'And you came here to find out?'

George nodded.

'Bravo…' Thanasi seemed impressed. 'It's one hell of a long way from Astypalea.'

'I've come from Athens.'

'Still a long way. How's it going?'

'This is my first day.'

Thanasi nodded thoughtfully. 'Gavrilis somehow got the idea you were a salesman.'

'Really? How did he work that out?'

'Used to be in sales himself. Anyone he likes, he thinks they're in sales.'

'Fair enough.'

'So what *is* your business?'

'I'm an investigator.'

Thanasi's eyebrows shot up. 'Insurance, police, private?'

'Private.'

'Oh… That explains your interest in the gold.'

'I told you. Mario was my friend. My dear friend.'

'I understand.'

But Thanasi seemed troubled and distracted. He glanced over his shoulder. 'Give me a few minutes. I need to give those guys their food.'

'Why are they here?'

'I'll tell you in a while.'

George waited. Thanasi hurried into the kitchen, came out with glasses, wine and food on a tray, and, with a glance in George's direction, sat down to talk to the two men. They spoke in undertones but the body language was clear. They were putting Thanasi under pressure. He gesticulated. They stared at him coldly. He talked rapidly. They looked bored. At last, with an exasperated shrug of his shoulders, Thanasi stood up and walked into the kitchen. The two men began picking at their food.

George waited a while longer. He checked his watch. Four o'clock. Time to go. Thanasi had not reappeared, so he went to the kitchen to find him.

An argument was raging. A woman, presumably Thanasi's wife, was saying, 'I'll put poison in their food!'

'Don't be so stupid,' said Thanasi.

'I'll do it. You watch me.'

George said, 'Excuse me, Thanasi, I'd like to pay the bill.'

Thanasi turned, his cheeks flushed with anger.

'OK,' he said. 'Just give me two minutes.'

Thanasi's wife slipped past him, muttering, 'I'm going to talk to those bastards.'

'No, Rena, don't do that!'

She was already out of the door.

'I've got to stop her,' he said and hurried past.

George followed them. Rena had already started giving the men a verbal savaging. They tried to maintain a look of indifference, but they were clearly alarmed.

'You two are a disgrace! You know what business is like these days. How many customers do you see here? One? Two? So what the hell do you want? Go and do some honest work! We have nothing more to give! Nothing, do you hear? You can tell Kokoras from me that if he comes here again, or sends you, I'm going to kill him. Do you understand? I'll tear his eyes out and then I'll kill him!'

'Don't talk like that,' said one of the men. 'The boss...'

'The boss! I know where he lives and I'll go there personally with a knife and stick it in his heart. Just watch me.'

The other man said, 'Stop it, Rena. This is not a joke. You know how it works.'

'It doesn't work any more! Can't you see that? Everything's going to pieces. Even your shitty business.'

'Let's go,' said the other, pushing back his chair.

'I'll kill you too! Both of you!'

Ignoring her, they made for the street.

Thanasis watched them go, his face pale with worry.

'You shouldn't talk to them like that,' he said.

'They can go to hell and so can you! They can't do anything to us.'

'They can close us down just like that.'

'Then where do they get their payments? Wake up, Thanasi! They're not stupid.'

'You shouldn't threaten them.'

'They don't frighten me. I'll kill them if they come back.'

Thanasis turned to George. 'I'm sorry,' he said. 'This is a very difficult time for us.'

'I can see that,' said George.
'Rena gets upset…'
'Rightly.'
'But it's not a solution.'
'Don't be so sure,' said George.
'These guys are trouble.'
'They only exist because we allow them to,' said Rena furiously.

Thanasis shook his head. 'If you saw what they've done to others. Restaurants burnt down, windows smashed, robberies. It's not as easy as that.'

'They need us, Thanasi! If we die, they die! Get that into your head!'

It was dark by the time he left the taverna. The three of them sat, drinking coffee and *tsipouro,* lamenting the state of the country. George learned how Kokoras operated, lending money, calling in favours, threatening, corrupting, destroying. His two enforcers were feared and hated across the region.

George wondered if there were connections to his cousins and their hotel. The couple knew of no such schemes, but it would not be surprising. Anything to do with building and property was up his street.

And archaeology? Selling stolen goods?

'Why not?' said Rena. 'Property is dead, let's face it. He has to find new ways to make money. Drugs, arms dealing, he probably does the lot. Refugees will be his next thing. You watch.'

George drove back to the hotel and made phone calls to Zoe and Dimitri in Athens. All seemed to be well there. Then he rang Haris and asked him to find out what he could about the illegal trade in antiquities. See if someone called *Kokoras* was ever mentioned. He could almost hear Haris rubbing his hands.

'With pleasure!' he said.

George went downstairs to the bar. Gavrilis was deep in a telephone conversation, which he interrupted for George to order a bottle of beer and a plate of bread, cheese and smoked sausage.

'Here or in your room?' asked Gavrilis.

'My room,' said George.

'I'll send it right up.'

George left him to his call, and went back up the stairs. The place was silent, and he could hear Gavrilis's voice, though he spoke softly, over the sound of his footsteps.

Five minutes later there was a knock on the door. An elderly lady stood with a tray on the threshold.

'Thank you,' said George. 'Where is Gavrilis?'

'He's gone out.'

He poured a glass of beer and settled down to read his new book.

He was soon absorbed in the drama of the Vergina excavations. A young French archaeologist, Léon Heuzey, had first found the palace at Vergina while wandering in northern Greece in 1855. He had returned to dig there for six weeks with a gang of sailors in 1861 and written a book about his discoveries, *Mission Archéologique de Macédoine,* published in Paris in 1876. This contained prophetic words: 'Whatever the name of this unknown city, the importance of its ruins for Macedonia will be comparable to those of Pompeii.' The site was ignored by archaeologists and continued to be used as a source of building materials by local villagers for the next sixty years. Subsequent excavations were slow and intermittent. In the early 1950s, Andronicos had started working there alone, acting as 'draughtsman, photographer, accountant and foreman' as well as archaeologist. In 1957 he brought along students and university staff as volunteers. They explored the city, its temples and cemetery, sensing its grandeur but unable to get a historical fix. Then in 1976 the site yielded a spectacular find: the tomb of a king – almost certainly that of Philip II of Macedonia, father of Alexander the Great. The city must surely be his capital, Aegae. Andronicos, a scholar of the highest order, permitted himself a moment of speculation: he was sure that some obscure force, beyond rational understanding, had guided him.

For George, engaged in excavations of a different kind, there was a mysterious satisfaction in this story.

21 Into the City

Next morning he drove to Thessaloniki. A good fast country road, through golden autumn landscapes. Then a jumble of petrol stations, body repair shops, supermarkets and bathroom stores before he came into the old city: the long, curved promenade gazing south into the sea, the hills studded with churches and synagogues with red-tiled roofs.

He had an appointment with the Deputy Inspector of Antiquities, Dr Mylona, in a building beside the Archaeological Museum. She kept him waiting three quarters of an hour with no apology; a middle-aged woman with yellow skin and a worn, distracted, self-pitying air. She must have possessed an office of her own, but she chose to meet him in a corridor where staff came and went to make coffee, smoke and chat. Four office doors were open onto their conversation. There was no question of privacy.

George explained what he was trying to discover: the trail that led from an ancient goldsmith's workshop in Pella to a funeral parlour in Brooklyn and a graveyard in Astypalea.

Dr Mylona listened with no sign of interest. She frowned. Then sighed deeply. This was a complex issue, she declared. Many questions arose, with many obstacles to answering them.

George asked her to expand on this. Again she frowned.

The matter was under police investigation, she said. Moreover the objects had not been officially catalogued, so their physical dimensions, condition, provenance, status, etc, were not defined. An undefined object obviously cannot be the subject of an inquiry. Unfortunately there would be a delay in defining the objects, as the department had been re-organised by ministerial decree, with the Byzantine and Classical Inspectorates in the process of being combined into one. In the present economic crisis, staff numbers were being reduced and everything was moving more slowly than usual. In addition the archaeologist with responsibility for Pella was currently unavailable – she was on extended leave, with health and family problems. The documents in her office could not of course be touched because of the investigation. Dr Mylona was unable to say anything about the police enquiries at the Inspectorate as these were a separate and confidential business. Was there, she asked with an exhausted look, anything else she could help him with?

George said there was. As far as he understood, the objects found in Mario's coffin had been remarkably similar to a number of treasures unearthed by Professor Andronicos at Vergina in 1976. What did she think of this?

Dr Mylona winced at this. '*Similar* is a very approximate term!' she said irritably. 'Perhaps one might say there are *certain similarities*, but similar overall? That would be overstating it.'

'It was the opinion of one of your colleagues.'

'I cannot answer for a colleague!'

'Have you seen the objects in question?'

She hesitated before answering. 'I have seen photographs,' she said.

'What surprises me,' said George, 'is the number of these things. The golden wreaths were thought to be individual masterpieces, created specially for King Philip and his Queen. Why was this workshop creating multiple versions of them?'

'Possibly for export? Or some non-funerary use?'

'Such as?'

'Crowning victors in battle, or in civic games?'

'It seems odd to use royal wreaths. Golden ones too!'

'Gold became more plentiful following Alexander's conquests.'

'Perhaps it did, but still, most ancient wreaths for athletic and military honours were made of laurel and olive leaves, which cost nothing to make. It's a big jump from that to gold.'

For a moment, the archaeologist became animated. 'I see you have been doing some research,' she said. 'But remember, these might also be Roman. We know that the Emperor Nero liked to take part in Greek games. Naturally he won every event. He may well have insisted on golden wreaths.'

'How much time separates Alexander the Great from Nero?'

'About four centuries.'

'Can you date the objects precisely?'

The frown returned. 'That's difficult. The question of dating is one of many which we are hoping to study. But with a shortage of staff, budget cuts and a workload that just seems to go on increasing we are extremely restricted in what we can do.'

'I understand. It must be very frustrating.'

'I have not been much help.'

George waved away the apology. 'You have already told me a lot,' he said.

She reacted with a jolt of surprise. Really? She felt that she had not told him very much at all. No, George insisted, this had all been most revealing.

Dr Mylona was nonplussed. He could see her replaying the

conversation in her mind, to find the scrap of useful information that she might, by some terrible oversight, have allowed to escape. George stood up, and at once turned sideways to allow a man in a lab coat to hurry past. He was about to leave when a final question occurred to him.

'Do you know of anyone, locally or elsewhere, who deals in these treasures?'

Dr Mylona shuddered. 'I cannot begin to answer that! Such barbaric people must exist, but I have never come across them. Not consciously at least. It's a crime, as I'm sure you know, to buy and sell antiquities.'

'I know,' said George, eyeing her firmly. 'A serious crime. One possible explanation for the presence of these items in a coffin is that they were intended for illegal export.'

'I have no doubt about that!'

'The question is, who in Thessaloniki organises this trade.'

'I am not the person to ask.'

'Then who is?'

She seemed astonished by the question. 'This is absolutely not my field! Go to the police. Or to the *antiquaires* in the old town. They must have a circuit…'

'You've never had any contact with these people?'

'Absolutely not! I'm a scholar, Mr Zafiris! Those people are traders in illegal goods. You might as well ask me if I can recommend a drug dealer.'

George noted the aggressive character of her indignation and wondered if it was a sign of guilt. He thanked her for her time – although she had given little enough of it – and left the shadow of the building for the glare of the street.

His next stop was the undertakers. The address was not far from the archaeological museum, but their shop was closed.

A notice taped to the window gave a telephone number for inquiries. George called it and left a message on the answering machine. He tried asking in the shops nearby whether the owner had been seen recently. Not for a few days was the answer. Was this unusual? It was. They were normally open every day. When he asked further questions he met the inevitable suspicion. What do you want them for? Is there some kind of problem? Has someone died? Who are you?

Frustrated in his quest, George walked along the seafront until he found a café without the distracting frazzle of pop music where he could sit and think. He ordered a bottle of beer and a *mezé* of grilled octopus, opened his notebook and jotted down some thoughts. He had drawn a blank on archaeology, but that was probably peripheral. He doubted whether Mario's death had anything to do with smuggled goods. Much more likely was a connection with the mysterious project he was setting up with Dr Skouras – probably something medical – but until he knew more he could go no further with that line of thought.

Finally there was Paris. George hoped the musician would be in touch with his father soon, and that his message would be passed on.

On impulse he decided to call the old music professor, who said, 'As it happens, I have just been speaking to my son.'

'Did you tell him to get in touch with me?'

'I did.'

'And?'

'He was unwilling.'

'Did he say why?'

'He described you as aggressive.'

'Really? Zealous perhaps, but…'

'No. *Aggressive* was his word.'

'I see. And what did you say?'

'I encouraged him to contact you all the same. For the reasons you gave me.'

'That was kind of you. Is he back in Greece?'

'Not yet.'

'Do you know when he's coming back?'

'This evening.'

'To you or to Athens?'

'Neither.'

'So where?'

'He's planning to go to Mount Athos.'

Mount Athos? George immediately thought the worst. The Athos peninsula, known as the Holy Mountain, was extraterritorial: physically part of Greece but legally separate, an ecclesiastical domain beyond the reach of state law. Within its twenty monasteries it was said to harbour several criminals who preferred a life of prayer and fasting to the confinement of prison.

'Did he say why he's going there?'

'He goes every year.'

'Which monastery?'

'I don't know… although…' The professor seemed to hesitate. 'Mr Zafiris I am not entirely happy with the way this conversation is going.'

'I'm sorry. Why is that?'

'I have to be sure that you are not seeking to entrap him or endanger him.'

'He's endangering himself by hiding. I think I made that clear.'

'Do you suspect him of killing Keti?'

George felt unable to reply.

'Tell me straight, Mr Zafiris! Do you suspect him of killing

Keti?...Your silence is ominous.'

'There is evidence...'

'Evidence! Why don't you answer me directly?'

'I am trying to do that. There is evidence that links him to her death. There may be an innocent explanation for it, but that evidence and his behaviour – disappearing to Bucharest, his hostility to questions, now going off to the Holy Mountain – this combination suggests guilt. If he's innocent he must come forward and explain himself.'

'Who possesses this evidence?'

'The police.'

'I see...'

'And they will go after him.'

'If they know where to go.'

'That's right.'

The professor sighed. 'I find myself in an impossible position,' he said. 'I can't tell you any more.'

'I understand.'

George ended the call and watched the traffic go by, ghostly in the sun's glare. The father's impossible position was one thing, the death of an innocent woman another. He telephoned Anna.

'Did Paris ever go to Mount Athos?'

'Every year.'

'Do you happen to know which monastery?'

'Osiou Grigoriou.'

'He has friends there?'

'I believe so. And a spiritual adviser. Why do you ask? Have you found him?'

'Still looking. But this might give me a lead.'

Driving back into Edessa that afternoon, he got a call from Haris. He pulled over and opened his notebook. Haris had two names to give him: Christophe Lakiotis, based in Geneva, and Philip Ventouris, based in New York. Both dealers in antiquities. The similarity of the New York dealer's name struck him at once. Ventouris and Medouris were almost identical. Haris had noticed this too.

'OK,' said George. 'Tell me what else. These two deal in Greek artefacts?'

'They're well known for it. Top end of the market. Christie's, Sotheby's, Dorotheum…'

'Do they compete or work together?'

'Both.'

'They must have agents in Greece?'

'Surely.'

'Can you contact them? Find out how they operate?'

'How am I going to do that?'

George hesitated. 'I'm not sure. Try to sell them something?'

'Like what?'

'Those golden wreaths that were in Mario's coffin.'

'No chance,' said Haris. 'If they're any good they'll know exactly what happened to those things. They'll see through me straight away.'

'You could say you have some other material from the same source.'

'That's even worse! I don't even know what the source was.'

'Maybe try an indirect approach?'

'Listen, Zafiris, these are hasty ideas. You can't bluff with the big boys. We need something fresh, something really tempting. Let me work on it.'

'OK, Haris. You work on it. Call me when you're ready.'

22 Kokoras I

Driving into Edessa he saw signs for the hospital and on impulse decided to take a look. It was an impressive new building on the edge of town, surrounded by a vast car park, unfinished but already in use. Doctors hurried through the enormous lobby where wires poked out of bare plaster walls. Patients and visitors wandered about looking lost. A deserted information desk offered no help. Only the bar, a lively little room stacked with sandwiches, bottles and cakes, made any sense.

George walked in and ordered coffee from the barman, a stout bearded fellow with long curly hair who broke off a phone conversation to serve him.

'Is this the only hospital in town?' asked George.
'You want two?' said the barman with a loud laugh.
'I didn't know about this one.'
'It's new.'
'I can see that. Is there an old one?'
'In the centre.'
'What's happened to that?'
'Finished. Demolition job.'
'And private hospitals?'
'In Edessa? You're joking.'
'If I wanted to find a private hospital, where would I have

to go?'

The barman shrugged his shoulders. 'Ioannina? Thessaloniki?'

George took a sip of coffee.

'Are there any plans to build a private hospital?' he asked.

'I don't know. You should ask at the Town Hall.'

'I thought you might have heard something.'

'If you need a hospital, why not come here? It's good. And it's free.'

George waved away the suggestion. The man regarded him strangely. 'Unless you have some rare disease that needs the top specialists.'

'It's OK,' said George, 'there's nothing wrong with me.'

'So what's the problem?'

'No problem at all.'

'Then why are you interested?'

George was starting to wish he had never started this conversation. 'It's my work,' he said vaguely.

With a sharp look the barman said, 'Really? What's your business?'

'Construction.'

The barman seemed satisfied.

'This one doesn't look quite finished,' said George.

'It's not. The contractor's still waiting for the final payment, the government's bust, you know the rest.'

'Who's the contractor?'

The barman stopped what he was doing. 'Why do you want to know that?'

'I'm just asking.'

'I don't believe that.'

George shrugged his shoulders. 'It makes no difference. Must be public knowledge anyway.'

'There's only one contractor for big jobs like this. If you were local you'd know that.'

'I'm just visiting.'

'Then don't ask too many questions.'

'How about a few names?'

The barman did not reply. He began unpacking glasses from the dishwasher.

'Well?'

'There are names, but some are public and some are not. I don't want to get it wrong.'

'Is Kokoras one of them?'

The barman gave him a heavy look. 'If you know that name,' he said, 'you're not as ignorant as you make out.'

'Is he one of them?'

'Why don't you ask him yourself?'

'How would I do that?'

'He's over there in the lobby. In the red shirt.'

George glanced over his shoulder and saw a heavily built man in his sixties, red-faced, dressed like a farmer: check shirt, baggy jeans, workman's boots.

'That's Kokoras?'

'Don't tell him I told you.'

George put a ten-euro note on the counter.

'Thank you,' he said. 'Keep the change.'

Kokoras did not look pleased to be accosted.

George put on a smile and chanced it. 'George Zafiris, International Health Care,' he said. 'We met a couple of years ago.'

The other man's eyes narrowed. 'International Health Care. What the hell is that?'

'We build clinics and medical facilities worldwide.'

'What are you doing here?'

'I'm here for private reasons, but I just saw you and thought I'd say hello, it's Mr...?'

'I don't know you or your company.'

'We talked about joint ventures in Greece.'

'I don't remember.'

'I remember it clearly. Here in Edessa, also in Ioannina and Thessaloniki.'

'Must have been pre-crisis.'

'It was. But my company is still interested. They take a long view.'

Kokoras gave a twisted smirk. 'Good luck to them!'

George battled on. 'With Greece at the bottom of a cycle, the prices are low and the opportunities big. That's the way we see it. But everyone here is so depressed they think it's going to stay like this forever. We need people with vision, with connections, who can lift us out of this mess. I have foreign investors ready to go in.'

Past the mean and suspicious glint in the man's eyes George could see that something was registering.

'Give me your card,' said Kokoras coldly.

'I don't have one with me. But I'm staying at a little place in town, the Pindos Hotel. You can catch me there this evening.'

'Your name again?'

'George Zafiris. And yours?'

'I'll get someone to call you,' said Kokoras. 'And don't ask my name again.'

'I've forgotten it, I'm sorry...'

'No, you haven't forgotten, because you never knew it. Now leave me alone, I'm busy.'

George took him at his word. As he walked out of the lobby into the blazing sunshine, he wondered uneasily if he had just done something stupid. It would not take Kokoras long to find out he was lying. Then what? He didn't like to think what might happen next. He unlocked his Alfa, started the engine and backed out of his parking space, still wondering. Then he noticed the black Skoda waiting.

In the seven minutes it took him to drive back to the hotel, the Skoda in his mirror all the way, George forced himself to think of a plan. He needed a hell of a good story, or a plausible threat, to see him through.

'Gavrilis,' he said, as he picked up his key, 'can you make me a coffee?'

'Of course. Right now?'

'In ten minutes. I just need to make a phone call.'

He went up to his room and opened the shutters. Down in the street he saw the Skoda parked a few spaces behind the Alfa. Staying at the window, watching the Skoda, he telephoned Sotiriou.

The Colonel was sceptical. He could see no connection between Kokoras and Mario, only suppositions. George said that was not the point. He just wanted to know that he would be protected if Kokoras turned vicious. Again the Colonel gave nothing away. 'You are protected as an ordinary citizen,' was all he would say.

George replied angrily, 'I'm just telling you where the hell I've gone if you can't find me.'

'That's noted,' said Sotiriou. 'Let us know if you find anything.'

George was still fuming when he walked into the kitchen. Gavrilis was charging the coffee machine.

'I need to go back to the conversation we had about my

cousins,' said George. 'You said they trod on people's toes. Was one of those people Kokoras?'

Instead of replying, Gavrilis asked, 'Where did you hear that name?'

'I seem to hear it everywhere.'

Gavrilis frowned. 'Is it just your cousins or some other matter that concerns you?'

'What began with my cousins now seems part of a larger problem.'

'Why don't you tell me about it?'

'I don't want to compromise you.'

'That's not an issue.'

'I think it could very well be.'

'I promise you it's not.'

George thought about this. Gavrilis seemed to enjoy a privileged connection to this man. He told him what he had told Thanasi. Then he added, 'I've just met Kokoras, and his men followed me here.'

Gavrilis listened gravely. Then said, 'I don't think you have a problem. Unless you're trying to pin a specific crime on him, of course?'

'I don't pin crimes on innocent people,' said George.

'OK, so you think he's guilty…'

'My mind is open. But when I hear the words *construction* and *public works,* or I see men putting the frighteners on a couple running a taverna, I fear the worst.'

'He's not a bad man,' said Gavrilis pensively.

'You know him then?'

'Everyone knows him.'

'But you better than most…'

'Why do you say that?'

'I sense a connection.'

Gavrilis did not reply directly. 'The problem with Kokoras is that he sometimes keeps bad company.'

'For example?'

Gavrilis said nothing.

'People who keep bad company eventually become bad themselves,' said George.

'Let me call someone,' Gavrilis said and stood up. He went into the next room and closed the door.

George waited until he returned, still with an unsettled expression.

'I've explained what you're doing,' he said.

'To Kokoras?'

His mouth tightened.

'I'll take that as a yes,' said George. 'What did he say?'

'He has nothing to hide.'

'What about the company he keeps?'

'I didn't ask about that.'

'How did he react when you told him about me?'

'He said he knew at once you were lying.'

'OK... So how does that leave us?'

'He's happy to let the matter drop.'

'That's big of him. And if not?'

Gavrilis tensed again. 'There's no *if not.*'

'What do you mean?'

'I mean you should not even think that thought.'

'I've already thought it.'

Gavrilis shook his head. 'You have to get one thing clear. Kokoras is a provincial businessman. No more no less. To survive he has to be connected. He doesn't ask too many questions, and it's best if you don't either.'

'Connected? With whom?'

'I have no idea. But I repeat: stop asking questions. He

can't help you. Nor can I.'

'Tell me what the problem is.'

'Oh come on!'

'No,' said George, 'I'd like you to spell it out.'

'OK. It threatens his business.'

'Only if that business is illegal.'

'No! His whole model is at risk. It's a system. Break one part and the whole thing fails.'

'In other words, mafia.'

'Kokoras is not mafia! And he's a hell of a lot better than the alternatives.'

'What evidence do you have for that?'

'Plenty.'

'Give me an example.'

'You'll have to take my word.'

'I saw how Thanasi and his wife were treated,' said George. 'That did not look like the work of a man with a conscience.'

'He won't press them any further. He knows they're in difficulties.'

George bridled at this. 'What business does he have pressing them in the first place? He runs a protection racket!'

'If we lived in an organised country like Sweden,' said Gavrilis, 'I would agree. But things are different here. It's a jungle. You know that. Everyone needs protection.'

George laughed bitterly. 'Only from the so-called protectors!'

Gavrilis did not seem amused. 'If you keep asking questions, Mr Zafiris, you will get into trouble.'

'Like my friend Mario?'

'I don't know about your friend Mario. I'm talking about you.'

George considered this. It was getting interesting. A threat, no less.

'I appreciate what you're telling me,' he said.

'That's wise,' said Gavrilis.

'If you could tell me the names of the people Kokoras deals with –'

'You've got to be joking!'

'No. I mean it… I can leave him and you out of it.'

Gavrilis seemed exasperated. 'You must be crazy. Even if I knew I wouldn't tell you.'

'Do you know?'

'Absolutely not!'

'I don't believe you.'

'It makes no difference. I'll prepare your bill.'

'I'm not leaving today.'

'Yes you are.'

'I was planning…'

'Forget your plans. It's time to go.'

'I see. If I move to another hotel…?'

'You'll find they're full.'

'Really? Your friend Mr Kokoras takes no risks.'

Gavrilis nodded. 'That's his style. And by the way he's not my friend.'

'Oh? A relative perhaps?'

Gavrilis smiled, an image of innocent goodwill. 'Never mind what he is to me. The important thing is not to be his enemy.'

23 The Holy Mountain

Like a weakening radio signal, the authority of Kokoras faded out sixty kilometres east of Edessa. It held good up to that point, however. George tried twice in quiet provincial hotels – shuttered, deserted, their owners deep in a narcosis of boredom and idleness – only to be told that every room was full. In the end, beyond the circle of his power, he found a guest house in a village where they let him stay the night. When he asked if there was a *taverna* nearby the owner's wife said no, but she offered him a share of their supper – cockerel stewed in red wine, *kokoras krasatos,* which George took as a sign from God. Next morning, after a cup of coffee, a rusk and a piece of cheese, he continued east for Mount Athos.

He had no idea what to expect when he arrived. Images flitted through his mind: monasteries clinging like swallows' nests to cliffs above the sea, bearded young monks in whitewashed cells, candle-lit chapels, mule tracks through the forest. He did not expect an office stamping visitors' permits with brusque efficiency. Or a sea journey in a rumbling old *kaïki*, with monks chatting to the pilgrims, a prayer book in one pocket, a phone in the other. They called in at several places: a little wooden jetty by a wooded beach, a solid stone harbour built out from a vast fortress-like monastery, a quayside with ramshackle sheds and a train of mules being unloaded by the water's edge. Grigoriou was the fourth stop. When the *kaïki* tied up, three other travellers jumped off with him. They climbed a steep, stone-paved ramp to the monastery gate, its massive wooden doors standing open. Below them the sounds of the slapping waves grew fainter while the *kaïki's* engine thudded away.

A handsome ginger-haired monk with an eastern European accent welcomed them and walked with them to their dormitory. He gave them the timetable for meals and church services, and said, 'Don't leave any valuables in this room. We have recovering drug addicts working here and we don't like to tempt them.' He walked off briskly, leaving the visitors to unpack.

'What happens now?' said one of them.

'I'm going to have a cigarette,' said another.

'Let's go together.'

That left one other man in the room with George, a sallow, droopy fellow, who glanced nervously at him three or four times, as if sizing him up.

'They shouldn't smoke here,' he said. 'Shame on them. It's not respectful.'

George shrugged his shoulders. He couldn't care less if they smoked or not. He was more concerned about finding Paris Aliveris.

'Have you been here before?' he asked.

'Many times.' The man offered his hand. 'My name is Stephanos. I'm from Preveza.'

'George. Athens.'

'Ah, Athens.' There was an almost accusing note to this. 'Athens, Athens…'

George sensed that this man had problems. Best to keep the

conversation light.

'So what does one do now?' George asked. 'It's three hours till supper.'

'Oh there's plenty to do. Walk, think, read, talk to one of the Holy Fathers...'

'Where would I find them?'

'They're all around. It's a working monastery, so there will be some in the vegetable garden, some in the kitchen, some repairing the buildings, some praying or studying or taking confession. Are you here for a special reason?'

'Meeting a friend,' said George.

'A monk?'

'No, a visitor. In fact I'm wondering how to contact him.'

'How about his phone?'

'Is there a signal?'

'Should be.'

George checked his phone, and found to his surprise that the signal was strong.

'I can show you round,' said Stephanos. 'We'll probably meet him.'

George said, 'I would appreciate that.'

They walked up through a series of courtyards, past the chapel, the refectory and kitchens, the library, offices and cells. Solidly built, monumental, well-maintained. Beyond all these lay immense gardens and orchards, terraced and fertile, tended by monks with their cassocks tucked into the belts of their trousers. Among them, labouring with a less willing air, were a dozen civilians, scrawny young men that you might see begging in the streets of cities. These, said Stephanos, were the 'children reclaimed by God'.

They began to talk. In this unworldly medieval atmosphere George already felt disconnected from the rest of his existence.

Work, family, home – he found himself mentioning these as if they belonged to someone else. He was not allowed to talk for long, however. It soon became clear that Stephanos had a story he was burning to tell.

'I was a school teacher in Preveza,' he said. 'I taught biology and gymnastics. But I lost my job.'

George said nothing.

'Do you want to know how I lost my job?'

George did not want to know. He said nothing.

'I lost it because I made sexual advances to a fifteen-year-old girl.'

George's heart sank.

'I was helping her recover from an injury. I'm a qualified physiotherapist as well. I had to adjust her posture, help her to straighten her back, her neck... The fact is she led me on.'

'Really?' George could not prevent himself objecting. 'That sounds like an excuse.'

'No, she did. Definitely. She was a little *poutana*. But I should have been in control of the situation, and I wasn't. I kissed her.'

'That was a mistake.'

'It certainly was. Not on the mouth! Just once, lightly, on the back of her neck. She reported me, there was an inquiry, and my career was finished.'

'I hope you don't blame her,' said George.

'Not as much as I blame myself. She was confused. Mature physically, a woman to look at, well-developed and seductive in the way even the youngest girls can be, but she was a child inside. I believe she lacked affection at home. Unlucky that she found me at a weak moment. I'll never work again. What a waste! I'm forty-five, I have twenty good years of working life ahead of me and no future. Can you imagine how that feels?'

'A lot of people in Greece have that problem now. Through no fault of their own.'

Stephanos seemed to droop even more, his mouth downturned, his cheeks hollow, a haunted self-pitying glitter in his eyes.

'I feel like a piece of rubbish,' he said, 'just waiting to be thrown into the flames.'

'Is that why you come here?'

Stephanos nodded. 'On Athos I am not judged by the standards of this world. All are equal before God.'

'You want forgiveness?'

'Who will be forgiven if not the sinner?'

'I hope you find it,' said George. 'But if you don't accept responsibility for what you've done, all the forgiveness on the Holy Mountain won't help you.'

Stephanos shifted about uncomfortably. He did not appear to find the conversation palatable.

'Is your friend here?' he asked.

'I haven't seen him.'

George had been keeping a look-out for Aliveris, whose sin was beyond even the most extreme Christian mercy. But the musician was nowhere in sight. George could only hope he was at confession, facing the horror of what he had done, guided by the stern wisdom of a priest.

'Shall we walk some more?' suggested Stephanos.

'I'd like to be alone for a while,' said George.

The teacher smiled weakly. 'I'll see you later.'

George walked on through the gardens, enjoying the autumn colours and scents. The land faced west and the afternoon sun gilded every tree, every leaf, as if the whole scene were transforming itself into one of those wreaths from ancient

Macedonia. He felt the peace of this strange peninsula – a place dedicated to God yet forbidden to women, mysteriously attractive to both saints and sinners. Already it was calming his mind, emptying it of troublesome thoughts, filling it with a deep, tranquil sense of acceptance.

Then, just at the moment when he seemed to hold the secret in the palm of his hand, his phone pinged. George did nothing for a while. Then, inevitably, his curiosity overcame him. He pressed the *On* button. A message was flashing from Colonel Sotiriou. 'Here is the recording you wanted.'

George plugged in a set of earphones. Bracing himself for he knew not what, he pressed *Play*.

'Why are you following me?' A girl's accusing voice.

'Because you're cheating on me.' The man's reply, menacing and cold.

'I'm not and I never would.'

'I don't believe you.'

'You think I come out here to meet my lover?'

'I don't know any more. You've changed so much.'

'I haven't changed. You have! You're suspicious, you're jealous, you frighten me.'

'If you're frightened it can only mean you're guilty.'

'Don't be stupid! I'm afraid because you're mad with jealousy, because... what are you doing?'

'I want one last kiss.'

'What do you mean? Don't look at me like that! You're crazy.'

'Come here.'

'Paris, don't!'

A gasp, the sounds of a struggle, a stifled scream, then silence.

George slowly unplugged his earphones. He stared into the chasm of light that expanded beyond the gardens to the sea. He felt polluted. He should not have heard this dialogue. No one should. It was intimate and terrible. Yet here was proof of a rare kind.

Gone was his sense of peace and acceptance. His mind was in turmoil again. Now the deep silence of this place become a vacuum waiting to be filled, a question demanding an answer: *how will you find this evil man?*

A moment later the vacuum was filled. Paris was walking quickly along a path about twenty metres below him, hurrying towards the monastery as if late for an appointment. Between them stood a long row of cypress trees, which shielded him from view every few seconds. George saw a diagonal path leading down about a hundred metres ahead. He pocketed his phone and set off in pursuit.

Paris was moving fast, not glancing behind. George had to run to catch up with him. By the time Paris reached the main buildings, George was still some way behind. He entered the courtyard and found it empty. Rows of closed cell doors. A hot, blank stillness. Nothing to say where Paris had gone.

George hesitated for a few moments and ran on. The next courtyard was also deserted.

He tried knocking on a cell door. Getting no answer, he tried another. This was opened by a sleepy monk who was angry at being disturbed.

'You don't knock on the monks' doors!' he said.

George apologised and walked slowly back to the gardens. He sat for a while thinking about what he had seen.

24 A Monk's Life

The evening meal, known as *trapeza*, was a hasty business. Monks and pilgrims sat at long tables, where plates of vegetable stew were laid out among baskets of roughly chopped bread. A grace was intoned, a bell rang, and everyone began eating, quickly and hungrily, eyes down, without ceremony or conversation, while a monk at a lectern read in a loud monotonous voice from the life of a saint. Ten minutes later the bell rang again. Spoons clattered on empty plates. The meal was over. George felt like an inmate in a prison. He scanned the crowd of faces in the refectory. Paris was not there.

Strolling after supper, in the courtyards and gardens, he continued his search. There was no sign of him. He grew more and more convinced that Paris was avoiding him, no doubt alerted by his father.

At nine, George went to bed – the feeling of imprisonment still strong within him.

Some time later, George was woken up by a hand shaking him eagerly.

Bewildered and heavy with sleep he mumbled, 'Who is it?'

'It's me, Stephanos! I'm going to the early morning service.

Will you come?'

'Did I say I would?'

'I thought you did.'

George rubbed his eyes. 'I don't remember.'

'Come! It will help you.'

'Help me? How?'

'Just come!'

'What's the time?'

'Almost three o'clock.'

George could not see how losing half a night's sleep would help anyone and dropped back onto his pillow.

'Are you coming?'

'Let me think about it.'

'Come.' Stephanos was insistent, yapping like a little dog.

George was dimly conscious of other sleepers stirring. There was an air of almost military purpose about them, of a team preparing for action.

Still clouded with sleep, he said, 'OK. Let me get dressed.'

The night was still black outside, the stars casting a faint silvery light on the stones of the courtyard and silhouetting the monastery buildings against the sky. Ahead, through an open doorway, a single candle burned in the darkness. George and Stephanos stumbled stiffly towards it, their footfalls loud in the nocturnal silence.

Inside the chapel, George could dimly make out the wooden stalls that lined the walls, each one inhabited by a bearded figure. The candle-flame burned steadily over a lectern where a young monk chanted from the gospel, his voice echoing in the vaulted obscurity. Stephanos led him to an empty stall. 'Go there,' he whispered.

George squeezed himself into the narrow curve of wood

with its shoulder-height elbow-rests and its awkward little shelf of a seat. Stephanos took the stall next to him and flashed a smile of triumph.

George nodded grimly. Four hours of chanting was not his idea of a good use of the night. Still, he was prepared to try it once, if only to experience for himself one of the realities of monastic life. Already he could see how harsh it must be, mentally and physically, and how false were those accounts that portrayed it as 'stress-free'. With no more than five hours sleep each night the mind and body would create stress enough for a lifetime with its own desperate hunger for rest.

As his eyes grew accustomed to the darkness he began to see the painted images of saints on the walls, their harsh faces and stiff robes blackened by smoke and time. Above them floated the giant face of Christ in mosaics on the dome. George was struck by the power of the single candle. It was all stage-managed for maximum effect: the light of truth scattering the night of ignorance, the Holy Fathers hovering in the shadows, their faces reflecting the candle's rays, while Christ gazed down from the heavens. Beyond the walls of the church lay the world, unseen, unknown, an immense and incomprehensible universe.

Still, this chanting seemed endless! *Kyrie eleison, Kyrie eleison, Kyrie eleison...* The slow unwinding of an enormous reel of thread. Time barely seemed to move.

Maybe an hour later, having dozed off, George opened his eyes and was startled to find himself looking at the face of Paris, in the stalls on the far side of the church. He had been dimly aware of monks and pilgrims occasionally moving in and out, of newcomers entering the church. And suddenly there was the man he was looking for, eyes downcast, apparently deep in contemplation.

Paris did not look up. George watched him steadily.

The chanting continued. Another candle was lit on the far side of the church and a second monk added his voice. The effect was dramatic. Suddenly there was a dialogue. The two melodies alternated, joined, drew apart, curled around each other like the tendrils of a vine. George was lulled into a state that resembled hallucination, where one sense entered his mind in the guise of another. Sound became colour. The smoke of incense, burning every day here for centuries, became his own memories. Past and present fused in a molten river of darkness and gilded flames.

When he woke up again, stiff and hunched in the stall, he glanced up and saw that Paris had gone. A wave of anger shook him from his lethargy. He hurried out of the church.

In the courtyard day had risen, painting the world with surprising colour. Birds were singing. The sun's first rays lit the sky beyond the high monastery walls. He glanced at his watch. Seven o'clock. He was no nearer to finding Paris, but at least breakfast could not be far off.

He breathed deeply, drinking in the cool morning air.

Back inside, he whispered to Stephanos: 'How much longer does this last?'

'Until breakfast.'

'I know, but when's that?'

'It depends. Seven-thirty some days, eight-thirty on others.'

'And today?'

'We'll see.'

'What does it depend on?'

'The saint's day. If it's a feast, the service is longer and they eat later.'

'I'm hungry,' said George.

'This is the food of eternal life,' said Stephanos.

'Of course,' said George. 'I was forgetting.'

He leaned back in the stall, rolling his shoulders to ease his aching joints.

At last the service ended, and the monks flowed out through the church doorway, a river of black ink. George watched the congregation leave, monks then visitors. Paris was not among them.

Nor was he visible at breakfast time. George began to suspect again that Paris was avoiding him, perhaps already planning to escape. He asked a monk what time the first boat would come in.

'They arrive all the time,' was the reply.

George asked how he could find a fellow visitor.

The monk seemed puzzled. 'There are many visitors,' he said.

'I know. There's a particular one I need to talk to.'

'Do you have his name?'

'Paris Aliveris.'

There was not even a flicker of recognition. 'What do you want with him?'

'I have to ask him something.'

The monk looked firmly into George's eyes. 'This is a place of prayer, not of worldly affairs. If you need to talk to a man, you should do it on the mainland.'

'This is for his own safety.'

'You have a message for him?'

'Can you pass it on?'

'If I can find him I will.'

'And if I told you he was wanted by the police?'

'I would expect the police to speak to the monastery through official channels.'

'So you offer sanctuary to criminals?'
'You appear to be in some confusion.'
'Perhaps. Or perhaps not. If I had a murderer as a guest in my house I would like to know about it.'

The monk was taken aback at this. He reflected for a few moments before speaking.

'That is a serious matter.'
'You see why I'm concerned.'
'I will speak to the Abbot as soon as he returns.'
'Where is he?'
'On his way from Thessaloniki. He has been in hospital.'
'It's quite possible that Mr Aliveris will try to escape.'
'In that case he will meet his destiny elsewhere.'
'That destiny could be very unpleasant indeed.'
'If he has taken life, God will punish him. In just measure.'
'You're happy to leave it to God?'
'We're all in His hands.'

George took a notebook from his pocket, scribbled 'Paris Aliveris' on a fresh page and tore it out.

'What's that?' asked the monk.
'His name.'
'No need.' He tapped his skull with a forefinger. 'I've got it in here.'

George thanked him. The monk said, 'Try to leave your business behind when you come here.'

'I wish I could,' said George.
'Come to the sea gate in an hour.'
'Why?'
'We are welcoming the Abbot. If I find Aliveris I'll tell him to come too.'

'Thank you,' said George.

Shortly after breakfast a buzz of expectation began spreading through the monastery. Heavy wooden doors opened. Monks stepped out of their shadowy cells into the sunshine, formally robed, their stovepipe hats draped with black cloth. They greeted each other, gathering in small groups along the alley that led down to the port. There they waited, saying little, quietly excited. Soon the whole monastery had turned out, maybe two hundred people. Stephanos the gym teacher was standing with a trio of older monks, talking, gesticulating nervously. They listened with solemn faces to his desperate tale.

Paris Aliveris was not there. George walked among the crowd, working his way slowly towards the port, searching for that elusive face.

As he reached the sea gate, he saw a neat little coaster approaching, its blue and white smokestack puffing dark smoke. A shiny black jeep was parked on its quarter deck. The ship slowed, dropped anchor, hooted three times and backed carefully onto the jetty. A wheeled metal ramp was rolled out from her stern and the jeep lumbered off. It turned up the hill, its windows down. George glimpsed a smiling grey-bearded old cleric waving from the front passenger seat. The monks cheered and crossed themselves as he drove slowly past. 'Welcome back, Father!' they cried. *'I ora kali!'*

George was surprised by their enthusiasm. Until now they had seemed emotionless creatures, pure spirit, going efficiently about their business, their minds rigorously bent on duty. Yet here they were in the grip of their feelings: loyalty, admiration, love. It seemed miraculous that a leader could inspire such devotion in a community.

So absorbed was George in his thoughts that he failed to notice two figures approaching. One of them took him by the elbow. He jumped with surprise. It was the monk he had spoken to earlier.

'Mr Zafiris, Father Seraphim. I have brought the man you were looking for.'

'Oh?'

He turned, and found himself face to face with Paris Aliveris.

George offered his hand, which the musician refused to take.

'You wanted to see me?' he said coldly.

'Can we talk in private?'

Paris glanced at Father Seraphim. 'I prefer to have my confessor present.'

'Makes a change from a lawyer,' said George.

Father Seraphim said, 'Let's go to my room.'

He led them to the innermost courtyard, where they climbed a staircase to the first floor. Father Seraphim extracted a bunch of keys from his pocket and let them into a large study made smaller by hundreds of books on the walls and in piles on tables. A desk in one corner faced a pair of straight-backed wooden benches.

'Sit down,' said Father Seraphim. 'I'll make some coffee.'

He vanished through a doorway behind the desk. George and Paris sat tensely side by side, not speaking.

Father Seraphim returned but did not sit down. 'Did you come to Athos just to see Mr Aliveris?' he asked.

'I did.'

'But you also attended morning service.'

'I thought I might see him there.'

'Are you a Christian?'

'In a general way, yes.'

'What do you mean by that?'

'I don't reject the claims of Christianity, nor do I accept

them uncritically.'

'For example?'

'The miracles.'

'And the resurrection, the greatest miracle of all?'

'Strangely enough I can believe that.'

'I see.' He looked displeased. 'Still, it's a start.'

'What are you trying to tell me?'

The monk gave him a long, level look. Slightly pitying, George thought. Slightly ironic.

'I'll get the coffee,' he said.

He returned with three little cups on a tray.

'I'm going to get straight to the point,' said George.

'Fine,' said Father Seraphim.

'Mr Aliveris, I came to your home to question you about your wife's death. You received me with hostility, and a few hours later you vanished. People who run away are assumed to be guilty.'

'I didn't run away.'

'You flew to Bucharest.'

'For good reason.'

'Please explain.'

'I was exhausted and harassed. I needed a break.'

'Why Bucharest?'

'I have friends there. Friends who are not Athenian, people of faith who could help me.'

'Did they?'

'Greatly.'

'After Bucharest you came here?'

'As you see.'

'Why did you do that?'

'To talk to Father Seraphim. To take strength from this community.'

'And to seek forgiveness?'
'Always.'
'What do you mean "always"?'
'I come here every year. And confession is a sacrament.'
'Did you feel in particular need of confession?'
'Yes.'
'Why?'
'My mind was polluted with bad thoughts.'
'What kind of thoughts?'
'Revenge, hatred, regret…'
'Directed at anyone in particular?'
'At my wife's killers.'
'Why regret?'

For a moment or two he seemed too distressed to reply. Then he gathered himself. 'I believe I failed to protect her. Failed to love her enough.'

'Let's be clear about this. You say regret, not guilt?'
'I leave guilt to the evil souls who destroyed her life.'

George watched him closely as he spoke. No sideways glances, no slippery replies. He seemed calm. That could mean innocence, or a psychopath's detachment. George had no doubt which it was. In his pocket was a phone with a recording on it. It lay there coiled like a snake. All he needed to do was press *Play*. That would be the end of it.

Before that, he wanted to see how far this cold-blooded liar was prepared to go in his denials.

'Does Mr Aliveris's story make sense to you?' he asked Father Seraphim.

'Complete sense,' said the monk.
'To me it's puzzling,' said George.
'You're not a confessor.'
'No, I'm an investigator. I know guilty behaviour when I

see it.'

'I wonder if you do, Mr Zafiris.'

Resenting the monk's tone, George reacted sharply. 'Really? That's amazing. How many criminals do you talk to every month?'

Father Seraphim replied calmly, 'As a confessor I am granted insight into people's souls.'

'Oh yes? I suppose they always tell you the truth?'

'Of course not. Some things are too unbearable to confront, impossible to put into words. And yet, through God's grace, I can see, sometimes "through a glass darkly", as St Paul says, but often face to face.'

George could sense where this was leading. Higher truth, mystical knowledge, a swamp of mumbo-jumbo. 'The fact is, though, Father, you are bound by the secrecy of confession. Even if Mr Aliveris had killed his wife and admitted it to you, you would never tell me.'

'That is correct. But since he did not kill his wife, that painful contradiction between earthly justice and heavenly mercy does not arise.'

'If he had killed her would you grant absolution?'

'I cannot possibly answer that. It depends on the individual. Normally I would encourage a person who has committed a crime to surrender himself to the police and pay the penalty. I am not in favour of avoiding responsibility.'

'In what circumstances would you allow them to take sanctuary here?'

Father Seraphim frowned, his eyes two glittering black pools.

'Exceptional circumstances,' he said.

'Such as?'

'We cannot know the mind of God, but occasionally

His purpose requires us to allow a sinner to redeem himself through work, prayer and fasting.'

'Work for the monastery? Like the addicts in rehab?'

'That's the general idea, but it would be a much more intense and complicated process.'

'And how do you judge who is suitable?'

'That is up to God.'

'But you must decide?'

'We would examine the case with the Abbot, with the Council of the monastery, and pray for enlightenment.'

'Even against the law of the land?'

'Only if a higher law sanctions it.'

'What is that higher law?'

'The law of God's mercy. We are all sinners, Mr Zafiris. Every one of us lives or dies by that law.'

'That's convenient.'

'I assure you it's anything but. There is no hiding from divine justice.'

'How often do you grant sanctuary to a criminal?'

'Very rarely.'

'Once a year? Once a month?'

'No. I have known it perhaps three times in thirty years.'

George put his hand into his pocket. 'I'd like you to listen to something,' he said. He placed the phone on the desk in front of them and, watching Paris attentively, let the recording play:

'Why are you following me?'

'Because you're cheating on me.'

'I'm not and I never would.'

'I don't believe you.'

'You think I come out here to meet my lover?'

'I don't know any more. You've changed so much.'

'I haven't changed. You have! You're suspicious, you're

jealous, you frighten me.'

'If you're frightened it can only mean you're guilty.'

'Don't be stupid! I'm afraid because you're mad with jealousy, because... what are you doing?'

'I want one last kiss.'

'What do you mean? Don't look at me like that! You're crazy.'

'Come here.'

'Paris, don't!'

George compared the two men's reactions. The monk was watchful, calm, expressionless. Paris was increasingly agitated.

'Well?' said George. 'What do you say to that?'

Paris could hardly speak. His eyes blazed with rage. 'Where... how did you get that?'

'From the police.'

'And where did they get it?'

'They found Keti's phone.'

'Where?'

'In the bushes.'

'So long after the murder?'

'It happens.'

Paris looked devastated. His face crumpled. Tears flooded his eyes and he shook with sobs.

'Time for a confession?' said George.

Father Seraphim raised his hand in a gesture of restraint.

Paris sat with his head in his hands, shaking as if gripped by a fever. George waited patiently. He felt his goal was in sight.

His eyes wandered along the bookshelves. There were the expected volumes on prayer, the gospels, the lives of the saints, the history of the church. But there were other books too: paperbacks with titles in French and Italian, on art, psychology and philosophy. Orthodox monks did not usually possess such secular works. They were trained in a certain way of thinking and were expected to stick to it. Very occasionally one stumbled across an exceptional character, a refugee from some other way of life – business, science, the arts – intriguing figures who had known the world they renounced and chosen the cloistered life in the light of experience.

He was curious about Seraphim, but this was not a moment for curiosity. Paris had stopped shaking. Slowly, he raised his head. He glanced first at Seraphim, then at George, his eyes distant and scared. There was something childlike in that look, like a boy who has climbed a tree and is frightened to come down.

Seraphim folded his hands.

'Come on, Mr Aliveris,' said George. 'You're safe here. Not even the police can get to you. But you must tell us the truth.'

Seraphim nodded.

Paris made an obvious effort, struggling with some unseen difficulty. 'I don't know what to say,' he mumbled. 'It's such a grotesque fake…'

'A fake?' cried George. 'How could it be?'

'Listen to the voices. That's not me or Keti.'

'Don't give me that, Paris! It's your wife's phone. It's clear-cut evidence, and you're using any…'

'Listen to them!' Paris insisted. 'Listen to them!'

'All right,' said George, 'I will.'

He pressed the little white triangle on the screen of his phone and the dialogue began again. Paris winced as it played.

'Does that sound like me?' he said.

'Voices change under stress,' said George.

'Not that much. I tell you, it's not me, and it's not Keti. This is some obscene trick.'

'Unless you can prove it you won't convince me or the police.'

'Check the recording! When was it made?'

'That's obvious.'

'You must check it.'

'I don't have the original file.'

'Find the person who does. It will have a date and time.'

'I'm sure the police checked that.'

'Are you? You've asked them?'

'No.'

'Please do that.'

George dialled Sotiriou's number. When the Colonel answered, George put the question to him. The Colonel told him to wait, ruffled some papers, muttered something insulting about his colleagues, then said irritably, 'I'll have to check this.'

'Please do.'

'Is it urgent?'

'Extremely.'

'Why?'

'I'm with Mr Aliveris now.'

'Ah.' The Colonel said nothing for a moment or two.

'Where are you?' he asked.

'Mount Athos.'

'You've tracked him down. Good work.'

'How soon can you check this?'

'A few hours.'

'I prefer minutes.'

'We all prefer minutes, Mr Zafiris! But they are in short supply.'

'Try to find some. I suggest you check all the settings on that phone, and fingerprint it.'

'I shall do a lot more than that, I assure you.'

George slowly put his own phone down.

'Well?' said Aliveris.

'No answer yet,' said George. 'But they're checking… Now tell me, why would anyone fake a thing like that?'

'To incriminate me,' said Aliveris.

'I find that impossible to believe.'

'I tell you, Keti was spending time with thoroughly unpleasant people.'

'But not stupid people.'

'What difference does that make? This is a question of evil, not intelligence.'

'All right. The trouble is, it fits with other evidence.'

'What are you referring to?'

'Your jealousy, for example.'

'Who told you about that?'

'Do you deny it?'

'I do!'

'But you behaved like a jealous man, following her about, listening to her phone calls…'

'Ah, it's Anna, isn't it? Angel-faced Anna! With a snake's heart!'

George did not reply.

'All I did,' said Paris, 'was protect her from exploitation.'

'What do you mean?'

'She was a serious musician, a fine soloist, and she wanted to throw all that away for a show-business career.'

'She wouldn't be the first.'

'I know, but it's a mistake. A terrible mistake.'

'Mistake or not, it was her decision,' said George.

'One that needs to be taken very carefully!'
'She wanted money presumably?'
'And fame.'
'Nothing wrong with that.'
'Her reputation would be ruined.'
'So you tried to stop her?'
'I did my best.'
'By stalking her?'
Paris winced. 'Who said I did that?'
'I have witnesses.'
'I did not stalk her. How do you "stalk" your own wife?'
'You did exactly that.'
'I followed her on a couple of occasions.'
'And checked her phone, diary, emails?'
Paris did not reply.
'Do you know who she was seeing in the last days of her life?' asked George.
'Of course.'
'Can you give me names?'
Paris stopped short. 'Names?'
'That's what I want.'
He seemed lost for a moment or two, 'Why do you want names?'
'If you didn't kill your wife, Mr Aliveris, I need to know who else it might have been. Who was around her? Who might have had a motive? Without names I keep coming back to just one suspect: you!'
Paris sighed and looked to Father Seraphim, who sat with his eyes downcast.
'This is incredibly painful,' said Paris.
'No doubt,' said George. He took a notebook from his pocket. 'Let's get on with it, shall we?'

Paris began. Three night-club owners, a stylist, a business consultant, a concert promoter, a journalist, a photographer, a director of TV commercials. He spoke each name with clarity and contempt.

Two names, different from the others, attracted George's attention. Vladimir Merkulov, one of the night-club owners, and Stelios, the photographer.

'Tell me what you know about Merkulov,' he said.

'He owns a big night-club in Glyfada. Also a hotel in Halkidiki. And businesses in Russia.'

'Do you know him personally?'

'Not at all.'

'And Stelios?'

'Nothing.'

'Does he have a surname?'

'He does. I forget it. Stelios is his professional name. A sure sign of pretentiousness.'

'You seem to dislike these people.'

'I am trying to moderate my feelings.'

George took a last sip of coffee and closed his notebook.

'Thank you, Father,' he said. 'I'll leave you to your work now.'

George shook hands with them both, saying to Paris, 'Please answer your phone in future.'

Paris gave a tense little nod in reply. Father Seraphim opened the door.

Back in his dormitory he met Stephanos the gym teacher packing his bag.

'Are you leaving too?' he asked.

'No,' said Stephanos. 'I'm staying.'

'You seem to be getting ready to go.'

'They're giving me my own room.'

'How come?'

'They've asked me to stay!' There was a childish excitement in his voice.

'How did that come about?'

'The Abbot has trouble with his knees. He can't walk. They've asked me to look after him, get him walking again.'

'That's a stroke of luck.'

'It's all I could have hoped for. A gift from God. A reward for my faith and a sign of His mercy. The age of miracles is not over!'

George offered his hand. Stephanos grabbed him by the shoulders and kissed him on both cheeks. 'My friend!' he said, tears glinting in his eyes. 'You have witnessed the miracle. You have seen God's work. Now go out and spread the word!'

George frowned. 'And you, my friend, make sure you behave yourself. I don't know about God, but man will not forgive you a second time.'

'I hear your wise words!' Stephanos patted his heart. 'God bless you, dear friend!'

25 Kokoras II

Two hours later, George walked through the frontier town of Ouranopolis in a daze of mental re-adjustment. Everything jangled, all things seemed garish and strange. Butcher's shops, motorbikes, racks full of magazines, advertisements for ice cream, fast food, insurance. The colours so bright! The women so sensuous! Their hair so extravagant! He felt like an astronaut returning to earth: out of place, heavy-limbed, not quite in control.

He needed a coffee, some means of rooting himself to the ground. In a quiet place, off the main street, where brash sensations were muted. He found an alley with a stone building at the far end. Wooden shutters, vines over the door. As he walked in a few fat raindrops started to fall.

He ordered a big black coffee. He wanted more than anything to sleep now, but that would have to wait. He took his phone from his pocket and dialled Gavrilis in Edessa.

'I know Kokoras wants to be left in peace,' he said, 'but tell him I have to see him.'

Gavrilis was brusque. 'He won't like it.'

'I know. Just tell him it has to happen.'

'No one says that to him.'

'He'll have the police all over him.'

'He has good relations with the police.'

'Listen, my friend, I'm not pissing about. I'm talking about the Athens police. Tough bastards. They like nothing better than stitching up an out-of-town villain.'

'What have they got on him?'

'Plenty.'

'Thanks to you?'

'No thanks to me.'

'I hope you're not bluffing, Mr Zafiris. If you are…' His voice trailed off, allowing George to imagine the rest.

George said, 'I have to see him this evening.'

'What time?'

'Around seven. Not before. I'm about three hours away.'

'I'll call him.'

Fifteen minutes later, as he set off for Edessa, he had the return call. Kokoras would see him in the Waterfalls Park at 7.30 pm. He checked his watch. He should just make it.

By the time he walked into the park he had it clear in his mind. He had phoned Colonel Sotiriou and told him what he was up to. Sotiriou was typically parsimonious in his support. 'If you disappear,' he said, 'we'll know where to look.'

'Nothing until then?'

'I've told you from the start, you're on your own.'

George thought a little more about it, then phoned Haris Pezas. 'God knows what I'm getting into here,' he said, 'but if I don't call you by 9.00 pm get yourself up to Edessa at once and find Gavrilis at the Pindos Hotel. He might have an idea where I am. Meanwhile call Sotiriou, tell him I've disappeared.'

'Got that,' said Haris. 'It sounds like you're taking your usual risks.'

'I don't know how else to do this,' said George.

He found Kokoras sitting at a table in the shadows, his lieutenants on either side of him, flicking their worry beads with a bored and stupefied air of self-importance.

George introduced himself.

'I remember you,' said Kokoras, giving the phrase a sinister intonation.

'I remember you too,' said George.

They eyed each other coldly.

A waiter appeared, asking, 'What will you have, gentlemen?'

'We don't want anything,' said Kokoras. 'Clear òff.'

'Hold on,' said George. 'I'd like a beer. A Fix. And a little *mezé*.' At the back of his mind was the thought that the bottle might come in handy if things got rough.

The waiter nodded and moved away.

Kokoras wasted no time getting to the point.

'What the hell is this about?' he demanded.

'It's about my friend Mario Filiotis.'

'I don't know him.'

'You've missed your chance now. He's dead.'

Kokoras said nothing.

'He tried to build a medical school here. He had several partners, including Dr Skouras in Athens.'

Kokoras glanced at one of his lieutenants. 'Is that who sent you? Skouras?'

'No,' said George. 'Skouras is not involved.'

'Who then? One of the investors?'

'You seem to know what I'm talking about all of a sudden,' said George.

'It's coming back,' said Kokoras, a smirk twisting his narrow strip of moustache.

'OK,' said George. 'Filiotis was prevented from building a

teaching hospital, here in Edessa, by people who had their own alternative project.'

'So?'

'You're one of those people.'

'What's the problem?'

'Filiotis was murdered.'

'Not by me.'

'By one of your partners perhaps.'

'Why? He was no threat to anyone.'

'I'm not so sure.'

Kokoras dismissed this with an impatient flick of his hand.

'I want to know the names of your partners,' said George. 'The backers for the new hospital here.'

'What did you say?'

George repeated the question slowly.

Instead of replying, Kokoras said, 'Who are *your* partners, asshole?'

George felt like putting a fist into that drooping mouth. 'I'm asking the questions,' he said brusquely.

'You want information for nothing?'

'Tell me the names of your partners and I'll tell you the names of mine.'

'Bullshit,' said Kokoras. 'Who sent you? Some cocksucker in the Athens police?'

'I'm not giving names,' said George.

'Neither am I. You're wasting my time.' He signalled to his men. 'Let's go.'

The two lieutenants began lifting themselves out of their chairs.

George said, 'Take it easy. No rush. I've ordered a beer and I'd like to drink it.' He turned to Kokoras and said softly, 'Why don't you ask your friends to go and pose somewhere else?'

One of the lieutenants said, 'Get up, *pousti!*'

George addressed Kokoras again. 'I want to talk to you privately,' he said.

Kokoras thought about this, his face unmoving. Then the gold rings flashed on his left hand.

'Go and look at the waterfall, lads,' he said. Then, turning to George, 'This had better be good.'

'That's up to you,' said George.

'What's that supposed to mean?'

'The people I work for know exactly where I am, who I'm with. They have you in their sights. They're prepared to destroy you.'

Kokoras did not seem unduly worried.

George cranked up the pressure. 'They'll start with a tax check, a full one. They'll move on to a criminal investigation, looking into a pile of complaints about intimidation, extortion, restraint of trade, and all your other nasty habits. With two investigations running, bank accounts frozen, you'll find it hard to do business. You'll be a wounded animal, and your rivals will know all about it. Everything you've built up will fall apart.'

Kokoras glared at him, his eyes two fiery slits.

'I've never had a problem with the tax authorities. Or the police.'

'I forgot something else,' said George. 'Bribing public officials. They're getting tough on that now. You're probably looking at ten years in prison. Plus confiscation of property.'

George was bluffing, but decided to risk it. No Greek feels immune from prosecution. Everyone is in tax jeopardy. What is untaxed today may be taxed tomorrow. What is legal today may be illegal tomorrow.

If Kokoras was vulnerable, though, he never showed it.

George needed to work harder.

'All I have to do,' he said, 'is say the word. In fact, I don't even need to do that. This process is ready to start. And it will start unless I put the brakes on.'

Kokoras remained unperturbed. 'Leave out the bullshit. What do you want?'

'I repeat. The names of your fellow investors in the hospital.'

'No way.'

'In return for protection. A word you understand.'

'No tax investigation?'

'That can be arranged.'

'If you're spinning me a line, Zafiris, you're dead.'

'Of course.'

'And I will find out.'

'It doesn't worry me.'

Kokoras took a phone from his pocket and called a number.

'Stavro? Just check something for me. I've got a private dick from Athens trying to threaten me with tax and police trouble. Can you just run a check for me? See if there's anything pending on my name?'

He listened to the reply, his face unchanging.

'OK,' he said. 'I've got that.'

Again he listened.

'Right, thank you, Stavro. This guy's name is Zafiris. He claims to have high-level contacts in Athens. Sounds like grade one bullshit to me. Let me know as soon as you find out for sure.'

He put away the phone, resting pitiless eyes on George.

'He doesn't know of any such plans. And if he doesn't, no one does.'

'Who is he?'

'Never mind who he is. Who are you?'
'I've told you who I am.'
'We'll see about that.'
Kokoras waved a hand above his head. His lieutenants approached. Behind them came the waiter.
'When I've checked you out one hundred per cent, then we'll talk.'
'How long will that take?'
'Who knows? A few hours? A few days? I'm in no hurry.'
'But I am.'
'Hurry kills.'
'So what am I supposed to do?'
'Whatever you like.'
'I need to get back to Athens tonight.'
'Go.'
'I need results now.'
'No you don't, Mr Detective! All you need is life insurance. Now piss off.'
'You don't even have my number.'
'I'll find you.'
The waiter, sensing the tension, hung back. Kokoras stood up and threw a twenty-euro note disdainfully on the table. 'That's for the beer.'
'It's too much,' said the waiter.
'Then bring him another one! Bring him ten. Let him drown in it.'
Kokoras moved off into the darkness, his lieutenants ambling after him as if every step was an effort.

26 Unexpected Quarter

As the waiter levered the top off the beer bottle, George said, 'You can keep the change.'

'Thank you,' said the waiter. 'Give it to a beggar.'

'Really?' said George, surprised. 'Are you paid so well?'

'This is dirty money.'

'In what way?'

The waiter moved closer, lowering his voice.

'I don't know what your business is with that man, but be careful.'

'I'm always careful,' said George.

'You're from out of town, aren't you?'

'I am.'

'Can I ask what you want from him?'

'I can't see how that's any business of yours.'

'None at all. But I have some pride in this town and I don't want you to think that everyone here is crooked.'

'I promise you I don't.'

'I was Mayor here once.'

George was suddenly more attentive. 'Really? Mayor? And now…?'

'I know,' said the waiter. 'It's a long way down. But it's a job.'

'What happened?'

'It's a long story,'

'Does it involve Kokoras?'

'Partly. But that's all in the past now. The point is, if you want to do business here I can tell you who to go to and who to avoid.'

'That could be useful.'

'What business are you in?' asked the waiter.

'I'm an investigator.'

'Oh.' This did not seem to be welcome news. 'What kind of investigator?'

'Private.'

'What are you investigating?'

'I can't tell you the specific case. But I suspect some irregularity.'

'That's a sure bet. But if you gave me some indication, I might be able to help.'

George thought for a moment. This might be a trap or a golden opportunity. 'I'm interested in his building projects, particularly the hospital.'

'I see,' said the waiter. 'You've got plenty to investigate there.'

'Really?'

'That was big money. From public funds, Europe, charities. All into his pocket.'

'*His* pocket? No one else's?'

'Of course there were others. The politicians who did the deal, the lawyers who fixed the paperwork, the businessmen who funnelled the bribes to foreign accounts… He was the front man. It's what they call teamwork.'

'If you're prepared to give me the names of those associates I will make it worth your while.'

'I have to be sure the information can't be traced back to me.'

'Your name will not be mentioned.'

George took a pen and notebook from his briefcase. 'I'm ready,' he said.

'OK. Give me your card. I will check that you are who you say you are, and then I'll contact you with the names.'

'I wish you'd tell me now,' said George.

'I'm sure you do,' said the waiter, 'but what little I have I want to protect. You can understand that.'

'I can, but I'm in a hurry.'

'That's a mistake.'

'It's not my choice.'

'Make it your choice. Enjoy your beer.'

George did his best to relax for a few minutes even while a time bomb was ticking in his head. He tried closing his eyes and listening to the sounds that marked the distances around him: a pair of boys kicking a football, a motorbike roaring away into the night, people talking, glasses clinking, traffic rumbling, the river swirling towards its death-leap over the cliff. His mind refused to settle. Everything pressed in on him. Thoughts of home, the monastery, the chanting by candlelight... He needed to call Sotiriou, get a police file going on Kokoras. If not, his bluff would be exposed. And he needed to set off for Athens before the night got much older. He had been up since 3.00 am and waves of fatigue had started to wash over him.

He pulled out his phone, called Sotiriou first, and cut through the Colonel's customary objections with a sharp demand: 'Do this for me or I'm off the job.'

Sotiriou tried to salvage a little self-esteem by informing

him that public denunciations took time to be registered on the system, were subject to verification, witness interviews and other processes, and that all this could take several weeks. George stopped him. 'You've got to short-cut all that. He's threatened to kill me. I believe he means it.'

'All right,' said Sotiriou. 'If it's so urgent…'

'Right now,' said George. 'Or you and I have had our last conversation.'

'How peaceful that would be!'

'I'll leave a note in my pocket saying you sent me,' said George. 'So if he kills me, you'll be next.'

Sotiriou laughed drily.

27 Anna II

George slept for a couple of hours parked on a farm track in Thessaly, never finding a comfortable position, woken periodically by animal shrieks and the distant thunder of trucks. He crawled into Athens at dawn, longing for his bed.

Waking at noon, he made a pot of coffee and padded around the apartment in his shorts, trying to get into focus. He watered the plants, checked phone messages, opened his mail. Zoe was in Andros wanting to fix a date for the olive harvest, his son Nick in England saying winter was late this year. 'If you're not wearing a coat in Newcastle by the first of October,' he wrote, 'global warming has definitely reached danger level.' Meanwhile Haris Pezas had called to check that he was back safely. Anna Kenteri had phoned twice, leaving no message.

He contacted Anna first, telling her he had seen Paris Aliveris on Mount Athos. She was excited to hear it, and asked if George had confronted him with the recording.

George was taken aback at the question.

'How the hell do you know about the recording?'

'I gave it to the police,' she said.

'You? But how did you get it?'

'Someone put Keti's phone through my letterbox.'

'When was this?'

'Four or five days ago.'

'You don't know who?'

'No idea.'

'That is strange,' said George.

'I assume it was one of Keti's friends, who doesn't want all the fuss of going to the police.'

George thought about this. It was almost plausible, but something jarred.

'According to the police the phone was found in the bushes at the quarry. Near her body.'

'That's right.'

'How do they know that?'

'There was a note with the phone.'

'That's the only evidence?'

'As far as I know.'

'So it could have been found somewhere else?'

'Could it?' She seemed nonplussed.

'Of course,' said George. 'If it was really in the bushes, the police would have found it.'

'Not necessarily.'

'I'm sure they would. This doesn't sound right.'

'Yet the police accepted it.'

'Supposedly.'

'Why would anyone lie about it?'

'Good question,' said George. 'Spot the lies and they lead you to the truth.'

'You're being enigmatic,' she said irritably.

'People are enigmatic,' he replied. 'But everything has a meaning. Especially lies. They tell you a great deal.'

She said nothing for a while. Then, 'How did Paris react?'

'He was appalled,' said George.

'I should think so! Did he confess?'

'No.'

'What did he say?'

'He denied it.'

Anna reacted angrily. 'How the hell could he do that? With the evidence in front of him!'

'I gave him every opportunity,' said George. 'He was in a place of sanctuary. He had his confessor with him. But he claimed he was innocent.'

'He's got a nerve.'

'You could say that. Unless he's telling the truth.'

'Really? So she fell by accident?'

'He doesn't even say that.'

'What does he say?'

'He says he wasn't at the quarry.'

'Then who the hell was?'

'That's the big question.'

A note of bitterness entered Anna's voice. 'Mr Zafiris, I think you've got this wrong. Paris is an extremely persuasive man. I think he's fooled you with his charm.'

'I promise you he has not.'

'Don't be so sure. He's sly. And he was watching her like a hawk. Don't forget that! He could tell you exactly where she was at any time of day. And he says he doesn't know who was with her at the quarry! Bullshit!'

George decided to move the conversation on. 'OK, Anna, I take that point. But I need to look at other possibilities.'

'Why? When the facts are so obvious!'

'I need to know more about this new career she was planning. Who she was seeing, how often…'

Anna struck back fiercely. 'You even sound like him now! What the hell do you need to know that for? You're just creating more work for yourself, more hours, more business.'

'Absolutely not.'

'I've found the piece of shit that did this horrible thing, but that's too quick for you, too easy.'

'Fine,' said George. 'Let's stop the investigation. It's no problem for me.'

'Then what happens?' asked Anna indignantly.

'It's up to the police.'

'The police?' She seemed to consider this for a few moments, then switched tack again. 'Why this sudden interest in Keti's career?'

'That's where the answer might lie.'

'Why do you think that?'

'She was seeing night-club people, media, show-business agents…'

'So?'

'Not the most reputable characters on earth.'

'That's a hell of a presumption!'

'I know. But one of these presumptions will turn out to be right.'

'It's just what Paris would say. Such a bloody snob! The people in classical music are no better, I can tell you! There are plenty of self-serving shits among them! Don't think that because they dress up in –'

George interrupted. 'Listen, Anna, just decide. Do I go on with this investigation, or stop? It makes no difference to me.'

'How can I decide just like that?'

'Take your time,' said George. 'You know where I am.'

George put the phone down and closed his eyes. The accusation of 'creating work' was a familiar one; a certain type of client made it regularly. The impatient, the self-centred, the neurotic. He remembered her first phone message, how her voice had put him off, some hidden tone alerting him to unseen problems in the future. And then Paris's words – how had he described her? 'A snake.' Was that the word?

Or was she right? Had he fallen under Paris's spell?

Thinking back to the monastery, that weird suspended state he had been in, hungry and sleepless, cut off from the world, among monks who spent their days and nights fasting and praying, a place where justice could be obscured by mysterious concepts like divine grace – his judgement could very easily have been impaired.

Yet there was one fact that could not be twisted or changed. If he could get hold of it. The date of the recording on Keti's phone.

It was time to see Colonel Sotiriou again.

28 The Diarist

At the Colonel's insistence they met in a different place, the ground-floor bar at the Hilton Hotel. Spacious, cool, well-lit, a place where the optimism of the 1960s had been preserved miraculously intact. You would not be surprised to see Audrey Hepburn or Jacqueline Kennedy walk in and order a dry martini from the bow-tied barman.

Sotiriou was already there, at a corner table, writing thoughtfully in a small, elegant notebook which he put away the moment he saw George.

'Your private journal?' George enquired.

'Private yes, journal no.'

This was an unusually informative statement.

'Tell me,' said George.

'It's nothing special.' The Colonel took the notebook from his inner pocket and showed it, without opening it, to George. It had a floral silk cover with a Chinese symbol in the centre.

'From the east?' said George.

'In every way. Open it.'

George did so. He found page after page covered in three-line sequences of characters, written in a script he did not recognise.

'What language is this?' he asked.

'Greek, although you may not recognise it.'
'I sure as hell don't.'
'It's Linear B.'
'Which is ancient Minoan? Mycenaean?'
'Correct.'
'And you know how to write it?'
'As you can see.'
'That's quite something.'
'It's no big deal. Just a different alphabet.'
'And these are what? Notes, ideas, epigrams?'
'Haiku. A short Japanese verse form which I find particularly congenial.'

George flicked through the pages, spikily adorned with the archaic script.

'It's an exercise in brevity,' said the Colonel. 'One has to concentrate everything into seventeen syllables distributed over three lines.'

'Does it help with your work?'
'Not at all!'
'Why do it?'
'To relax. To observe. To reflect. The last five years of my life are in this book. Coded, distilled, bottled like summer fruit.'

George handed the notebook back. 'I wish I could read it,' he said.

'There's nothing of interest. I do it for myself. Possibly my grandchildren.' He slipped it back into his pocket. 'Tell me how I can help.'

George was struck again by the gulf between the man's vile telephone manner and his far more congenial presence. They were two different people.

'First the Kenteri death,' George began. 'You need to verify the time and date settings on Keti's phone.'

Sotiriou nodded. 'That's done. It's all consistent.'

'With what?'

'What we suspected – an attempt to plant evidence.'

'Really? You suspected that?'

'Of course.'

'Fingerprints?'

'Nothing. It was wiped clean.'

'Which is also consistent.'

'Exactly.'

'How about the contacts list?'

'We have the names and we're checking them.'

'Was anything deleted from that?'

'How would you know?'

'Check the phone's memory. Failing that go to the phone company.'

'I don't see the point.'

'It would be the first thing to do,' said George. 'If you were on the contacts list and you tampered with the phone, you would delete yourself from the list.'

Sotiriou considered this. 'I confess I had not thought of that,' he said.

'There are two names I would be particularly interested in.' George took out his own notebook, found the page he had written yesterday afternoon in Father Seraphim's room.

'Vladimir Merkulov, a Russian businessman, and a photographer called Stelios.'

'Surname?'

'Doesn't use one.'

'Huh. *Très artiste*. Why those two?'

'They were seeing a lot of Keti, helping her start a career in show business.'

'How do you know that?'

'Paris Aliveris gave me their names.'

'I see,' said the Colonel, but he looked puzzled. 'You don't want to do this yourself?'

'The sister has taken me off the case.'

'Ah.' He swirled the coffee in his cup. 'So the urgency has gone out of it?'

'Maybe for her,' said George, 'but not for me. I sense there's something else going on.'

'For example?'

'I'm not sure. Something hidden. Just out of sight. There's a battle between her and Paris.'

'Over what?'

'She was in favour of her sister's move into show business, Paris was against it.'

'That's all over now. How does it help us?'

'I can't be sure. But I notice she's very defensive.'

'Normal in a battle.'

'She won't hear anything against the show business people.'

'Is she connected with them?'

'She doesn't say. That's another problem. I sense a hidden agenda.'

'We can look into it. I'll put our rugby-playing friend onto it.'

'Good.'

George was hungry and tired. He looked around for a waiter. 'Excuse me,' he called over to the bar. 'Can you bring me a French coffee and a toasted cheese sandwich?' He turned back to Sotiriou. 'I drove from Edessa last night. I need a shot of something to stir myself up.'

'Unquestionably,' he said. Then, 'Tell me about this fellow Kokoras. Is he as ridiculous as his name suggests?'

'No. He's far from ridiculous. You shouldn't underestimate him.'

'A man who calls himself the Cock is inviting a certain amount of amusement.'

'Of course. But he runs Edessa. And the surrounding province.'

'Really?' said Sotiriou. 'I would be surprised.'

'I'm telling you what I saw. On the spot.'

Sotiriou seemed unconvinced. 'There must be other forces at work.'

'Perhaps,' said George. 'But Kokoras does the dirty stuff.'

'Then he should call himself the Pig.'

George was beginning to get irritated. 'Never mind his name. He's an ugly customer.'

'Don't worry,' said Sotiriou. 'I get the picture. By the way, I did as you asked. His name is live on police files. You're covered.'

'I'm grateful.'

'I should hope so. At some point I'll have to back up the alert with evidence.'

'You'll get it,' said George.

He told the Colonel what he knew about Kokoras: the protection racket, the construction business, the hospital, the heavies.

Sotiriou said, 'He still sounds to me like a middle-ranker. There has to be money behind him.'

'Of course,' said George, and he mentioned the promise of more information from an unnamed source.

Sotiriou said, '*That's* where you'll score. If your informant ever gets back to you. He may think better of it.'

'I offered him cash.'

Sotiriou nodded. 'That should help. Who is this man?'

'Someone who knows all the facts.'
'How come?'
'He was once an official in the town hall.'
'Senior?'
'I'm not saying any more.'
'Oh come on!'
'No. I have to protect him.'
'From me?' Sotiriou seemed astonished.
George frowned. 'Yes, Colonel, even from you.'
Sotiriou shrugged it off. 'He must have been senior to know the facts. Easy enough for me to trace if I wanted to.'
'I'm not saying any more.'
'That's fine,' said the Colonel. 'Trust no one, give nothing away. It's the correct approach. A policy that has served me well in public service.' He became distracted for a moment. Suddenly he snapped back into focus. 'Edessa was useful, definitely. But the obvious place for what you want is not there.'
'Where is it?'
'Astypalea.'
'I could have told you that.'
'So? Do what you have to do! Go there!'
George shook his head. 'Mario's wife has handed over his papers to the Town Hall. I can't get at them because I'm not officially on the case. Unless we do this through the police or some other official channel we're stuck.'
'Forget that,' said the Colonel. 'An official approach is impossible.'
'You never explained why.'
'Some things cannot be said.'
'Pressure from above?'
The Colonel's face turned to stone.

'Too much to resist?' said George.

'I can resist anything. If I wish to spend the rest of my life writing haiku, on a microscopic pension. I have enemies enough without making more.'

'But this is obstruction of justice!'

'Exactly.'

'And you do nothing.'

'Nothing until the right moment. When I have enough evidence to go for the kill, I shall swoop. Without mercy.'

'Until then?'

'Patience. You talk to your unnamed source. Think of a way of getting at Mario's papers. You say his wife won't help?'

'She's impossible.'

'Any close family?'

'Only Andreas, his brother.'

'What's he like?'

'Makes enemies of everyone.'

'Perfect! He can demand to see his brother's papers.'

'On what pretext?'

'Financial, legal, it doesn't matter. He needs to assess the size of the estate for the purposes of executing the will – something like that. A lawyer will give you the words.'

'Andreas is a lawyer.'

'Even better! Get him on the case at once.'

'I wonder if I should go with him.'

'No. Send your assistant.'

'All this costs money.'

'I know.'

'We're still within the budget?'

The Colonel looked pained. 'Tell your man to stay in a cheap hotel.'

'We know no others,' said George.

'That's what I like to hear.'

George's toasted sandwich arrived. 'Do you mind?' he said.

'Go ahead,' said the Colonel mildly. 'You must keep up your strength.'

'Oh. You give health advice now?'

The Colonel looked stern. 'Eat,' he said.

29 Untouchable

George rang Andreas Filiotis and asked him if he would consider a trip to Astypalea. The response was immediate. He had been looking for a reason to visit, he said. His brother's estate needed investigating. It was too easy for things to get lost or swallowed up by greedy advisers. 'Eleni will do something stupid. It's inevitable. She'll let some madman talk her into an investment scheme or a lunatic charitable cause. I need to get in there and stop her.'

'I want you to take a man with you,' said George.
'Who?'
'My assistant, Haris Pezas.'
'Absolutely not.'
'You'll need help.'
'No I won't.'

George pointed out that there would be a huge number of documents to go through, too many for one man with only a few days at his disposal. Andreas countered that he was a lawyer and well used to finding what he wanted in mountains of papers. George vouched for the man's intelligence and his surprising array of talents. 'I promise you he will be useful,' he said, 'and in ways you won't even imagine.' Irritated more than convinced, Andreas grudgingly acquiesced, adding that he would send Haris back to Athens on the next flight if he turned out to be useless.

George briefed them on what to look for among Mario's papers and wished them a good trip. He would have liked to go along too, but recognised that Sotiriou was probably right to discourage it. He had plenty to do in Athens anyway. Feeling calmer than he had for months, he set off down the stairs for some lunch and his daily dose of news and gossip at the Café Agamemnon.

It was a bright day, the air scoured by twenty-four hours of wind, the sunlight sharp and dazzling. Dimitri was cheerful, people walked purposefully by, you could almost forget the gloom of politics and the crushing atmosphere of cynicism and lost hope. George ordered a beer and a plate of *souvlaki* and salad which Dimitri called in from the taverna round the corner.

Seeing no one he knew, George picked up the newspaper. This soon darkened his happy mood. Farmers were blockading main roads, civil servants planning new strikes, and the government still trying to sidestep the obligations of its reform programme. Meanwhile the Russians were bombing Syria and the number of flimsy inflatable boats crammed with refugees crossing the straits from Turkey had scarcely dropped since the end of summer. Cold weather had not stopped them. Yet the families who hazarded the trip were rapidly running out of places to go. Germany had taken as many as it could, Macedonia had closed its southern border. Greece was forced to look after them until a solution could be found.

Who were these people? Not all, it seemed, were victims of the civil war in Syria. Many came from Iraq and Afghanistan. These, said experts in Europe, were 'economic migrants' with no right of asylum. Some could even be terrorists, using the humanitarian route into a society they had sworn to destroy. Most Greeks, however, felt there was only one decent response: to take them in. Whether their future was wrecked instantly by a bomb or slowly by a failed society, despair was despair. Distinctions between grades and speeds of personal disaster seemed callous, typical of observers seated in comfort many hundreds of miles away.

Inside the paper he came upon worse news: 'Ex-Mayor found dead in waterfall.'

Next to the headline, a photograph of the waiter from Edessa. Not as George had met him, humbled and unsure of himself, but as he had once been, in his days of power, wearing a smart suit, smiling and waving to supporters. He read the short article about him. He had been found in the pool at the bottom of the waterfall, having disappeared at the end of his shift in the café at the top. A colleague said that he had seemed depressed recently. He left behind a wife and three teenage children.

George was sceptical. Kokoras's men could easily have noticed them talking. It would have been a simple matter to knock him into the river in the darkness. He was unable to stop himself visualising the grim spectacle: the man falling into the fast-flowing water, scrabbling for a grip on the slippery concrete sides of the channel, and then flung still conscious into space, electric with terror and the certainty of death. He pitied the man. Yet he wished he had managed at least a phone call before ending his life.

Feeling guilty for this thought, he turned the page and tried to read an article about the state of the nation's roads, where potholes were multiplying as fast as the government's debts. A minute or two later he found himself staring at the print, seeing nothing, taking nothing in, while his mind worked over that waiter's miserable death.

He cast his mind back to the table under the trees, the way Kokoras had walked off, his lieutenants slouching in his wake. They had slipped away into the darkness and he hadn't given them another thought. They could easily have stopped, turned, and seen enough to get suspicious. The sight of George handing over his business card would have clinched it.

George took his phone from his jacket pocket and called Sotiriou. He told the Colonel to look at page three of today's *Kathimerini*. The man described there, he added, would have been one of his most crucial informants. The Colonel said, 'I don't have time to waste reading newspapers,' and hung up.

Accustomed as he was to the Colonel's filthy manners on the phone, he did not bother to take this as a rebuff. If the Colonel wanted to take note he would. If not, too bad.

His food arrived, and he ate hungrily. Dimitri stood by, telling him the latest from the neighbourhood. The story of the week was the woman on the fifth floor, known to be slightly soft in the head, a believer in astrology and obscure 'energies' who had been evicted from her apartment by her own brother. This cruel man had no need of the rent or the space, but was simply exercising his rights. She had nowhere to go. Dimitri was trying to help. If George knew of anyone with a good flat to let, at a reasonable rate... Meanwhile Olga, who ran the kiosk on the corner selling newspapers, magazines, drinks, chocolate, batteries, crisps and cigarettes, had been told by the council that her rent would double in June. She too was packing up. Dimitri began one of his homilies on the state of society. 'We need solidarity, but what do we see? People trying to destroy each other! No one wins by this. And it's all done according to the law! Which does nothing to protect the innocent!'

George nodded, agreeing. Dimitri was a Greek 'Everyman', an honest soul driven to fury by the rottenness of his country's institutions. If he needed to blast off a salvo of anger from time to time, let him do it. One day, perhaps, enough of these good souls would gather and organise themselves into a political movement. Then something might change. It was, of course, precisely what Mario had been attempting.

He finished his lunch while Dimitri, with perfect timing, wound up his speech. It ended, in the usual way, with an apology: '*Se éprixa!* I've bored you rigid.'

'Not at all,' said George. 'You're absolutely right. In everything you say. But now I'm going upstairs. I had a hell of a journey last night. I need to catch up on sleep.'

George collapsed into bed and slept heavily for two hours. The ringing of the telephone woke him, a surreal rush of kaleidoscopic images spinning through his brain as he stumbled across the darkened bedroom to pick it up. The voice on the phone startled him. It was Anna Kenteri.

'Who the hell have you been talking to?' she demanded.

'Sorry, I don't understand.'

'A friend of mine has been interviewed by the police.'

'So?'

'How did they get his name?'

'I don't know,' said George. 'Why not ask them?'

'I told you to stop working on this.'

'I have stopped.'

'But you've spoken to the police?'

'I've done that from the start.'

'Since we last talked?'

'Only to tell them I'm off the case.'

'You took Paris's side.'

'No. Just gave the facts.'
'His "facts" are lies.'
'That's your understanding.'
'What do you mean "my understanding"? I'm Keti's sister! You think I don't understand?'
'I don't think anything. The police and magistrates will make up their own minds.'
'So you poison them with lies from Paris.'
'No,' said George wearily. 'I just gave them the evidence.'
'What is this evidence?'
'The phone recording is part of it,' said George.
'That says it all!'
'If it's genuine.'
'What do you mean? It's obviously genuine.'
'There is some doubt.'
'Just from the fact that Paris denies it?'
'No, there are other problems.'
'What are they?'
'I'm not going to discuss this. I'm off the case, remember?'
'Andonis is very upset.'
'Who's Andonis?'
'My friend.'
'If he's not involved he's got nothing to worry about. It's a routine enquiry.'
'You should tell them to leave him alone.'
'I can't.'
'Of course you can!'
'They'll regard it as interference.'
'They'll get a lot more interference if they carry on bothering him!'
'What do you mean?'
'The police need to treat him with great respect.'

'I'm sure they will.'
'Don't give me that horse-shit! He's not a man to provoke!'
'I don't understand why you're so worried.'
'My God! Are you stupid?'
'Could be. Why don't you just explain?'
'Oh come on! These are things which are not "explained". If you know what you're doing you don't go near certain people.'
'Why not?'
'Because they are who they are!'
'OK, so who are they?'
'Don't give me that, Mr Zafiris! You know what I'm talking about and don't pretend you don't!'

George made an effort to remain calm.

'I can't see into your head,' he said. 'If I could, I wouldn't need to ask. Just make yourself clear.'

'Talk to the police,' she said dismissively. 'You'll find out soon enough.'

'Is he one of the night club people?'
'Ah, the man's brain works!'
'That's all you needed to say. Keti was involved with him?'
'Only in the business sense.'
'I see… And he's dangerous?'
'Only to people who cause him trouble.'
'In other words he's dangerous.'
'Use any words you like.'
'I want to make sure I've got this straight.'
'Whatever!'

George flared up. 'No, not "whatever"! Either you're trying to tell me something or you're not. If it's important, take a little trouble over it! But don't piss me about with these stupid catchphrases.'

Anna gabbled on harshly. 'You know what these people are like, the circles they move in... People get hurt. If you've got any sense you'll stay out of it, and tell the police to stay out too.'

George listened, thinking about what she was saying. 'It's odd,' he said, 'that you wanted your sister to go into that world you're describing. Did you ever think about that?'

She slammed down the phone.

30 The Crop

With both investigations now in other people's hands, George decided to spend a few days on Andros. His wife had asked him to come over and help with the olive harvest. 'We'll all be together,' she said.

He asked what she meant.

'Nick's coming,' she replied. 'He found a cheap flight from Newcastle.'

George threw a few things into a bag – book, shaving kit, a change of clothes – and rang the garage to get the Alfa ready.

By evening he was on the island, rooting about in a shed for the harvest equipment: nets for spreading under the trees, little rakes for combing the olives off the branches, a ladder, a pruning saw, sacks for collecting the fruit. Zoe was in a peaceful mood and cooked one of her favourite recipes: rabbit with green olives. George asked how things were going, although he did not need to. Her body language was clear. She was all energy.

Early the next morning, they drove out to the olive grove on a hillside overlooking the sea. They spread nets under the first of their trees and started work. In the absence of traffic George noticed a host of unexpected sounds: birds whistling and chirping in the branches, waves breaking on the shore far below, the buzz of machinery on a distant slope. With the abrasive touch of the twigs in his left hand, the pulling with his right, the stretching up and the bending down, the silvery green of the leaves at every angle, the colours of the olives darkening from green to red, blue to purple and black, he was soon enveloped in a small but self-sufficient space. They picked and spoke little, each absorbed in the satisfaction of the task, the berries clattering down around their shoulders like heavy drops of rain.

They continued stripping the tree until the branches were bare and the ground carpeted in fruit. Lifting the corners of each net they rolled the olives into a heap, then sat and sorted them from the leaves and twigs that had come down with them. This was a restful half hour, chatting and feeling good in the sun.

They poured the olives into sacks till they were full and almost too heavy to carry.

Nick arrived at noon. They spent an hour having coffee and hearing his news, then started work again, laying out the nets under the next tree. George felt himself reconnecting with his body, his family, their little piece of land and all the generations that had lived on it. He forgot about the city.

That evening he soaked away the day's labours in a bath and thought with pleasure of the good things in his life; a pleasure that seemed to grow without effort from the sensory impressions of the day, the fatigue in his muscles, and the luxurious dissolution of all contradictions and pain in the steaming water.

At the same time he could not quite keep out this happy thought's ugly companion: all the things that were wrong and unsettled, the tangle of menace, brutality and greed that awaited him in Athens. Things were moving forward at last, but to what end? If all his efforts were leading him back into that horrible arena where he was required to fight against the unseen potentates, people protected by money and influence, people who had no need of others, no belief in anything but their own advancement, he felt sick at heart. Why was he doing this? For justice? Money? Job satisfaction? There was precious little of any of that.

They had dinner that night in a local taverna, where Nick commented on the poor quality of the meat and wine. Zoe said she had not noticed, but she did not recall the food in England being anything to boast of. Nick agreed. 'Besides, it costs twice as much to eat out there.'

Zoe pressed him, as if the subject was preying on her. 'You don't prefer it there do you?'

Nick said, 'No,' decisively but his voice left doubt in the air.

'Why not?' she asked.

'It's cold,' he said, 'it's grey, everyone's stressed. It's not too bad if you have money, but the poor really lead wretched lives, drowning in debt... And I miss your cooking.'

Zoe took his hand and squeezed it. 'My boy! I miss having you here to eat it. But I would understand if you preferred England. We're going deeper and deeper into depression over here. The future is worse than the past, and each step forward is like a step back, a step down. No matter how cold you are in Newcastle, how much you miss your family, you have hope, there's a future.'

Nick nodded sadly. 'It seems so odd to me.'

'What exactly?' asked George.

'How can everything just degrade?'

'Very easily,' said Zoe. 'All you need is leaders who don't care.'

And at once George thought of Mario again, his attempts to raise his island out of the morass of neglect, the way he was punished for his efforts.

The next two days passed quickly. On Monday at lunchtime they finished picking. In the afternoon they loaded the car and drove to the olive press. The atmosphere was hot and pungent, noisy with machines, misty with the vapour of crushed olives. The sacks of fruit were weighed and emptied into a hopper, washed, sieved, chopped into pulp, pressed and centrifuged. Glasses of *tsipouro* were gulped, yields and acidity discussed. At last the oil, a bright grass-green fluid, poured from a spout into a steel barrel. They dipped their fingers in. It was warm and tasted of the summer.

They carried their oil home in big square seventeen-litre cans and had a last harvest supper in front of the fire, feeling happy and hopeful. The next morning the party broke up. George and Nick took the ferry to the mainland and drove on to the airport. With tears in his eyes and a knot of foreboding in his heart he kissed his son goodbye and turned towards the centre of town.

Part Three

The Package

31 Hospital Papers

When George switched on his computer he found an email from Haris inviting him to download a file of documents from an online transfer site. A covering note said, 'We've made progress. Take a look at this.'

George watched the file download over several minutes. It was enormous, fifteen gigabytes. He had time to make a cup of coffee and drink it before the download was complete. When he clicked it open, it revealed a single folder with the name 'ASK'. This contained eight more folders with geographical names, including Athens and Edessa. He tried 'Edessa' and found six hundred and fifty documents. 'Athens' had more than a thousand.

He sampled a few, finding letters from ministries and municipalities, photographs, architect's plans, emails from university professors, banks, educational charities and European funding bodies. Buried among them lay a typical cross-section of Mario's interests: environmental, economic, social, scientific. There was no summary, no guide. Just vast quantities of words and images. How could Mario stay on top of all this? How could anyone?

He phoned Haris.

'What's this you've sent me?' asked George.

'It could be what we're looking for,' said Haris.

'How?'

'It comes from Mario's laptop, and it explains what he was up to.'

'Looks like everything under the sun. I can't get a handle on it.'

'It all centres on a special project.'

'ASK?'

'That's it.'

'What's ASK?'

'A medical school.'

'Where? Edessa?'

Haris grunted. 'And a few other places!'

'I don't understand,' said George.

'Filiotis and a man called Skouras were in discussion for years about it.'

'Skouras? At the Red Cross in Athens?'

'That's the one.'

'I've met him. He shut up like a clam when I mentioned Mario.'

'He's probably scared.'

'That's what I thought. What else do you know about this project?'

Haris said, 'The idea was to set up a new teaching hospital and medical school in Greece with the help of London University. Top class, fully funded, open to anyone, not just the sons and daughters of the rich.'

'Sounds dangerous. I can see the enemies massing already. What happened?'

'They tried various locations: Athens, Ioannina, Edessa, Corfu, Crete, Kos. For some reason it failed everywhere.'

'What was the problem?'

'We don't know. But it doesn't seem to have been a question of money.'

'How do you know that?'

'They had plenty.'

'Money does everything in Greece,' said George.

'You would think so.'

'What's the connection with Mario's death?'

'There may be none at all, but I noticed he was starting to get somewhere in Astypalea. He was raising money to buy an old factory.'

'Who the hell would want to build a medical school in Astypalea? It's a lump of dusty rock fourteen hours by ferry from Athens. And who would bother to stop you? There'd be no need. Climate and geography would kill the project stone dead within a couple of years.'

'He was Mayor here. There's an airport, a reasonable town…'

'And a population of less than fifteen hundred. It doesn't make sense. Either to build a hospital or to get killed over it. This isn't what we're after.'

'Why don't you read the file?'

'Why don't I *not* read it?' said George.

'Up to you, but Andreas thinks this is gold. I'm reading it again. More carefully.'

'Where's Andreas?'

'Asleep.'

'The layabout! It's not even lunch time.'

'He's exhausted. He was up half the night reading that stuff, after six hours non-stop with Eleni.'

'Non-stop what?'

'Fighting.'

George was pained but not surprised. 'What were they

fighting about?' he asked.

'I didn't pay much attention, but it seemed to be houses and bank accounts.'

'Anything you could possibly relate to his death?'

'No.' Haris checked himself. 'Unless…'

'Go on,' said George.

'I did wonder if he might have killed himself.'

'On a bicycle? Unlikely.'

'Not as a direct suicide, more like the kind of recklessness that sets in when you don't care any more if you live or die.'

'What makes you think that?'

'I'm not sure I should say.'

'Go ahead!'

'Is Eleni a close friend of yours?'

'No.'

'What do you think of her?'

'I find her difficult.'

'Exactly.'

'So?'

'Imagine living with her!'

George tried for a few moments. It was not pleasant.

'You mean she drove him to it?'

'It's possible.'

'If she did,' said George, 'our job is done.'

'But was he the type to kill himself?' said Haris. 'From what I understand he was a highly energetic man. Fully committed.'

'That can have its dark side.'

'Was he up and down a lot?'

'Didn't seem to be. Though you can't always tell.'

'There's another thing,' said Haris. 'Debt. Have you thought of that? It can be a killer.'

'Don't I know it.'

'The whole country's drowning in post-dated cheques.'
'I asked Eleni if Mario had any problems of that kind.'
'And what did she say?'
'She said it was none of my business.'
'Which means he probably did.'

George took a deep breath. 'In normal circumstances I would agree,' he said. 'But we can't make assumptions. We need evidence.'

'I need to go through his emails,' said Haris. 'And a few thousand other files.'

George thought about this. 'Can you put it all on a hard drive?'

'I've done that.'
'So you could come back to Athens?'
'I could. But I thought I would give it another day, go and look at the factory…'
'What does Andreas say?'
'I told you, he's asleep.'
'Ask him when he wakes up.'
'OK. I'll let you know.'

*

George opened his laptop and clicked on 'Astypalea'. Another vast and thickly populated file. He arranged the documents in order of date, plunged in at the beginning and was soon deep in his friend's affairs. Despite the doubts he had expressed to Haris, he found himself impressed by the project, surprised by the energy and goodwill it had attracted. Retired professors ready to work for nothing, Greek financiers in New York and London, bankers and shipping people who wanted to help, Brussels bureaucrats with funds to spend, secretive private donors... The very improbability of launching a new medical faculty on a remote island seemed to catch people's imagination. If it worked, it would transform the place. The Aegean, Mario had once said, should become 'a living museum, a buzzing market-place of culture and creative exchange'. It was a bold impulse. Hundreds of people could benefit, thousands more could be inspired, but George knew too well how these things tend to go in Greece. The more beautiful the dream, the more brutal the awakening.

The ancient Greeks had a terrifying story of the Titan Prometheus, who stole fire from Mount Olympus and gave it to mankind, against the wishes of the gods. As a punishment Zeus had him chained for eternity to a rock, where an eagle visited him daily to eat his liver, which grew back again every night. It was a disgusting and demoralising tale, but it played out a pattern that was all too easy to recognise in daily life.

Weary of his black thoughts, George stood up from his desk and stretched. His neck and shoulders were stiff from sitting too long. He rolled his head around, loosened his joints, walked into the corridor, the kitchen, the bedroom, back into his study. He stared out of the window, his eyes on the garden of the church opposite, his mind floating elsewhere. Drawing comparisons with ancient myths is all very well, he told himself, but it didn't get him any further with this case. What had Mario done to deserve a death sentence? Building a hospital might spoil a rival developer's plans, but a *medical school?* Who could possibly object to that? Yet somebody had objected. Repeatedly. Then fatally.

Or was his death unconnected with the medical school?

He turned away from the window, thinking he must speak to Dr Skouras again. Or, if Skouras was still reluctant, one of the English partners in the scheme. One of them must know what had been going on. Perhaps they would not be so afraid to talk.

As he moved towards his desk, something made him stop. Something unusual in the scene outside had caught his eye. He returned to the window, looked back at the church garden, down into the street. Among the cars parked on the far side was a black Mercedes with tinted windows. That was the jarring detail: in this ordinary Athens street, the preferred vehicle of the politician, the tycoon, the gangster.

George picked up his keys and went downstairs. It was still early, the Café Agamemnon was empty, Dimitri sitting inside, watching television.

'Do me a favour, Dimitri. Keep an eye on the black Mercedes on the far side of the street. I'm going for a short walk. Let me know if anyone gets out of that car and follows me.'

'OK,' said Dimitri, who was used to these odd requests. 'Which way are you heading?'

'Up the hill. Against the traffic. They'll have to follow me on foot.'

Dimitri nodded and switched off the TV. 'I'm ready.'

George walked briskly, not looking back. It was a cool day, with a touch of winter in the air. He buttoned his jacket and turned up the collar. At Evantheia's flower shop on the corner he paused to examine the display. Despite six years of declining business and a depressive husband, she kept the shop going, always with a cheerful smile, riding the crisis, offering affordable flowers: chrysanthemums, sunflowers, hyacinths, little potted violets and azaleas. The days of lilies and gardenias, of extravagant bouquets, had long gone. George wondered how much longer her shop would survive, selling even this modest luxury in grim times. He waved to her but did not go in.

Turning left into Smyrna Street, he called in at the fruit and vegetable shop and bought a kilo of oranges and a piece of broccoli for lunch. He turned left again down Filis, then Epirou, and back into Aristotle Street, where he found Dimitri at the Agamemnon wiping the tables and arranging the chairs outside.

George walked into the café and sat down. Dimitri followed him in.

'You're right,' he said. 'A short fellow in a leather jacket got out of the car. Fortyish. Bald. Tough guy. I expect he'll come by in a moment.'

'Anyone else in the car?'

'Yes, but I couldn't see a face.'

'Just one?'

'Not sure. They usually go in twos, don't they...? There he is now!'

George saw the man walk past without a glance into the café. Very cool. He was wearing an earpiece for a mobile phone. Only that and his lithe gait, perhaps also the slightly bulging leather *blouson,* marked him out from an ordinary passer-by.

'Watch my back,' said George. 'I'll try and talk to him.'

He went out into the street again, crossed to the Mercedes and knocked on the driver's window. There was no response. He knocked again.

A voice behind him said, 'What do you want?'

George turned and saw the short man standing in front of him. He had a hard, serious face and calm blue eyes.

'Why are you following me?' asked George.

'I'm not following you,' said the man calmly.

'Yes you are.'

'You're making a mistake.'
'I've got your number plate and a photo of you.'
'Doesn't bother me.'
'It will.'
The man shrugged his shoulders. 'Can I get to my car?'
George did not budge. The man began to go past him. George felt the steely muscles of the arm moving him aside. The door opened and he caught a glimpse of another figure in the passenger seat, sitting quite still. Then the door closed again and was locked from the inside.

George wanted to put some heat on them, hustle them out of the street, but he remembered Haris's dictum about knowing your target. If a fight started it would be two against one. He was also unarmed.

He returned to the Café Agamemnon and let Dimitri serve him coffee.

'In trouble again?' said Dimitri.
'Looks like it,' said George.
'Who are they?'
'God knows.'

*

Back at his desk he found a new thread in the hospital story. At a certain point in the negotiations, in July, the price of the disused factory in Astypalea had suddenly shot up by seven hundred and fifty thousand euros – an enormous hike justified by the inclusion of a piece of adjoining land. This was odd. It could either be due to a spoiling bid by Mario's enemies or perhaps spectacular greed on the part of the seller.

George read the correspondence. It looked more like greed. Unusually successful greed in this case because Mario, instead of pulling out as he should have, had calmly increased his offer. The reason for this cool response was clear: he had recently made a successful application for crowdfunding, raising over one million euros, which more than covered the new price. Even if Mario's enemies were on the case, it seemed there was no stopping him.

Now, though, another obstacle appeared. With the good news about crowdfunding came a blow from one of the investors. Due to 'global uncertainty in the markets' a London-based fund called Worldwide Ethos had decided to pull out. This suddenly took two million euros away. So now the project was one and three-quarter million euros worse off than before. This was the situation the day before Mario left for Athens.

Had he gone there to raise more money? Did he need it so fast that he went to a 'no questions asked' lender?

With a shudder George remembered that unpleasant man at EAP, who purported to deal in finance. It seemed unlikely that such a man would ever tell the truth about anything, but perhaps in this case he had.

George read the last few documents in the folder: a note of regret from his financial adviser about the situation; a request to the owner of the factory about paying in instalments; a reply from the owner's lawyer saying the price had been agreed on the understanding that the full amount would be paid on the date of transfer of ownership; finally a plea from Mario for flexibility, which remained unanswered.

Reading these emails, George felt Mario's desperation. His friend was frustrated, impatient, fed up. As a result he had let himself be cornered. Anyone offering to buy a ruined factory at a time like this should have been in a commanding position. With the national economy in meltdown, no other buyer would be likely to appear for five, ten, maybe twenty years. Mario had all the cards in his hand. Why was he allowing himself to be outplayed?

George stood up from his desk and took a turn around the room. There was something wrong here. If Mario was in such a weak position, why had his enemies found it necessary to kill him? Why not simply exploit his weakness?

Perhaps he had some kind of hold over them? Some compromising knowledge? Had he threatened to expose them? That was the usual way in Greece. Everyone who runs a business, builds a house, lives any kind of active life, is forced by the complexity of the law and the malevolence of the state bureaucracy to work outside it, in the fast-moving unofficial economy of cash payments and favours. Everyone is vulnerable, so they leave each other in peace. A hostile peace, always in danger of exploding...

He returned to his desk and checked again through the last few emails. Maybe he should talk to the other people in these exchanges? The financial adviser, the owner of the factory, the lawyer? Maybe, too, he should ask Haris and Andreas to look for other clues.

He picked up the phone.

32 The Two Andonis

Before he could bring up Haris's name on his phone he had an incoming call. This showed as a 'private number'. He answered, and a voice he did not recognise, a smooth, confident voice, used to giving orders, said, 'Don't upset my men, Mr Zafiris. They are there to protect you.'

'Really? I find that hard to believe.'

'That's your problem.'

'Who are they protecting me from?'

'A lot of people. And yourself.'

'In other words this is a threat.'

'I don't deal in threats, Mr Zafiris. I deal in self-preservation.'

'Did Mario Filiotis get one of your phone calls? Offering self-preservation? If he did I don't think much of your services.'

'Watch your step, Mr Zafiris.' The voice was suddenly harsher. 'You're starting to annoy me.'

The phone went dead. George pushed it away in disgust. He fetched a can of beer from the fridge and snapped it open. He thought about what had just happened. This was not good. On the other hand if he was receiving calls like that he must be getting close to the bone.

He picked up the phone again and called Haris. He would surely have something helpful to say.

He began with the black Mercedes, and was about to move on to the threatening phone call when Haris brusquely interrupted him.

'Listen, Mr Zafiris, I can't discuss this now, I'm running out of battery.'

'Plug in your charger!'

'I can't, I'm out in the country.'

'Where? At the factory?'

'I'll call you back later. Bye.'

George was puzzled. This was not like Haris, either to be caught short of battery – he used to run an electrical shop for heaven's sake – or to cut off a conversation so abruptly. Something else was going on.

He gulped his beer, feeling frustrated, wishing he had a cigarette.

A knock on the front door made him jump. Sliding open the top drawer of his desk he found his Beretta. He slipped off the safety catch and walked softly to the door. He put his eye to the keyhole.

It was not the bald man or his companion. It was Dimitri from the café downstairs. He let him in at once.

'What's up?' George asked, laying the Beretta on the hall table.

Dimitri closed the front door behind him. 'Haris Pezas has just called me. He says your phone is being monitored. That's why he cut you off.'

'How does he know all this?'

'He didn't explain. He said you should ask me to go out and buy you another phone so that you can talk freely. Meanwhile watch what you say.'

'I could go and buy a new phone myself.'

'You could, but you have to give your name and address.'

George laughed uneasily. 'He's paranoid!'

'I don't know. Only you can judge…' Dimitri looked embarrassed. 'Excuse me, there's no one in the café. If you don't mind I'd better go.'

'Of course,' said George. 'Thank you for the message.'

'What about the new phone?'

'I'll think about that. You need to go now.'

He saw Dimitri out.

George considered his options. If Haris was right it would be impossible for him to do anything without being followed, listened to, observed. His effectiveness would be drastically reduced, with every move signalled in advance to his so-called 'protectors'. The new phone was an easy solution to the problem. Even if Haris was wrong he would only have wasted a few euros. He would ask Dimitri to buy one for him.

Meanwhile he needed to see Colonel Sotiriou. No call in advance, just turn up at his office unannounced. He picked up his keys and descended to the street.

Leaving the dusty brown lobby, he stopped briefly at the Café Agamemnon to give Dimitri fifty euros for a cheap phone and some pay-as-you-go credit. Emerging again, he walked quickly against the traffic for a couple of hundred metres, past the first side street, then hailed the first taxi that approached. He told the driver to take an immediate right, then right again towards Leoforos Alexandras. The black Mercedes and its crew could not possibly follow him, but still he took no chances. About half a kilometre beyond the police headquarters he asked to be dropped off. They were at the junction with Panormou, where dozens of little streets spread out in every direction.

He paid off the taxi, crossed the busy avenue and slipped

into an alley between two bars. At the far end was Ambelakion Street, with the traffic running one way towards him. He took it, walking against the flow, until he reached the junction with Dimitsanas. The side entrance to the police headquarters was on the left. He had not been followed on foot, and it would have been impossible to follow him by car. He entered the building with a sense of relief.

The policewoman on the door, a young blonde with big, handsome eyes, took his name in a businesslike fashion and telephoned Sotiriou's office. As she waited for a reply, George glanced outside. A black Mercedes with tinted windows was pulling up at the kerb. The front door opened and the bald man in the leather jacket stepped out. He glanced about, adjusted the earpiece on his wire, and headed straight for the entrance to the police building.

George's heart tightened with fear. How had they traced him? The thought flickered instantaneously through his mind even as his eyes darted about the small entrance lobby searching for an escape. To the left was a closed door. Ahead a dark corridor. To the right the lift. The policewoman was still waiting on the phone, peering distractedly at something on her desk. George made for the corridor, entering its shadow as the street door opened, sending a beam of reflected light sweeping across the floor. George flattened himself against the wall and listened. He heard the policewoman begin to say, 'His office is not answering…' then stop with a gasp of surprise.

'A man just came in,' said a male voice. 'Where did he go?'
'Who are you?'
'What did he say to you?'
'What do you want?'

George heard nothing for a few seconds. Then the man's voice spoke more softly in words George could not make out. The street door opened again, the beam of light swung across the floor, just catching the toes of George's shoes. He waited a little longer before emerging from the shadows. The policewoman was at her desk, wide-eyed and bewildered.

As George approached they fired questions at each other.

'Where did you go?'

'What happened?'

'Who are you?'

'What did that man say to you?'

'Stop asking questions! You need to tell me what you're doing here.'

'I'm looking for Colonel Sotiriou. I have urgent information for him. Please try his office again.'

She pressed her lips together, glanced nervously to one side, back at her desk and computer screen, then picked up the phone.

'Is Colonel Sotiriou there? I have someone downstairs to see him.' She looked up at George. 'Your name?'

'George Zafiris.'

She repeated the name to the phone. 'Wait here. He's coming down.'

George tried one more time to prise some information from her. 'That man who just came in,' he said, 'works for a criminal organisation. If you want promotion from this janitor's position you'd be wise to tell Colonel Sotiriou what he said to you.'

She gave him a heavily sceptical look.

'Wait just there,' she said, pointing. 'In the light, where I can see you.'

The lift doors opened and Colonel Sotiriou appeared.

'Let's go out and get some coffee,' he said briskly.

George stopped him. 'I've been followed here,' he said. 'I don't know how they managed it. Haris Pezas says my phone's bugged, but they must have it on a tracker system.'

Sotiriou was listening carefully. 'Where are they now?'

'Outside in a black Mercedes. One of the men came in and spoke to the girl on the door. She won't say anything about it.'

'Hold on,' said Sotiriou.

The Colonel went over to the girl and exchanged a few words. When he came back he said, 'We'll use another entrance.'

Sotiriou called the lift and pressed the button for the fifth floor.

'Strange place for an entrance,' said George.

The Colonel ignored the remark. 'Give me your phone,' he said.

George handed it over and they rode up the rest of the way in silence.

At the fifth floor the Colonel led the way along a corridor to a door with a number on it. He knocked and went in, indicating to George to stay outside. A minute later he was back with a car key in his hand.

They rode the lift down again to the basement, where a police mechanic showed them to a scruffy blue Citroën. The Colonel reached into the glove compartment, found a baseball cap and gave it to George. 'Put that on,' he said, 'and shades if you have them.'

He drove up the ramp to street level, directly onto Leoforos Alexandras, avoiding Dimitsanas Street where the black Mercedes must still be waiting.

'If they're tracking your phone,' said Sotiriou, 'they'll think you're on the fifth floor. If they follow us it means they've planted some other device and we'll need to have you X-rayed.'

'Suppose someone needs to get in touch with me?'
'That's the least of your problems.'
'What are you trying to tell me?'
'You've got all kinds of trouble on your tail,' said Sotiriou. 'And it's going to be on mine soon if I'm not careful. So we're going to be quick and minimal.'

Spotting a parking space he switched on his flashers and reversed in.

'Got a notebook?' the Colonel inquired, turning off the engine.

George took one from his pocket.

'Get this down. I've looked into Stelios and Merkulov as you requested.'

'And?'

'Both highly interesting characters, although not quite my department as they're not involved in violent crime.'

'What about someone called Andonis? A friend of Anna Kenteri?'

'I don't know him.'

'She said the police had interviewed him, and he cut up rough.'

'I only know about Stelios and Merkulov.'

'So who the hell is Andonis?'

'I've no idea. May I continue with what I was saying?'

'Go ahead.'

'Stelios is a photographer. Or should I say *pornographer*?'

'Illegal stuff? Under age?'

'No. Just vulgar. He exploits and corrupts girls. He also owns a collection of nightclubs and casinos. The police spend a lot of time on call-outs to these places. They're associated with prostitution, drugs, money laundering, stolen goods and vehicles, insurance fraud... We have to keep rotating our personnel to prevent them getting sucked into the system. Even then we're never sure.'

'You should close those places down.'

'That's difficult. Stelios knows the law and stays inside it. The dirty stuff is done at arm's length. You can't pin anything on him. He's also well connected. Once or twice he's been in danger of being busted, and a word comes from on high to leave him alone.'

'What's the connection? Family?'

'His daughter is married to the son of the Minister of Justice.'

'Who's that?'

'Byron Kakridis.'

'That bastard!'

'Watch what you say about him!'

'I thought he was PASOK. How did he get into a SYRIZA government?'

'Switched parties when he saw the way things were going.'

'He killed my friend Hector Pezas, not to mention his own wife.'

'Steady on!' said Sotiriou. 'None of that is known for a fact. It's your theory.'

'Come on, you were there! It may have been his Georgian friends who did the shooting, but he was responsible.'

'I'm not going to argue that with you. Believe it if you want to, but keep quiet about it. For your own safety.'

George struggled to suppress his anger. 'You're so bloody legalistic sometimes.'

Sotiriou bristled. 'Someone has to uphold the law!'

'OK,' said George, 'let's get back to Stelios. He's a pornographer and pimp, and well connected. What else do we know about him?'

'He's in his late fifties, drives a Bentley convertible, has a yacht, what else? Models himself on James Bond…'

'Oh, it gets worse.'

'In spite of the glamorous lifestyle he's very private. He did not take kindly to being interviewed by the police.'

'Who questioned him?'

'Our friend Karás, the rugby player.'

'That's good. I'll talk to him. Tell me about Merkulov.'

'He's an investor.'

'In what?'

'Hotels, resorts, shopping malls. Various other things.'

'Any criminal connections?'

'Nothing known. In fact he dabbles in philanthropy, although that could be a front, cultivated for public relations purposes. He was described to me by one informant as the underground spring that supplies the wells.'

'What does that mean? A kind of bank?'

'Like a bank, but totally unregulated and on his terms.'

'High interest rates?'

'Or a slice of the action.'

'Where does he get his money?'

'He's a Russian oligarch.'

'Is he a friend of Stelios?'

'That's what you told me.'

'Did I?' George was surprised.

'You said he and Stelios were both close to Keti Kenteri. That was information from her husband, Paris Aliveris.'

'I remember that,' said George. 'But they might be friends of hers without knowing each other.'

'Good point,' said Sotiriou. He sat back. 'You can stop taking notes now. That's all I've managed to gather… By the way, I've been watching the street. We weren't followed.'

'Good,' said George distractedly. He was still thinking about 'Andonis'.

'I remember Anna telling me he was not a man to provoke,' he said.

'Who?'

'Andonis.'

'True of both, I would say.'

'Can we get a search order for either of them?'

'That will be difficult.'

'Why?'

Sotiriou's phone rang. 'Excuse me.'

As he answered the call, the Colonel's manner altered. His eyes narrowed, his brow contracted, his mouth compressed into a thin downward curve. The confident set of his features was suddenly gone. He must be talking to someone above him in the hierarchy, and in a nasty mood. He spoke very little.

Eventually he said, 'Very well, sir, I will do as you ask,' before laying down his phone.

It took him a few moments to compose himself.

'Trouble?' said George.

'Trouble,' said the Colonel. 'I left your phone with the secretary of the Chief of Police.'

'So?'

'He found out.'

'Did she tell him?'

'No. I asked her not to mention it.'

'Maybe she did anyway.'

'No. I trust her.'

'How then?'

Sotiriou sighed. 'I left it there as a kind of trap.'

'To catch the people who are tailing me?'

'Exactly.'

'Only now you've caught yourself in it?'

'You could say that...' Sotiriou placed the palms of his hands over his face and rubbed his eyes.

'Well?' said George. 'What's happened?'

Sotiriou looked at him heavily, without hope.

'They've put me in an impossible position.'

'Tell me.'

'I've been ordered to arrest you.'

'Arrest me? What the hell for?'

'Harassment. More serious crimes will no doubt be added before long.'

'Where has this come from?'

'The Chief of Police.'

'Himself?'

'He had a visit from the men in the Mercedes. They're Special Security, by the way, not gangsters.'

'Special Security? On whose orders?'

'We don't know. But it's likely to be at a high level, and connected with your friend Andonis. Whoever he is.'

'Anna wasn't bluffing then.'

'It seems not.'

'But how has this suddenly led to an order for my arrest?'

'The Mercedes men wanted to see you. The Chief of Police said he knew nothing about you and they proceeded to humiliate him by locating your phone in the secretary's desk.'

'OK. Unpleasant but effective.'

'Doing their job, that's all. The Chief of Police forced his secretary to say who'd left the phone there, and then he called me. My official duty now is, as I say, to arrest you.'

'But I'm acting on your orders.'

'That's right. If they find out about that, I'm finished too.'

'What do you mean you're finished *too*?'

Sotiriou did not answer. George knew what he meant.

'So what the hell do we do now?'

'In sixty seconds from now you get out of this car and start walking. Go home, collect what you need, and disappear.'

'Just like that? Walk out of my own life?'

'Not forever. A week or two will be a good start. Give me time to work on this and get the order lifted.'

'Then what happens to the investigation? All this work?'

'We'll come back to it.'

'When?'

'When we have more evidence.'

'They'll be destroying it as we speak!'

'They can't destroy everything. Something will remain. Some trace. It always does.'

George felt a surge of frustration and anger.

'The longer we leave it, Colonel, the less will remain! And now they know we're on to them.'

Sotiriou placed a hand on George's shoulder. 'We can't discuss this now,' he said. 'You must go.'

'Where?' cried George. 'I can't just snap my fingers and create a new life!'

'Go anywhere you like. Go abroad. Just don't tell me your plans.'

'That'll be easy! I don't have any.'

'Fine,' said Sotiriou lightly. He offered his hand. 'Stay in touch.'

'Can't do that,' said George. 'You took my phone.'

'Buy a new one. And let's speak through your friend.'

'Haris Pezas?'

Sotiriou repeated the name. 'Pezas,' he murmured. 'Any relation of your last assistant?'

'That was Hector. His brother.'

'Is he any good?' asked the Colonel mildly.

'What?' exclaimed George. 'You've just turned my life inside out and you start a conversation about my assistant? Are you serious?'

'Relax,' said Sotiriou calmly. 'I presume you trust him?'

'Yes of course I trust him!'

'Excellent… Off you go now. I'll give you an hour.'

'Then what?'

'Then your home will be put under surveillance.'

'You realise this is an abuse of my rights, as well as an absurd waste of police time?'

'I couldn't agree more,' said the Colonel. 'It's a necessary evil.' He offered his hand again. 'Goodbye.'

George walked fast through the streets of Kolonaki. He had a lot to organise, starting with his own thoughts, which raged through his head like a torrent, chaotic, anxious, turbulent and vengeful. He must pick up some essential things from home – laptop, camera, passport, bank cards, a change of clothes. He must buy a phone, without which he couldn't function. And he must find somewhere to stay.

This was the big one. He could go to Zoe's house on Andros, or try to remain in Athens. Andros would be safer but too far from the action. He had no intention of being idle, knowing he had to step up the pressure on 'Andonis', keep him guessing, keep him on the defensive. In Andros the temptation would be to switch off. It would also expose Zoe to danger.

Athens, then. But where? Not a hotel, because his name would go to the police within twenty-four hours. It would have to be a friend, somewhere outside his neighbourhood. Kifissia came to mind. Or Piraeus. Or Maroussi, where Petros Karagounis had a house. Perhaps Maroussi was best.

Approaching Aristotle Street he grew tense and watchful. Colonel Sotiriou had promised him an hour, but time is notoriously elastic in Greece. An hour could mean the whole of the afternoon, or just fifteen minutes. The Chief of Police might be impatient for results. He might send men over at once, pre-empting Sotiriou's orders.

The street looked clear, however, and he slipped into the Café Agamemnon unseen.

'Dimitri,' he said, 'I need to talk urgently.'

'Take a seat. I'm making coffee for those ladies.'

George glanced over at a pair of well-heeled Kolonaki housewives. One was talking in a loud, confident voice about her difficulties with hair colouring. When the other protested that her hair was like a twenty-year-old girl's, she rejected the suggestion vigorously. 'No, *agapi mou*, just look at the parting! That's the weak point. It's supposed to be dark chestnut. Do you see dark chestnut? No. It's red. Bordeaux in fact. Bordeaux! How many twenty-year-olds do you know with Bordeaux roots? I'm sick of Bordeaux! I told Mihalis to use anything he likes, Kerastase, Clairol, never mind the cost. And he's tried them all! Every one! He might as well have used water!'

George would normally have been irritated by her self-obsessed jabbering. As a glimpse of ordinary life, however, a life suddenly beyond his reach, it seemed strangely touching. If women could sit in a café all afternoon talking passionately about hair dyes, things could not be so bad.

A minute later Dimitri was with him. 'What's up?' he asked.

George explained the situation. 'I'll have to make myself scarce,' he said.

'Where will you go?'

'I don't know yet. The police are bound to question you.

Don't tell them anything. But don't lie to them either.'

'Let me know if there's anything I can do.'

'You didn't buy me a phone by any chance?'

'I didn't have time. Let me give you your money back.'

'Hold on to it,' said George. 'I may have a favour to ask you.'

'Whatever you want.'

George thanked him and left the café. He climbed the stairs to his apartment.

It took him ten minutes to collect his necessary belongings into a shoulder bag. He was about to leave when he noticed the message light blinking on the telephone.

There were two messages. One from Zoe, asking him to call, the other from Evantheia at the flower shop, saying she had a bouquet for his wife's name day.

This was odd. Zoe's name day was in the spring. Several months away. This must be a mistake. Or something worse... He was puzzling over this when the telephone rang. 'Private number' said the caller display. He let it ring until the answering machine clicked on. He heard his own voice saying, 'Please leave a message.' Then that smooth, confident, menacing voice, saying, 'Mr Zafiris, I warned you.'

On impulse he snatched up the phone. 'Andonis?' he barked.

'Who's that?' The voice had a note of alarm.

'This is Zafiris. You're the one who's gone too far now. Your secret is out.'

'Stay where you are, Mr Zafiris. If you leave your apartment you are in mortal danger.'

'Thanks for the warning,' said George. 'But I'm telling you, you've lost the game.'

'Bullshit.'

'We'll see,' said George. Without waiting for a reply he unplugged the phone and let himself out of the door.

33 Pursuit

The word 'bullshit' rang in his ears as he descended the staircase. Why had Andonis told him to stay in his flat? Threatened to kill him if he left? There could only be one reason. Because he wanted him in there. Trapped. A fish in a barrel.

Bullshit to you, Andonis.

There was no one in the street, although he was sure the black Mercedes must already be on its way. He walked quickly up to Evantheia's and asked about the bouquet.

Evantheia took a package from a shelf behind her and placed it on the counter.

'Strange bouquet,' said George suspiciously.

'It's from your friend Mr Pezas,' she said. 'He told me to say it was flowers.'

George smiled. 'Thank you, Evantheia. Forgive me, I'm in a rush right now, but I'll see you very soon.'

He hurried out of the shop, peered anxiously up the street at the oncoming traffic. Seeing a taxi, he flagged it down.

'Where are we going?' asked the driver, a large, lazy-looking man smoking an electronic cigarette.

'Maroussi.'

'Address?'

'I'll tell you later.'
'I can type it into my GPS.'
'Just drive please!'

The driver seemed reluctant, or possibly slow-witted. George glanced over his shoulder, every black car looking like a Mercedes.

'Go!' said George angrily. 'I'm in a hurry.'

The taxi driver took a last puff of his e-cigarette and placed it on the passenger seat. He sighed and put the engine into gear. At last the car moved off. As it did so George, turning his neck uncomfortably, saw a black car stop. This one was a Mercedes. With tinted windows. One of the doors opened. The short bald man in the leather jacket got out, raised the dark glasses from his eyes, and searched both ways along the street. Catching sight of the taxi, he tensed like a wildcat.

'Shit,' muttered George. He cursed as he saw the Mercedes pull out and follow them down the street.

Now he was being tailed again and Maroussi seemed like a bad idea. He did not want to lead his pursuers there. But what was the alternative? Kifissia, Piraeus – wherever he went they would go too. Maybe even to Andros? As he contemplated what they might have in store for him he knotted up with anxiety. What could he do? Where could he go? He sat still for a minute, his hands gripping his bag, forcing himself to calm down. 'Concentrate on your breathing' – a phrase remembered from a yoga class, many years ago. It helped at times like this. Breathe in slowly, counting to eight, and let it slowly out. Once again. In and out. Four or five times more. Concentrate. Eliminate other thoughts. He became aware of his body, the shape it made in the car seat, the slump in his shoulders. His head, buzzing with possibilities. His hands, one on his left knee, the other clutching the package from Pezas...

Suddenly it occurred to him: time to open it. A few more breaths, this was doing him good... Inside the package was a new telephone. A note stuck to it said, 'Charged. Ready to use. Pin number 0951.'

George turned on the phone and keyed in the pass code. A text message was waiting. 'Hope you can use this. Arriving today 1530 Eleftherios Venizelos. Meet there. Haris.'

George checked the time. It was 3.15 pm.

'Change of plan,' he said to the driver. 'Take me to the airport.'

Twenty-five minutes later, speeding along the Attiki Odos, the Mercedes still visible fifty metres behind, George tried calling Haris.

'Just landed,' said Haris. 'Where are you?'

George explained the situation.

'How many in the Mercedes?' asked Haris.

'Two, I think.'

'Right. Give me a few minutes. I'll call you back.'

George settled back in his seat and watched the countryside flash past. This conversation made him feel better. He was no longer alone.

Three minutes later his phone rang. George answered, and Haris said, 'Tell the driver to enter the short-term car park on the *Arrivals* level. He won't like it, because you have to pay to get out, but that's going to work in our favour. Tell him you'll add the parking fee to the fare. Is that clear?'

'Completely.'

'Leave the taxi there, with the packaging on the back seat, pay him what you owe so far and ask him to wait. Say you'll be back in twenty minutes.'

'Will I?'

'No.'

'Why do I leave the packaging?'

'So it looks as if you're coming back.'

'That won't fool him.'

'He won't care. He'll have his money. Cross the road to the airport, go up to the *Departures* level and make some enquiries about a ticket to anywhere you like, New York, Dubai, Frankfurt, whatever. Say you'll think about it. Do some shopping, have a coffee, use up twenty minutes. It can be more but no less than that. Then head for the taxi queue and take a cab to Markopoulo. There's a butcher's shop there, Margaritis, 24 Trikoupi Street. Margaritis is a friend. He's expecting you. Say you'd like to see me. He'll take you out through the back door of the shop to his house. We'll meet there.'

'I'll be followed.'

'Of course. One of the agents will follow you into the airport, on foot. The other will be stuck in the car park. After twenty minutes he'll have to pay to get out. That should delay him enough to keep him off our backs.'

'What about the one on foot?'

'I'll deal with him.'

'Be careful.'

'Of course.'

'He's Special Security, not some thug.'

'It's OK. I know what to do. Just play your part. And stay calm.'

'There's a warrant out for my arrest. Won't the airport police spot me?'

'That's my only worry. But there are hundreds of people wandering around. Just stick to the crowded places and don't draw attention to yourself.'

'Haris, this is scaring me. Is it going to work?'
'Of course it is.'
'What if the Merc doesn't follow us into the car park?'
'Call me if that happens.'
'Or the little bald guy talks to the police?'
'He won't.'
'Why not?'
'Because Special Security don't like the police.'
'He might still do it.'
'I'll be watching him. If he goes near the cops I'll let you know, and you head straight for the taxis.'

George paused a moment to consider the plan. It was not foolproof. Plenty could go wrong. But it was better than anything he had in mind.

'All right,' said George. 'Let's go for it. I'll be there in about ten minutes.'

As they came to the airport, George told the driver to head for *Arrivals*. Seeing the sign for the short-term car park he said, 'In there.' The taxi driver pulled over in a lane reserved for buses. 'I'm not going in there,' he said.
'I'll pay for the ticket.'
'No.'
'I'll pay you ten euros extra.'
'I'm not allowed in there.'
Bugger, thought George.
'I need you to wait for me.'
'I'll wait here.'
'You're not allowed here. It's for buses.'
'No problem.'
'OK,' said George. 'How much do I owe you?'
'Thirty-five euros.'

George paid.

'Do you want me to wait?'

'No.'

He opened the door and got out.

'Your bag?' said the driver.

'It's rubbish.'

'Take it with you.'

George reached in for the bag. As he straightened up he glanced to his left and saw the Mercedes parking. Also in the bus lane. The plan was not going well.

He dialled Haris again.

'Total mess so far,' he said. 'I'm feeling very unsafe.'

Haris asked what was wrong. When George explained, he said, 'All right, stay cool. Just walk into the airport and carry on as I said.'

'Airline desk, shopping...?'

'The twenty minutes is irrelevant now. Just make the airline enquiry and order a coffee. I need to be able to see you and the bald guy. We'll make it work.'

'I don't see how.'

'Don't worry.'

'I say again, Haris, take care! I don't want to lose you like I lost your brother.'

'Message understood. See you in Markopoulo.'

George took a deep breath and crossed the road. In the glass doors of the airport entrance he saw the bald man following him. George prayed that Haris knew what he was doing.

He took the lift up to *Departures* and looked around for an airline ticketing desk. Air France was the nearest, but there was no one near it. Stick to the crowd, he told himself. He joined a stream of people and wheeled suitcases drifting through the immense hall. There was some bland jazz playing on the public address system. A man selling lottery tickets crossed his path. George waved him aside and spotted the Aeroflot desk. An aircrew with Asiatic faces stood by it, waiting. There was one customer at the desk. George stood behind him, close to the aircrew.

The man was speaking in Russian. George heard the strange liquid syllables flowing between him and a fiercely impolite girl at the desk. They were arguing about something, the man in a surprisingly high musical voice, the girl periodically repeating *'Nyet!'* The man swore in Greek and turned away. Then, seeing George waiting behind him, said, 'Please! Go ahead. Maybe you can get some sense out of her.'

George realised as the man turned that he had seen him somewhere before. Forty-five or fifty, strongly built, well dressed, in a suit and plain silk tie. A round, well-fed, pleasant face. Where had they met? Did he recognise George?

'Yes?' said the girl in heavily accented Greek.

George turned to her. 'Can you get me on a flight to Moscow?' he asked.

'Economy or business?'

'Economy.'

'Next flight 6.40 pm.'

'Cost?'

'Three hundred and forty-five euros one way.'

'Return?'

'Six hundred and fifty euros.'

'Try Aegean,' said the man. 'You'll find them cheaper.'

'Mr Merkulov!' exclaimed the girl. 'You are not very patriotic!'

George tensed at the name. Merkulov. The underground spring that supplies the wells, banker to white-collar criminals...

'Thank you,' said George. 'I'll do that.'

'It's a pleasure,' said Merkulov. Then, to the girl, in Greek: 'When you learn about helping your customers instead of treating them as an irritation, I'll be more patriotic.'

She scowled at him and said something in Russian, which made Merkulov laugh.

George decided to take a chance. 'Vladimir Antonovich Merkulov?'

'Do we know each other?'

'George Zafiris.'

'How do you know my name?'

'Courtesy of Aeroflot…'

'Ah.'

George pushed a little harder. 'You knew Keti Kenteri?'

Merkulov's face became solemn. 'That's where I've seen you,' he said. 'I couldn't put my finger on it. Keti's funeral.'

'You're right.'

'What a terrible day!' said Merkulov. 'I'll never forget it.'

'No…'

'Just one small step separates life from death. And then the door is closed forever. You must have known her?'

'Only the family. Her husband Paris, sister Anna…'

'Keti was beyond them all. A fine musician, a genius. Lovely in her thinking, her feelings, her movements…'

'How did you meet her?'

'She performed at one of my parties. Several parties in fact. And we became friends.'

'Did I hear someone call you Andonis?' asked George.

'Not me!'

'I was sure I heard that.'

'No. You're mixing me up with someone else.'

'So who is Andonis?'

'It could be many people. It's a common name.'

George's phone rang. 'Excuse me,' he said.
'What the hell are you doing?' asked Haris.
'I'm having a conversation.'
'I can see that. It's not in the plan.'
'I know.'
'You need to get moving.'
'Why?'
'Baldy's getting restless. He's talking to someone on his wire. Something's up.'
'OK. I'll get on with it.'
George turned back to Merkulov, who was checking something on his phone.
'You have business in Moscow?' asked the Russian.
'Possibly.'
'If you do, give me a call.' Merkulov handed him a business card. 'You need allies there. It's a tough environment. Even tougher than Athens.'
'Thank you,' said George.
He was surprised by Merkulov's manner. He seemed mild, positively friendly. Normally these people bristled with menace. Still, George hesitated to give him a card with Private Investigator on it.
'What's your line of business?' asked Merkulov.
'Research,' George replied. 'I'm sorry I don't have a card on me.'
'No problem. I'll remember the name. George Zafiris.'
They shook hands.
'See you in Moscow!' said Merkulov.
As the Russian turned away, he was joined by a man with a wrestler's physique crammed into a badly cut black suit.
The bodyguard.
That was more like it.

He put his mind to Haris's plan. Taking the lift down to *Arrivals*, he walked out of the airport building to the taxi rank. There were four people ahead of him in the queue, but plenty of taxis in a steadily moving line. He could not see the bald man, but thirty metres away, on the parallel road, just by the entrance to the car park, the black Mercedes was waiting. One word from 'Baldy', the taxi number plate, and the Mercedes would be after him.

He looked around for Haris. No sign of him. Should he go or not?

He was now at the front of the queue. The taxi rolled forward and stopped. The driver got out, asking, 'Where to?'

Not knowing if the plan was working or not, George muttered, 'Markopoulo.'

'Address?'

'I'll tell you in a while.'

The driver opened a door for him.

During the journey George checked behind him several times for the black Mercedes. He was surprised not to see it. Haris must have done something – he wondered what. Still he felt uneasy as the taxi driver deposited him at the butcher's shop on Trikoupi Street. He hurried in, not wanting to be spotted in the street.

George told the girl at the counter that he was looking for Haris Pezas.

'Mr Pezas?' She gave him a special look. 'Of course.'

She turned to a dark doorway at the back of the shop and said a few words. A square-headed man came out to meet him. 'I'm Margaritis,' he said. 'Haris told me you were on your way. Everything's ready. Come with me.'

Margaritis was built like a bull, filling his blood-speckled white jacket with a bulging mass of muscles. He led George through the back room, past giant refrigerators, into a yard where a big Nissan pick-up was parked. It had heavy chrome roll bars and a radiator grille that looked ready to chew granite. It bulged in all directions, like its owner.

'In you get,' said Margaritis.

George opened the door. The smell of blood inside was intense.

Margaritis said, 'We clean it every day, but the smell lingers. You can't get rid of it.'

'It always leaves a trace…' said George.

His comment was drowned in the roar of the starting engine.

'Haris told me you're employing him,' said the butcher as they moved off. 'That's a kind thing to do.'

'Really? Why do you say that?'

'Business not going well, wife complaining. He needed a break. You gave it to him.'

'He's a decent man,' said George vaguely. He was searching along the street as he spoke, half afraid he would see the black Mercedes.

'Not just a decent man. One in a million.'

The Mercedes was nowhere in sight, but George now began wondering where Haris had got to. He thought of calling him. Then thought again. Give it a few more minutes.

'How do you know Haris?' asked George.

'From the Navy.'

'Special forces?'

'Correct. Started together, ended together.' He held up a pair of crossed fingers. 'We're like that.'

'I had that with his brother Hector.'

'It's rare. Not just in Greece. Anywhere. I'm sure you help your friends in trouble, your family, but it goes beyond that with us. Something you can't even speak about. In the heart.'

'I sometimes wonder about how they train you in that section.'

'The training is good. But Haris goes beyond it. He thinks fast. Thinks ahead.'

He slowed down. 'We've arrived.'

George saw a taxi parked in the road ahead. 'Would you mind driving on?' he asked.

'What's the problem?'

'Go slowly past that cab, then round the block.'

'OK.'

Margaritis picked up speed a little. George peered into the cab as they passed, saw Haris in the back seat and said, 'It's OK. We can stop.'

Margaritis parked the pick-up and climbed out. At the same time Haris emerged from the cab. The two men hugged each other. Margaritis beckoned to George and they hurried into the house.

Once inside, Margaritis led them into the kitchen and said, 'You know where everything is, Haris. The place is yours. Help yourself to anything you find. I need to get back to the shop, but I'll see you this evening.'

George thanked him for his help. He waved away the thanks.

Left alone, they heard the Nissan growl away into the distance. As the silence settled around them Haris said, 'I need a coffee. Want one?'

'I'd rather have a beer,' said George. 'I need to calm down.'

Haris opened the fridge. 'Relax. You're safe here.'

'I hope so. I was getting panicky. Couldn't form a plan.'

Haris pushed a bottle of Amstel towards him. 'It's OK. That's what I'm here for.'

'How did you get rid of Baldy?'

'I distracted him.'

'How?'

'Banknote.'

'Sorry?'

'I dropped a fifty-euro note on the pavement behind him. Asked him if it was his.'

'He fell for that?'

'He was focussed on you. Wasn't expecting anyone to talk to him. By the time he'd dealt with me, you were off. He didn't even get the number plate of your taxi.'

'How do you know?'

'He went crazy. Sprinted across the road to the Merc. They went shooting off, then stopped at the first junction and started arguing.'

'How do you know that?'

'I was following in a taxi. I saw them sitting at the place where the road divides, Markopoulo–Athens. They didn't know which way to go.'

'They didn't follow you?'

'No. Why should they?'

'Where did they go?'

'Who knows? Probably back to Athens. Anyway they're off our backs, and you're in the clear. For a few days at least. After that... Do you want a glass for that beer?'

'Please.'

34 Catch-Up

They spent the next two hours comparing notes. In Astypalea Haris had come across more material about the medical school. A long letter from Dr Skouras to a certain Professor Harrison in London was particularly revealing:

'For some reason this medical school offends a group of powerful people who in a neighbouring country we would not hesitate to call "the mafia". Their identity in Greece is more obscure, although I believe it must be an alliance of doctors, property speculators and financiers who have made fortunes out of private hospitals. For them social medicine is anathema. You are right, of course, in asking if we are a genuine threat to them. After all it will take years to educate a new generation of doctors, and all but the most dedicated of these will quickly be demoralised by working for the Greek state. But the "mafia", if that is who they are, are apparently not very subtle in their thinking. We are their rivals for business. We stand in their way.'

'If he thinks like that he should have talked to us,' said George.

'He's scared.'

'No doubt. But what he says is significant.'

'How does that lead to murder?'

'That's what I don't understand. OK, the fact is Mario was

getting somewhere at last. On Astypalea, his own island, it looks as if he's finally going to win. His enemies need to stop him. They've tried everything else. So they decide to kill him.'

'It's a bit extreme, isn't it?'

'Definitely. There must have been another reason. Something that pushed them over the edge.'

They were silent for a while, thinking it over.

'But we still don't know who *they* are!' said Haris.

'We start with the photographer called Stelios. Also known as Andonis.'

'What has a photographer got to do with the medical school?'

'I don't know,' said George. 'But the trail leads to him.'

'Which trail?'

'The trail of blood. And the trail of gold.'

'Kenteri or Filiotis?'

'That's a big question! The two trails cross. After a certain point you can't tell which is which.'

'But who is he? How do we find him? All we have is two first names, and they could be false.'

'Two first names is better than none. Let's talk to Karás.'

George opened his laptop and searched for the young policeman's number. He found a note made after rugby training a few weeks ago. 'Mother's flat. Visits her twice a day.'

The phone was answered by a female voice. He asked if Nikos was there. She enquired cautiously who was calling. When he gave his name she said, 'Here he is.'

After a brief exchange of news George asked Karás what he knew about 'Andonis' or 'Stelios'.

'They're the same person.'

'OK. I was starting to work that out for myself. You're sure?'

'Completely. Stelios is his professional name, as a film director and photographer.'

'Did you find out where he lives? Where he works?'

'No. We met in one of his nightclubs.'

'Name?'

'Black Velvet Privé.'

'The name alone…'

'Exactly. It gets worse.'

'Address?'

'Leoforos Poseidonos, 180. Glyfada.'

'Is that his main office?'

'It's not an office. It's a hangar. A big black room smelling of sweat and last night's beer.'

'OK. I get the picture.'

Haris asked, 'Can I talk to him?'

George put the call on loudspeaker.

'What's the set-up down there?' asked Haris. 'Lots of security?'

'Two men on the door,' said Karás. 'Plus personal bodyguards.'

'How many of them?'

'Three.'

'Armed?'

'Definitely.'

'Describe them to me.'

'Ex-army. Big guys, plenty of muscle.'

'Nationality?'

'Russian.'

'Interesting,' said Haris. 'But the man himself is Greek, not Russian?'

'Totally.'

'Where from? Any idea?'

'The north.'

'How do you know that?' asked George.

'I come from there myself. There are certain words, and the way they say them…'

'Did you pick up anything else about him?'

'He's a porno king and a pimp, and he dresses the part. Full length leather. Stench of cologne. Jewellery. And he makes nasty films.'

'Any family?'

'We didn't go into that.'

'No hints at all?'

'He has a brother. In fact more than one.'

'How did you pick that up?'

'He had a phone call while I was there. A girl brought him the phone saying, "It's your brother." And he asked, "Which one?" '

'What was the answer?'

'Mr Efstathios. Or Mr Efthimios. I forget which.'

'Any sign of a woman in his life?'

'Plenty! All sex-objects.'

'I don't mean strippers and prostitutes. I mean a wife, a girlfriend.'

'No sign.'

'You mention his films,' said Haris. 'How do you know they're nasty?'

'I watched one. On his website.'

'Free to watch?'

'No. You have to pay.'

'And you paid!?'

'I did.'

Haris laughed lewdly. 'Hot stuff, eh?'

Karás sounded offended. 'I did it for professional reasons.

It's not to my taste. Eastern European girls being screwed indiscriminately by some fat guy in a mask – almost certainly him. It's a big turn-off.'

'Can you arrange another meeting with him?'

'I doubt it.'

'Why?'

'He's already filed a complaint for harassment about the last visit. And he's got you down for arrest, Mr Zafiris, as I think you may be aware.'

'Well aware,' said George. 'I'm an exile in my own city.'

'Colonel Sotiriou is working on that.'

'So he tells me. I can't go home till this ends. But maybe we can use this to our advantage.'

'How?'

'Tell him you know where to find me.'

'You mean tempt him to a meeting?'

'Exactly.'

'What's in it for him?'

'Silence. Discretion.'

'He has that already.'

'Only up to a point. We're on his case. He knows that. He may be protected by a minister, but this government could fall any day. Try telling him he can buy us off.'

'I don't understand why you want to meet this guy,' said Karás. 'He's a pig with a persecution complex.'

'I suspect he's involved with the death of Mario Filiotis.'

'Really?' Karás was astonished.

'In fact I'm sure of it.'

'Can you prove that?'

'Only by getting to his studio, his computer, his phone.'

'That's not going to happen.'

'Maybe not now. But one day.'

'I don't think you realise, Mr Zafiris, how well-protected that man is.'

'Makes no difference. You're onto him. Sotiriou is onto him. His life is a disaster waiting to happen…'

'I'm not convinced,' said Karás.

'Will you give it a try?'

'If you wish.'

'Set up a meeting. Somewhere public. Not one of his nightclubs!'

'I'll do my best.'

'OK. Thanks for your help. Let me know what he says.'

George put down the phone.

'What do you plan to do now?' asked Haris.

'Right now? Have another beer. Sip it slowly with my feet up on that sofa. In fifteen minutes' time I want you to tell me how to get into that fortress on Leoforos Kymis where they tied you up in parcel tape and find the evidence I'm looking for.'

'You've lost me. What's this got to do with Leoforos Kymis?'

'EAP. Efthimios is E. Andonis is A. Pavlos, the lunatic, is P. Remember?'

'The car dealer?'

'Correct.'

'You want me to go back there?'

'We'll go together.'

'No.'

'Why not?'

Haris said, 'It's a death trap.'

'For the ignorant. But you've told me you know how to deal with those situations.'

'I do. But it's going to take a bigger team than we've got.'

289

George met his gaze. 'I want you to tell me how to do it,' he said. 'Whatever it takes.'

Haris fetched another beer for George and one for himself. Then he sat down with a pen and a sheet of paper. George closed his eyes and tried to relax.

Some time later Haris tapped him on the shoulder. The beer was untouched on the floor next to the sofa. He had fallen asleep.

'This is a plan of the premises. As I recall.'

George examined it. There was the showroom, the alley, the side door, the L-shaped corridor, Pavlos Marangos's office. Also shown were a pair of rooms and a door at the back which he had not seen.

'Where does the alley go?' asked George.

'There's a parking lot behind the building,' said Haris. 'And that connects with the woodyard. As do the offices.'

'Can we get in?'

'We can. The question is, can we get out again?'

'OK. Tell me, how many people do we need?'

'Depends. If all we want is hard drives, computers, documents, we should go in at night when they're on minimum staff. But we'll still need a safe-breaker and a computer engineer. Plus a vehicle, a driver on standby, a lookout, three or four guys to carry stuff, three or four to deal with the security. That's twelve. But if you want to go in during office hours and talk to these people, exercise any kind of leverage, we need more. Say fifteen.'

George waved these figures away. 'That's a full-scale raid. I'm thinking of a neater operation. At night. Three, four in the morning. Knock out the security guards, sneak in, spend a couple of hours in the offices, grab whatever looks good, and get out.'

Haris looked sceptical. 'That's you and how many others?'

'Two? Maybe even one.'

'No chance.'

'Why?'

'You don't spend two hours in a place. That's suicide. And they've got more security than you imagine. The Russians are the tip of the iceberg.'

'You mean electronic security? That can be jammed. Or we cut off the power supply.'

Haris gave him a pitying look. 'Ever heard of back-up systems?'

'Of course. But you're the electrical man. You know how these things work. You can disable the system.'

'With a plan of the installation, access to the wiring and plenty of time, I can do it. But they're not going to give us that, are they?'

'What about just going for the jugular? Find the main power supply? Cut that, and we're in business?'

'Man, I'm surprised you're not dead.'

'To be honest I've never tried anything like this before.'

'Really? You fooled me!'

'There's no need to be sarcastic.'

'OK, I'm telling you this is not a place for beginners. Start with an old people's home if you want to do housebreaking. I tell you, if the power supply goes down, that place is going to erupt like a volcano! Cutting the power will trigger an alarm run on a separate supply. You'll be toast before you've even got to the back door.'

'So what's it going to take? A full-scale police raid?'

'That would avoid the other major problem.'

'Which is?'

'The legal aspect. This is breaking and entering, to say the least of it. Even if you find the best proof in the world you'll be a criminal yourself. And that makes you vulnerable.'

'You may have a point there.'

'I have several points. This is a very bad idea, Mr Zafiris. It's crap, from end to end. Forget it!'

'I can't forget it,' said George. 'We're so close. Just to give up because of an alarm system is pathetic. It's defeatist.'

'The truth is,' said Haris, 'we're doing fine. Just by talking like this you and I have gained several decades of life.'

'I'll just have to go in and see the bastard myself,' said George.

'Please no!'

'Why not? I'll talk to him. After all, what can he do?'

'He's got quite a choice. Break your legs. Throw you out of a window. Tie your hands and drop you in the sea… Let's stop discussing this now. We've got it all upside down. You're suggesting such crazy things…'

'Since when was talking reasonably to a man a crazy thing?'

'These guys have no respect for life. Mario got in their way, they killed him. You get in their way, they'll kill you. There's no "talking reasonably". You're the enemy, you die.'

George considered this. Haris was right, but it annoyed him to admit it. His apprentice had taken charge. George felt the need to re-establish his authority.

'Listen, Haris, I appreciate your opinion, your concern. But what do you propose we do? Remember, I can't go home, can't work, can't do anything until these bastards are out of the way!'

'Of course,' Haris agreed. 'It's tricky. But Colonel Sotiriou has promised to get this arrest order lifted.'

'In a week or two. Which probably means a month or two, or even a year, the speed those guys work. So what do

I do while I'm waiting? Sit here and watch TV? Eating your friend's sausages?'

'No,' said Haris calmly. 'Go to Andros. You have a place there. Let your wife look after you. Get some rest. After a few days, start working on the case against Andonis and his brothers. Marshal your evidence. As soon as Sotiriou gives the all-clear you can reappear. Hand in your report. Let the police deal with it. That way we all survive.'

'That sounds absolutely fine, Haris, but there's a problem. A big problem. The evidence – if it exists at all – is in the hands of EAP. And they're not going to give it to us. In fact they're going to destroy it. As soon as they can. The clock is ticking.'

'So what do *you* think we should do?'

'Go in and turn the place over.'

'Despite the risks?'

'Either that or give up. And I'm not giving up.'

Haris seemed lost in thought.

George's phone rang.

'Mr Zafiris, it's Nikos Karás. I've spoken to Andonis.'

'What did he say?'

'Let me give you his exact words. "Zafiris can go to hell." '

'That's nice.'

'He also said, "If you really know where he is, Lieutenant Karás, and you're not pulling my dick, go and arrest him. That's your duty. He's on the run from the law." '

'I hope you told him where to stick his opinions.'

'I thought it best not to provoke him further,' said Karás earnestly.

Haris looked gloomy. 'This is getting worse and worse,' he said. 'He'll find you before long.'

'How?'

'Through your phone.'

'He doesn't have the number.'

'No, but he has a number for Karás, which will inevitably have a link to you.'

'How long will that take?'

'Not long. A few minutes.'

'So this safe house…?'

'Is not safe any more. Let's go. We're going to dump that phone and get you to Andros.'

'Now?'

'Right now!'

'I'd rather go after that bastard right now.'

Haris said, 'No!' Very firmly.

'Who the hell is in charge here?' cried George.

Haris stood up. 'Come on, Mr Zafiris. Get your bag. We're leaving.'

35 End Game

George was wondering what would happen next.

He found it hard to explain to Zoe why he was in Andros. At first he said he needed a rest. This was true enough, only he did not rest. She would find him awake in the early hours, agitated or staring at the ceiling in a trance of gloomy thought.

'You're worrying,' she said.

'It's nothing important.'

'Why don't you tell me about it?'

'You won't be able to help,' he said.

She did not press him, letting him talk or be silent as he chose.

Alone, he would go over the two cases, Filiotis and Kenteri, sometimes on paper, sometimes in his mind. There seemed to be an overlap between them, a join. The mysterious pornographer Stelios lived in that join, held the key to everything, but he was unapproachable. It was pointless, as Haris said, to risk their lives on an ill-planned raid, yet there was no sign of a better plan emerging. Haris was completely silent. George wondered what he was doing. He was used to taking action to solve problems and this idleness frustrated him.

One afternoon, thinking about what Karás had said, he decided to explore the website of *Black Velvet Privé* in case it gave him any help. Among endless shots of naked girls he was surprised to find a 'Tribute to the great musical artist Keti Kenteri'. When he clicked on this, a short film began. With a soundtrack of Bach, it showed various sunset scenes – the Acropolis of Athens, the theatre at Epidavros, the stadium at Olympia – dissolving in and out of a sequence of Keti playing her violin on a panoramic hill-top in Athens.

It was true, as Merkulov said, that she played exquisitely. And, allowing for the fact that this was the work of a director of pornography, the film was not too horrifying to watch. Keti's long backless dress emphasised her figure but was elegant rather than erotic. The hackneyed images of Greece did little except advertise the director's lack of imagination, yet the film somehow survived them. It was even quite moving. Only at the end did it strike a note of kitsch, as a title in gold copperplate spun across the screen giving Keti's year of birth, 1980, her death, 2015, and the traditional words of condolence, *zoe se mas*, 'life to us'.

George watched it through twice. At the end of the second viewing he was intrigued by a detail. The view of Athens from the hill-top. Which hill was it? He watched again. Behind Keti's head, for just a second as her hair moved, a distinctive form: the fez-shaped rock above the quarry in Psyhikó. He knew now exactly where that sequence was shot: the Tourkovounia, where Keti had died.

A thought occurred to him. He pursued it. There she was, walking along, playing her violin, near a cliff edge, at sunset. The great pornographer directing the action. With a sick feeling George imagined what happened next. Just one false step...

Someone had said that.
Who?
He racked his brains.

Who had he seen recently? Sotiriou? Haris? Dimitri?

Suddenly it came to him. Vladimir Merkulov... He had said virtually those words at the airport.

George grabbed his phone and called Anna Kenteri.

'I don't want to hear from you,' she said.

'Too bad. I have to tell you something.'

'If you want to talk to me, do it through a lawyer.'

'You don't need a lawyer for this,' he said. 'I'm telling you for your own good. I know how Keti died. Go to your friend Andonis and ask him. He saw it happen. Vladimir Merkulov also knows what happened. Ask him. Don't let Andonis fob you off with lies.'

'Paris killed her,' she said sullenly.

'Anna, that's not true. Andonis faked that recording.'

'Why would he do that?'

'Because he's a shit. A shit and a fool. That's the only explanation I can give you.'

'That's impossible,' she said.

'Just ask him! See what he says.'

She hung up.

He spoke next to Haris, and told him to contact Colonel Sotiriou. 'Ask him to ring me on this number. From a safe line. I have important news.'

The Colonel was on the phone within five minutes.

'What have you got?'

'Is it OK to talk?' asked George.

'Fine. This is a private line.'

George described the film and his recollection of Merkulov's words.

'It's not proof,' said the Colonel. 'As it stands, it's only your guess.'

'We may never get proof,' George replied. 'But a statement from Merkulov would come close.'

'We must talk to him. Can you arrange that?'

'I can try. But who should talk to him? You or me? Or Nikos Karás?'

'It should be you in the first instance. Not a police officer. That will put him on his guard.'

'I may have to come in to Athens in order to meet him.'

'Do it.'

'I don't want to be arrested.'

'You overestimate our powers. As long as you don't go home you'll be all right.'

'How much longer is this exile going to last?'

'I can't tell you. Be patient. Just get hold of Merkulov and let me know what he says.'

George found the Russian's business card among his papers and rang the phone number under his name.

'Hello?' A woman's voice answered.

'Vladimir Merkulov please.'

'Mr Merkulov is not here.'

'How do I reach him? This is very important. Urgent. My name is George Zafiris.'

'Wait please.'

A moment later Merkulov was on the phone.

'Mr Zafiris, what's the problem? Are you in Moscow?'

'No, still in Greece.'

'How can I help?'

'Are you in Russia or in Greece?'

'I'm in Athens.'

'Can we meet?'

'Do you have some business to discuss?'
'I do. And it's extremely urgent. How about this evening?'
'Can you tell me what it's about?'
'Keti Kenteri.'
'I see. Well, I have an hour to spare at 7.00 pm. I suggest the lobby of the Hilton Hotel.'

Merkulov was sitting in an easy chair, a pair of horn-rimmed spectacles on his nose, reading the *Financial Times*. George had been debating on the journey whether to tell him the truth. He heard two voices inside his head, one advising frankness, the other caution. As he entered the lobby he was still not sure which to choose.

They took a table in the bar and Merkulov asked how he could help.

George said, 'Before we talk business I need to know more about your operation.'

Merkulov looked surprised. 'You are in research, Mr Zafiris. I expect you to know everything before we meet.'

'Of course.' George was taken aback momentarily. 'I know about the hotels, resorts and malls.'

'And the philanthropic projects?'

'No. Tell me about those.'

'I focus on three areas. Green energy, education and health.'

'Was Keti Kenteri one of your philanthropic projects?'

'No. She was just…' He threw up his hands. 'Just Keti.'

The waiter approached their table.

Merkulov said, 'I like a glass of champagne at this time of day. Will you have one too, Mr Zafiris?'

'I'd prefer a beer. Fix please.'

'Of course. The bill to me please, waiter. And bring us some fresh pistachios. What were we saying? You asked about Keti.'

'Did you try to help her?'
'In what way?'
'With her career.'
'I hired her a few times, made some introductions, helped her think in a more commercial way.'
'Her husband was against that.'
'So it seems.'
'Did she talk about that to you?'
'Just once. It was clearly a problem between them. And the whole family.'
'I wondered if there was jealousy too.'
'Plenty! Everybody lusted after Keti.'
'Including you?'
Merkulov bristled slightly. 'I thought of her as a friend. And an artist. Did you ever hear her perform?'
'I've only seen a film of her.'
'Which one?'
'She's playing on top of a hill.'
Merkulov's look darkened. 'That film!'
'What's wrong? I thought it was pretty good.'
'Not when you know…' Merkulov stopped himself.
'Know what?' said George.
Merkulov sighed heavily. 'It's not worth going into now.'
'I know Andonis Marangós directed the film.'
'He did.'
'I thought maybe you worked with him and his brothers?'
Merkulov was becoming more cautious by the second. 'Why do you ask?'
'I've had dealings with them myself.'
'And?'
Now, George realised, his line of caution was getting harder to pursue.

'I don't like what I see,' he ventured.

Merkulov was neutral in his response. 'OK,' he said. 'We can talk about that if you like.'

'A friend of mine went to see them,' said George. 'And then he died on the way from their office. In suspicious circumstances.'

'Why suspicious?'

'He was hit by a truck. A truck from a woodyard. If you've ever been to EAP on Leoforos Kymis you'll know there is a woodyard next to their car showroom.'

'What was your friend's business with EAP?'

'I have no idea. Pavlos Marangós says my friend was looking for finance. I have my doubts.'

'What do you doubt about it?'

'Marangós is not the kind of person my friend would go to for a loan.'

'Why not?'

'Because he's a shark. An obvious shark.'

'Perhaps your friend was desperate.'

'Perhaps he was. But would you kill a man who comes to you to borrow money?'

'It would not be my first choice.'

'Precisely. So my friend must have had some hold over Marangós. He must have posed a threat.'

Merkulov said nothing.

'Well?' said George. 'Do you see why I don't trust them?'

'What was the name of your friend?'

'Mario Filiotis.'

Merkulov nodded. 'Mayor of Astypalea. The great eco-campaigner.'

'You're well informed.'

'Investors have to be.'

'Did you know him?'

'I met him a few times,' said Merkulov.

'On business?'

'On business.'

'How did that go?'

'I liked him. At first.'

'And then?'

'I decided that he was not on the side of the angels.'

'What do you mean?'

Merkulov frowned. 'He was too extreme. He opposed all development.'

'That's not true. He built the airport, roads, schools, a hospital…'

'Mr Zafiris, I don't know your politics. I believe in the free market. Filiotis was a typical socialist. All he knew was how to spend! Where is the return on investment? Of that he had no concept.'

'I'm sure the medical school would have earned money.'

'Very indirectly, very slowly. Always less than it spent.'

'If you want to be a philanthropist, Mr Merkulov, you'll have to adopt a less commercial philosophy.'

'Have you come to teach me about finance, Mr Zafiris?'

'No.'

'Good. Then I suggest we change the subject.'

'Did Filiotis come to you for money?'

Merkulov tensed visibly. 'I'm not prepared to discuss that.'

'I'm assuming he did.'

'We're getting off the point!' said Merkulov impatiently.

'I have a feeling,' said George, 'that we're coming right to it. I think you were about to finance the medical school, but EAP poisoned your mind against him.'

'Why would they do that?'

'Two very good reasons. One, they and their friends have been trying to stop him for years. Two, they wanted you to invest with them, not with him. Which I fear you may have done.'

'That's none of your business!'

'My friend was murdered, Mr Merkulov!'

'I'm sorry to hear it. It had nothing to do with me.'

'I feel there's a connection.'

'There is no connection at all! And why the hell are we talking about this? You wanted to talk about Keti.'

'I don't think much of your philanthropy, Mr Merkulov. The fact is, you're in bed with the Greek mafia.'

Merkulov did not reply. He was staring with surprise over George's shoulder at something on the far side of the room. George turned, saw only drinkers sitting at tables.

'What's up?'

'Talk of the devil,' said Merkulov. 'Look who's there.'

'Someone you know?'

'Someone we both know. Anna Kenteri.'

George looked again. There was Anna, with her back to him, sitting opposite a middle-aged man with a sharply clipped beard and long hair, in a tan leather suit.

'Who's the pimp?' asked George.

'Andonis Marangós.'

George observed him more closely. A man who had seen everything, or thought he had. Cynically putting up with a woman's tirade. Flashing an occasional look of injured innocence.

'You never know who you'll bump into at the Athens Hilton,' said George.

Merkulov nodded and raised his glass.

'What are they doing together?' asked George.

Merkulov frowned.

'You ask a lot of questions, but you learn too slowly.'

'Everyone has his own speed.'

'OK. Now let me ask you a question.'

'Go ahead,' said George.

'You describe your business as research. What kind of research?'

'General.'

Merkulov echoed him. 'General?'

'That's right.'

'What exactly do you mean by that?'

'Anything I'm paid to do.'

'I see. And who pays you?'

'Private customers.'

Merkulov drew his phone from his pocket and tapped it a few times. 'I find you evasive, Mr Zafiris. Let's see if I can do a little better than you. You live at 43 Aristotle Street, Exarchia. You were born 28th October 1969. You were educated at Athens College and the London School of Economics. You have a wife, Zoe, and a son, Nick, currently studying at Newcastle University. You worked for the National Bank of Greece for twelve years before moving to your current profession…' He paused for dramatic effect. 'Private Detective! Well, well, well! You didn't tell me that!'

'I didn't lie to you.'

'There's lying and there's evasion. They are very close. I don't care for either.'

'I'm not sure it matters any more,' said George.

'It always matters. Now let's go back to something you said earlier. You say I'm in bed with the mafia.'

'I do.'

'You're going to leave it at that?'

'Do you have anything to add?'
'It's a hell of an accusation!' said Merkulov.
'It's not an accusation. It's a warning.'
'I call it bullshit. I never dealt with this punk or his mad brother Pavlos. The one I know is Efthimios. He's worth the other two put together and multiplied by a thousand. I was going to invest in your friend Filiotis's scheme but Efthimios pointed out its weaknesses.'
'For his own purposes!'
'Maybe. But weaknesses nonetheless.'
'It was no reason to kill him.'
'Efthimios wouldn't have done that.'
'Pavlos?'
'Possibly,' said Merkulov. 'But I see no motive.'
'Maybe Filiotis threatened to expose them?'
'They wouldn't worry about that.'
'They would if it ruined things with you.'
Merkulov considered this.
'How much is at stake?' asked George.
'I'm not telling you that.'
'It's got to be a few million.'
'No comment.'
'I just hope you're in a position to get out.'
Merkulov tried not to react, but a slight flicker in his eyes told George the message had been received.

A moment later the atmosphere changed. Conversation died around the room.
'You're lying!' shouted Anna Kenteri.
'You've lost the plot!' said Marangós with scorn.
Anna picked up her cocktail glass and flung its contents in his face.

At first he did not react. Then he picked up a napkin from the table and calmly wiped his face, staring at her all the while with menacing intensity. He dropped the napkin into the empty glass. With lightning suddenness he gave her two violent slaps, left and right, jerking her head each time with the impact. She pulled back to avoid a third but he sat back casually, tapped a number into his phone and said, 'Come to the lobby, Ivan. I'm ready to leave. Miss Kenteri will not be coming with us.'

Anna reached for her handbag.

'Wait,' she said, and dipping her hand into the bag came up with a small pistol. Andonis reacted with a nervous laugh. She raised the gun, aimed at his chest and fired twice. Andonis's eyes widened in surprise, his body jolting. She fired again. He tried to stand up, but George could see the strength draining from him. He stiffened, tottered, clutched at the air for support, and collapsed on the floor. Anna stood over him. 'That was for Keti,' she said coldly. A rasping, gurgling sound came from Andonis. She raised the pistol and fired again. 'And that's for me!'

She dropped the gun back into her handbag, stepped over Andonis's body and walked haughtily towards the door.

At once the barman was on the phone.

Before she could reach the door, two security men ran in, guns raised, eyes darting. Quickly assessing the situation, one of them held his weapon on Anna while the other stepped forward and knelt over Andonis. He felt for a pulse.

'Call an ambulance,' he said to the barman. 'How did this happen?'

'I shot him,' said Anna.

'Where's the weapon?'

She offered her handbag. He took it carefully from her, glanced inside, and set it down it on the table next to him.

'OK listen everybody, we're all staying here until the police arrive.'

At once people began objecting. They had dinner appointments, meetings, places to be. The security man shouted over them, 'Forget it! This is going to take time, so you'd better be patient.'

George thought of his arrest order. If the police took his name, he'd be in difficulties. 'Can I make a call?' he asked.

The security man glanced at his colleague, who nodded.

George called Colonel Sotiriou.

'You'd better come to the Hilton bar,' he said. 'There's been a shooting.'

'I can't attend every shooting in Athens!'

'This is a big one.'

'Aren't they all.'

'Andonis Marangós.'

'I'm on my way,' said the Colonel.

George sat down again opposite Merkulov.

'What a mess,' said the Russian. 'What a bloody mess! I didn't like the man, but still! That's no way to go.'

'He shouldn't have hit her.'

'Bah! Made no difference. She was planning it. The gun was ready in her bag.' Merkulov formed a pistol with his fingers and mimed the shooting, with George as the victim. He dropped his hand to the table. 'I've seen some lovers' quarrels in my time, but this was something else.'

Taken aback, George said, 'What do you mean lovers' quarrels?'

Merkulov's eyes popped in disbelief. 'You don't know?'

'Why the hell would I ask if I knew?'

Merkulov shook his head. 'You don't know much, do you?'

'Who were the lovers?' George insisted. 'Keti and Andonis?

Anna and Andonis? All three?'

'Not all three.'

'Who then?'

Merkulov made a dismissive gesture with his hand. 'Those two.'

'Anna and Andonis?'

Merkulov nodded.

They sat in silence for a few minutes, lost in their own thoughts, until the wailing of police sirens and the pulsing of blue lights startled them back to the present. Car doors opened and slammed shut. A group of black-uniformed officers strode in, followed by Colonel Sotiriou in his grey suit. Behind him came two paramedics with resuscitation equipment.

As the paramedics got to work, Sotiriou spoke to the hotel security guards, his eyes calmly taking in the details of the scene. Customers in the bar began to press forward. Sotiriou held up his hands.

'Ladies and gentlemen, sit down! We have a procedure to go through. Disruption from you will merely delay things. My colleagues will take statements from you, starting with those nearest to the shooting. There will be no queue-jumping. I don't care who you are. Be patient and cooperative and you will be out of here in less than an hour. Make a fuss and you will be detained all night.'

A police photographer came in with other technical staff. Anna Kenteri was led away – her handbag, the cocktail glass, the wet napkin all sealed in separate plastic bags.

'Less than an hour!' said Merkulov. 'I don't believe that.'

Sotiriou directed the officers to the first four tables, where they began taking statements. He knelt by Andonis, lifted the flap of his jacket and saw the dark wet stain that had flooded his shirt. He glanced questioningly at the paramedics as they pumped oxygen into him and checked for signs of life. Their faces were stony, their actions automatic.

Sotiriou straightened up. He approached the table where George and Merkulov were sitting. Without a flicker of recognition, he sat down next to George, took out a pen and notebook and said, 'All right, gentlemen, please tell me from the beginning what you saw.'

36 News Bulletin

By eight-thirty, as Sotiriou had promised, the interviews were over. Merkulov gave his version of the events and was allowed to leave. George stayed on. There was no ferry back to Andros tonight, and he needed to talk to the Colonel.

Sotiriou was brusque. 'You'll have to wait until I've finished.'

'How long will that be?'

'A couple more hours. Tomorrow would be easier.'

'Where do I sleep tonight?' asked George. 'I presume I can't go home yet?'

'Stay here.'

'Do you know what that costs?'

'No. But your flat is still under surveillance. I can get that lifted in twenty-four hours.'

'I'd be grateful if you could speed that up.'

'Don't push your luck,' said Sotiriou.

George took the cheapest room he could get and ordered a club sandwich and a bottle of beer. As he waited for the order to arrive he phoned Zoe to say he was all right.

'Why shouldn't you be all right?' she asked, suspicion in her voice.

'No reason,' he said. 'Only I've just witnessed a shooting in the Hilton bar, and what with the police questions I've missed the last boat home.'
'Anyone injured?'
'A film director was shot. You'll see it on the news.'
'Why would anyone shoot a film director?'
'It seems to have been a lovers' quarrel.'
'Be careful, George!'
'It had nothing to do with me.'
'Why are you there?'
'It's a coincidence.'
'Are you coming back in the morning?'
'I'll need to stay a couple of days.'
'OK.' She sounded sleepy. 'Have a good night. Take care.'
'You too,' said George. 'I miss you.'
'That's nice,' she said.

There was a knock on the door. George got up to open it. A waiter stood there with a tray.

George signed the bill, took the tray and closed the door. He had plenty to think about, but he wanted to rest first. He poured the beer, pulled the cocktail sticks out of the club sandwich, laid them in a neat pile at the side of the plate, and took a big bite. It tasted delicious. 'I must be hungry,' he thought. He switched on the TV.

A news channel was showing images of police cars outside the hotel. This was the last thing he wanted to see, but a shot of the waterfall at Edessa seized his attention. *'This is the second suspicious death in this town in ten days,'* said the reporter. *'The police have so far confirmed only the names of the victims, but people are unofficially connecting the two. The latest death is Dimitrios Hatzifilippou known as Kokoras, a well-*

known local businessman. He owned construction companies, restaurants, bars and hotels, but he also had a darker side: protection, extortion, smuggling of people and goods. "He brought girls from the east to Greece, supposedly to work as maids," said one source, "but they ended up as prostitutes." His name is also linked with the illegal export of antiquities. Some say he was responsible for the recent raid on the home of an archaeologist in Thessaloniki. Rumours about him are legion, but one thing is clear: even a man as rich and ruthless as Kokoras was struggling in today's economic crisis. With businesses failing everywhere and construction at a standstill, his mafia-style model was becoming ever harder to sustain. Whether the finger that pulled the trigger on his revolver was his or someone else's is a question which the police, as much as anyone in this town, would very much like to answer.'

George listened in astonishment. Kokoras would surely not have killed himself? He was the classic bad dog, which according to the Greek proverb 'never dies'. So what had happened to his bodyguards? Why had they not protected him?

He was tempted to call Gavrilis, who would undoubtedly know more, but he thought better of it. The hunt would be on for the killer. It would not be too smart to remind Gavrilis of his existence. Since Kokoras had threatened George, and Gavrilis knew it, suspicion could easily fall on him.

He reached again for the sandwich. His phone rang. It was Haris.

'Forgive me if I eat while you talk,' said George. 'I'm hungry.'

'Fine,' said Haris. 'I just rang to say that I've been trying to work out how to get into that damned building without being killed.'

'Any luck?'

'Possibly.'
'Do you want to tell me about it?'
'Not on the phone. Where are you?'
'I'm in the city centre.'
'OK, I'll come in tomorrow.'
'You heard about Kokoras and Andonis?'
'No…'

George filled him in, adding the information he had picked up from Merkulov. 'Anna Kenteri and Andonis Marangós were lovers. I'm still trying to work out what that means, but it could explain a lot. Apart from that, Mario Filiotis was in line to get investment from the Russian. EAP poisoned the deal, presumably because they wanted Merkulov's money. Mario spotted what was going on and started fighting back. That's when they decided to act.'

'By killing him?'
'So it seems.'
'Can you prove that?'
'Only by getting in to EAP.'
'You still want to do that?'
'If we can get out alive.'
'Understood. I'm working on it. I'll come in and see you in the morning.'

37 The Death Trap

Early the next day George was woken by a call from Colonel Sotiriou. 'I've managed to get the arrest order lifted,' he said. 'You can go home.'

George asked him how he had achieved this, but the Colonel would say no more.

'How about the Kokoras killing? Any ideas on that?'

'A professional job.'

'Why?'

'Very quick and neat.'

'His bodyguards?'

'They played no part.'

'What do you mean?'

'No one has seen them or mentioned them.'

'They struck me as pretty useless.'

'A fair assessment, I would say.'

'So who could have done it?'

'Good question!'

'The TV report mentioned a raid on the home of an archaeologist.'

'That was Dr Mylona.'

'I met her! A dreadful woman.'

'Why do you say that?'

'She's a typical bureaucrat. Sitting like a spider in her web of regulations, waiting to catch unsuspecting victims.'

'What did you want from her?'

'Some help over those golden wreaths that were in Mario's coffin.'

'You never mentioned that to me.'

'You never showed any interest.'

'What was her involvement?' asked Sotiriou.

'I wish I knew. I thought she might have some ideas about where the stuff came from, where it was going, who the dealers are… She was even tighter with information than you are.'

'Did you find out any more?'

'The trail seemed to lead to New York. But I never got to the end of it.'

'Why not?'

'Not enough hours in the day.'

'Why New York?'

'Mario Filiotis ended up at a crematorium in Brooklyn. The name on the undertaker's waybill was Medouris. One of the biggest dealers in antiques from the classical world has a very similar name: Ventouris.'

'This is all most interesting,' said Sotiriou.

'Why?'

'You'll see.'

'Can't you tell me just one little thing for once?'

'Not now,' said the Colonel. 'As usual you have been most helpful.'

George paid his hotel bill and walked home through Kolonaki, past the Evangelismós hospital with patients in dressing gowns enjoying a contemplative smoke among the rubbish bins on the pavement, past the lost-world neoclassical beauty of the

Maraslion school, past the boutiques and cafés still clinging to their menaced old way of life. On the way he rang Haris and told him to come over as soon as he could. Haris said he would be there by eleven.

In the Café Agamemnon he ordered a fresh orange juice, coffee, toast and two fried eggs.

'American-style today?' said Dimitri.

'I'm hungry,' said George, 'but let's be patriotic. Fry the eggs in olive oil.'

'Very good,' said Dimitri. 'Do you want the news now or later?'

'Tell me now.'

Dimitri filled him in on the past few days in Aristotle Street.

'The police were in and out all the time,' he said. 'Uniform, plain clothes, asking questions, waiting in their cars, anyone would think you were a dangerous criminal.'

'They either do nothing or too much,' said George. 'It's insane. You never saw that bald man again?'

'Oh yes, he was around. Nasty piece of work. Never believed me when I said I hadn't seen you.'

'When was he last here?'

'A couple of days ago.'

'And the other plain clothes men? Who were they?'

Dimitri stared at him in disbelief. 'You think I asked them?'

'OK,' said George. 'I'm just a little surprised that they would have sent more than one team. Even by our crazy standards that's over the top.'

'I did what I could,' said Dimitri.

'You've done well,' said George.

Dimitri went off to fry the eggs and George picked up the newspaper. A short article confirmed all the details about Kokoras, adding that a neighbour had seen two men going into his home on the day of the killing. They had stayed about fifteen minutes, arriving and departing in a black Mercedes.

At half past ten George went upstairs. He let himself into his apartment and found a note scribbled on cardboard pushed under his door. As he tried to decipher it a sound behind him made him turn. He realised too late that someone had followed him in. Someone with a leather jacket, a bald head, and an automatic pistol.

'Put your hands on your head and walk slowly to your right.'

George obeyed. The door clicked shut.

'Keep walking. In there. Stop. Kneel on the floor.'

'Kneel?'

'You heard what I said.'

George knelt, facing the window of his study. He felt the barrel of a pistol pressing his neck.

'What do you want?' he asked.

'Don't talk. Hands behind your back!'

George waited, facing the window. He heard drawers opening in his desk, papers being checked and shoved aside. If Baldy was holding the pistol, he must have an accomplice.

'What's the password for this laptop?'

'Tell me what you're looking for,' said George, 'it will be quicker.'

The gun muzzle was jabbed into his neck. 'Password!'

'Karpenisi. All lower case.'

A finger tapped out the letters one by one.

'Are you in?' asked Baldy.

'I'm in,' said the other.

'OK. Take a look.'

George waited, listening to the sounds of fingers rattling

impatiently along a keyboard. In the street traffic rumbled through the sunshine. He wondered how long these men would keep him here, what they were planning to do.

After a few minutes the man on the laptop said, 'There's nothing here.'

'Give me your phone,' said Baldy.

George handed it over.

'Open the contacts.'

George did so and handed it back.

'What's this?' said the accomplice. 'Three names?'

'I've only had it a few days.'

'Where's your old one?'

'With the police.'

'Why?'

'Someone was using it to track me.'

'Oh, aren't we smart? Got a tablet?'

'What for? Headache?'

'I'll give you a headache, asshole! A tablet! An iPad?'

'No.'

'Where do you write down names, addresses, details of the people you see?'

'On my phone.' George lied. He also had his precious notebook, which they would certainly find if they made him empty his pockets.

'Look, guys, I don't know what you're after but if you just tell me what you want I can try to help you.'

'We know the kind of help you give, *maláka*. You're a waste of space.'

'OK, have it your way.'

'We will. What do you cook with, gas or electric?'

'Electric.'

'Loser!' He returned to the other man. 'Put some paper

under the sofa.'

George felt his hands grabbed and forced together. A cable tie was pulled tight around his wrists.

'Tell me what you want!' he shouted.

'Shut up, *maláka!*'

His feet were grabbed next, the ankles lashed together.

On the edge of his vision he saw the other man crumpling papers and tossing them into a pile under the sofa.

Then came a sound he particularly dreaded. Strips of parcel tape being torn from a reel. His head was seized and bent back, the tape wound in a gluey band round his eyes, shutting out the light.

'OK,' said Baldy. 'Do his mouth. Then light the fire and let's go.'

'Wait,' said George. 'This is crazy. You want something but you won't tell me what. You're going to burn the place down, you'll kill me and other people in this building. Why? What have we done? What are you looking for? Tell me, in the name of –'

The pistol was smashed into the side of his head and a ball of yellow light exploded in his brain. He toppled over against his desk, banging into it before hitting the floor. His head was roughly grabbed again and a band of sticky tape closed over his mouth and nose. Blinded, gagged, unable to breathe, he struggled to free himself.

'Let's go,' said Baldy.

George heard their footsteps crossing the floor, the front door closing behind them. Then silence.

The tape had cut off his air supply. In a mounting panic he twisted his mouth from side to side, up and down, wrenching in every direction, wrinkling his nose, working at the tape to get just a sliver of air, a wisp, a chink in the great wave of airless darkness that was engulfing him. He thrust out his lips, prodded with his tongue, levered with his jaw, chewed, spat, blew.

When a few molecules of air got through, they carried an ominous smell. Hot, rubbery, chokingly chemical. His sofa was starting to burn. He felt the heat increasing and knew that he must act now or die. It was an old foam rubber sofa. These things gave off poisonous black smoke. With his lungs bursting and his brain a flashing firework display he straightened his body and rolled sideways, against his instincts, towards the heat. He kicked out with his feet to scatter the fire beneath the sofa, but the heat continued to grow. He had to throw himself onto the sofa and smother the flames somehow, but roll and twist as he might he could not get to his feet. He tried his side, his back, his side again, ramming his fists against the floor to push himself up. All he could do was sit.

Then it occurred to him to use his legs in a different way. He lay back and shuffled as close to the fire as he could, feeling his shins and knees seared by the flames. Hoisting his legs he brought them crashing down on to the sofa, into the burning cushions, defying the pain, the stinging. He felt pieces of melting foam rubber stick to his legs, the stabbing sharpness as the flames scorched his skin. And that horrifying smell, the toxic smoke that he knew too well would kill him quicker than he could burn.

He was getting exhausted and the fire was still raging. He thought suddenly of the balcony doors. If he could break the glass he could let air into the room. It would feed the flames but at least give him some fresh air, and maybe someone in the street would see the smoke. He rolled away from the sofa, over towards the balcony. Four, five times: face to the floor, onto his side, his back, other side, face to the floor again.

When he reached the door he lifted his feet again and lashed out at the glass panes. They bounced off. He must have hit the woodwork between the doors. He dragged himself to the right and tried again, but his feet hit the glass at the wrong angle, too high and oblique, and slid down. His strength was almost gone. One more time, he told himself, one more time and a good one. Kick straight out, level and hard. He drew back his legs, the weight pressing painfully on his hands, crushing his clenched fingers, and hurled out with every shred of force he could muster. He felt his feet strike the glass, stop for a microsecond, then carry on, smashing through, a shower of splinters clattering onto the balcony and a sweet rivulet of air from the outside world pouring over his sweating face.

How good it was! But behind him the fire sucked in the draught, greedily, hotly drinking it in. Thinking he had made a mistake George gulped in the air, past caring, and let the blackness that had pressed in on him for so long come like a friend and close him in its arms.

38 The Other Side

George woke up in hospital, an oxygen mask over his face, his wrists and ankles raw, his throat and chest aching as if they had been slashed with hot knives. His mind was confused and hazy. Nothing was in focus. He tried waggling his fingers. They seemed to work. That was something. Even better, his hands were by his sides, no longer lashed together behind his back. His feet too, he found he could move separately. That was good. But this mask was awful. It had to go.

He raised a hand to remove it. A woman's voice said, 'No.'

He turned his head and saw Zoe sitting in a chair by the bed. Her left hand reached across to restrain him.

He tried to speak but the mask muffled everything. Zoe stroked his forehead.

'It's OK, George. We're in the Red Cross Hospital. There's poison in your blood. Your lungs are damaged. You must keep the mask on.'

He nodded, the tubes squeaking as he moved.

He wondered how Zoe had got there, what day it was, if the apartment had been destroyed... Questions gathered in his mind like clouds along the horizon, visible yet strangely distant. He realised that some medication must be keeping him hazy, detached, floating in mid-air.

She seemed to hear his thoughts. 'Don't worry, George, everything's OK. The old sofa was ruined but that's no bad thing. I've wanted to replace it for years.'

He tried smiling but his cheeks merely pushed against rubber. He raised his eyebrows instead.

Zoe smiled and reached for his hand. 'The important thing is you're still here.'

He closed his eyes and drifted away into sleep again.

The second waking was harsher. A doctor was standing by him pushing open his eyelids with his thumbs. He felt a stethoscope pressed against his chest. 'Just breathe normally. Don't force it. I'm listening.'

George tried once again to remove the mask. The doctor stopped him. 'Leave that alone. It's keeping you alive.'

A nurse was standing by the doctor. She handed him a clipboard, which he stared at for a while, then scribbled a few notes and handed it back. Without another word he left the room, followed by the nurse. George wondered how close to death he was.

A little later the door opened and Haris walked in. Behind him came Colonel Sotiriou. Haris looked worried, fraught and restless. Sotiriou was cool and detached as ever, noting the details of the room, the patient, the equipment, as if he was a technician checking that everything was functioning correctly.

It was Sotiriou who spoke.

'You owe your life to this man,' he said, placing a hand on Haris's shoulder.

Haris seemed embarrassed. 'Don't say that.'

Sotiriou insisted. 'He saw the smoke at your window. He called the fire brigade. In the fifteen minutes it took them to arrive he climbed over from your neighbour's balcony and dragged you out into the fresh air. He then put out the flames. By the time our distinguished colleagues from the fire department arrived the situation had been brought fully under control. And so it is that we visit you in hospital rather than the morgue. You are a very lucky man.'

George nodded.

'Mr Pezas, please say something.'

Haris cleared his throat. 'I arrived early for our appointment,' he said. 'And thank God I did. Dimitri let me into his apartment... You managed to break the glass in the balcony door?'

George nodded again.

'That's what saved you.'

'Nonsense,' said Sotiriou. 'A few more minutes and you would have been burnt alive as well as asphyxiated. Pezas saved you. That is indisputable!'

George gave his assistant a thumbs-up.

Haris said, 'You must know who did this?'

The Colonel held up a restraining hand. 'Let him recover.'

George shook his head angrily and wrenched off the mask.

'It was those...' his voice grated in his throat. Speaking was like vomiting sharp stones.

He waved towards the bedside table for some water. Haris poured a glass from a jug and brought it carefully to his lips. George took a sip. It burned like brandy as it went down.

'Don't talk,' said Haris. 'Put the mask back on.'

'It was those guys in the black Mercedes,' said George. 'They're not Special Security, they're...'

'I know,' said Sotiriou. 'Save your breath, Zafiris.'

Haris was puzzled. 'You *know*?' he said. 'How do you know?'

'It became obvious,' the Colonel replied.

'Who are they?'

'Private specialists.'

'You mean contract killers.'

'Potentially.'

'What do you mean "potentially"? This was attempted murder. Plain as day.'

'I repeat: *potentially!* Nothing is proved yet.'

'Two men walk into your apartment, tie you up, set fire to the place and nothing is proved? You have to be joking!'

'I proceed from fact to fact, Mr Pezas.'

'You have the facts, Colonel. I don't see you proceeding!'

'All in due course. I'll take a statement from Mr Zafiris, from you, from other potential witnesses…'

Haris waved this away angrily. 'Who's paying those men?' he asked brusquely.

Sotiriou's brow clouded. 'That would be most interesting to know.'

'Come on, Colonel! This isn't a court of law. We're colleagues. We need to share this information.'

Sotiriou thought about this for a few moments.

'I thought at first it must be your friends at EAP,' he said, 'but I'm starting to have my doubts.'

'Why?'

'Kokoras was in with EAP. He worked with them closely. He was their agent in Edessa. And yet these two fellows seem to have driven up there two days ago for the sole purpose of shooting him. Something odd there.'

'So Kokoras fell out with EAP?'

'Possibly. Over what, though? He was their faithful lieutenant. There was no sign of trouble. Our informers are as puzzled as we are. An alternative explanation is that Kokoras was killed on a contract for someone else, in order to weaken

EAP. In some ways I favour that scenario.'

'Why?'

'Because it is more chaotic. More bizarre. More Greek, if you like.'

'You talk about it as if it was some kind of show.'

'Things become savage when law and order breaks down.'

'It's your job to make sure it doesn't.'

'I do my best. But with a government run by communists and anarchist sympathisers, there are limits to my powers.'

George could not restrain himself any longer. He pulled away his oxygen mask and rasped, 'You know exactly what's going on, Colonel! Why don't you tell us?'

Haris moved to put the mask back on but George pushed his hand away.

'Tell us, Colonel! Those bastards nearly killed me! They were looking for something, a name, an address, they never said what. When they couldn't find it they set fire to the place. Presumably to destroy evidence. Or me. I want to know why!'

George coughed, which drove hot knives deep into his chest.

Sotiriou said, 'Put your mask back on, man, or you'll finish the job for them.'

'I'll do it when you tell me what's going on!'

'All right! Just put on that damned mask!'

George fumbled it back into place and breathed deeply.

Sotiriou folded his arms. 'Are we calmer now?'

George glared at him.

'Good,' said the Colonel. 'Let's get one thing clear. What I am about to say now is confidential. Totally confidential! Is that understood?'

Haris nodded. George continued to glare.

'I will take that ferocious expression as agreement,' said the

Colonel. 'Now, let me begin with Mario Filiotis. You spoke of him as a friend, Zafiris. He was also a friend of mine.'

George's fierce look turned to one of surprise.

'A friend and a kindred soul. Someone who was prepared to risk his peace of mind, his relationship with his wife, his family and friends, even his life as it turned out, in order to help his community and his country, to resist the appalling plague of self-interest and dishonesty that is destroying our society. He is one of a handful of mayors, teachers, doctors, journalists and other professionals who are prepared to do this. Admirable people, pitifully few in number. You, Zafiris, your friend Mr Pezas, *his* friend the butcher of Markopoulo, are also characters in this mould. There must be many thousands more who do not have the power to act on their beliefs. Ordinary people who recognise a simple truth: respect for the law, self-discipline, concern for our fellow human beings, our earth and our future – these are the foundations of civilisation. Our ideas are sound, they are unimpeachable, but we are not organised, we have no political power. We are fragmented, weak, demoralised. They can pick us off one by one.'

Sotiriou paused. 'Are you with me, Mr Pezas?'

'Completely,' said Haris.

'Let us look now at the opposite end of the moral spectrum. Mr Kokoras, the Marangós brothers, the men who drive the black Mercedes. They are well organised, politically connected, wealthy. Apparently unstoppable. But something has gone wrong. A piece has come loose in their satanic machine and it is starting to cause damage. What is this stray piece? We don't know. I believe the national economic crisis is playing a part. Businesses are failing everywhere, money is scarce, even the parasites are suffering. And along comes Mr Merkulov. He is the answer to everyone's prayers.'

'Where do you put him on the moral spectrum?' asked Haris.

'Good question! Hard to answer. He seems quite well-intentioned. But he doesn't know Greece, and his goodwill is easy to exploit. Mario Filiotis wanted his money for social projects, EAP wanted it for nightclubs. There was in effect a war between EAP and Mario for the soul of Mr Merkulov. Are you still with me?'

'Surely even a Russian can tell the difference between a nightclub and a medical school?' said Haris.

'Of course,' said Sotiriou. 'But I can't tell how EAP presented themselves. Efthimios, the clever one, is a highly capable man. He will have taken the measure of Merkulov at once and told him exactly what he wanted to hear. And remember, Merkulov is a businessman. To him, what makes money is good, even if it's a nightclub. What loses money is bad, even if it's a medical school. But I return to Mario Filiotis. After his death his body went missing, as you know. Mr Zafiris discovered that he was flown to New York and cremated. This sounds like an accident but I'm not so sure. The people in New York, the so-called family of "Mr Medouris" were expecting a casket full of ancient gold wreaths. They were not amused to find a dead body instead. Nor were they amused when the golden wreaths they had paid for were seized by police in Astypalea. They came looking for compensation. Their agents here were EAP, who said, "It's not our fault." The Americans asked a few questions, went to see that archaeologist you disliked so much in Thessaloniki, left her badly bruised, and then called on their agent Kokoras. He failed to show the proper respect and paid the price. Now they are in Athens and, if my theory is right, they will very soon be in conversation with E and P of EAP on Leoforos Kymis.'

Blood & Gold

George pulled off his mask again. 'Who are these Americans?'

'Oxygen, Mr Zafiris! I'll tell you. Although you know the answer because you yourself gave me the name. Philip Ventouris.'

'He's here in Athens?' asked Haris.

'He is.'

'And he's talking to EAP?'

'He and the two men who tried to set fire to your apartment.'

'Who are they working for, EAP or Ventouris?'

'That is the question! It is possible they were working for EAP but have just switched to Ventouris. Or they worked for both, and now that things have gone sour between Ventouris and EAP they have chosen Ventouris. But I repeat: all this is a hypothesis. I am uncomfortable even talking about it. I prefer proper evidence. But we will have that quite shortly.'

'How?'

'Someone will come out of that building on Leoforos Kymis. Either walking or carried out in rubbish sacks. Whichever it is, I shall make my move. Thanks to the disposal of Andonis Marangós, their ministerial protection has gone. I have men there ready to arrest whoever is the victor in this repulsive battle of snakes.'

'How can you arrest them? On what charges?'

Sotiriou tapped his briefcase. 'It's all in here.'

George was feeling weary again. He closed his eyes as the two men continued talking, their voices lulling him towards drowsiness. He was glad they had come to visit but now he wanted to be left alone.

The ringing of a phone snatched him back into wakefulness.

'Excuse me,' said Colonel Sotiriou. 'I must answer this.'

He stood up and left the room.

George sent Haris a sleepy glance.

'You have some rest,' said Haris. 'I'll go and get a coffee.'

George dozed off again, but uncomfortably. His mind wandered between levels of consciousness, never fully asleep nor fully awake, replaying scenes from the past few months like old films in a dusty provincial cinema. There was Kokoras with his twisted moustache. Eleni Filiotis like a poisoned ghost. Paris Aliveris darting through the monastery gardens. The calm voice of Father Seraphim. Andonis Marangós in his leather suit and blood-soaked shirt. And Mario Filiotis riding his bicycle on a journey to nowhere…

When he woke up again it was dark outside. A lamp was on beside his bed. At first he thought he was alone, but a young man's voice surprised him.

'Dad?'

He tried to speak but the oxygen mask still prevented him. He pulled it aside.

'Nick! What are you doing here?'

His joy at seeing his son was quickly replaced by dread as he realised what the answer must be.

'Mother told me I should…' Nick stopped, embarrassed.

'I understand,' said George. 'It's kind of you.'

'I had to come,' said Nick.

'I hope I'm not going to die,' said George.

'I'm sure you're not.'

'That's good. It helps.' He coughed painfully. 'Think positive.'

'How are you feeling, Dad?'

'I feel as if I've smoked about a million cigarettes.'

'Cigarettes made of foam rubber!'

'Not a brand I would recommend. And you, my boy, how are you?'

'I'm in good shape. But you mustn't talk. You have to keep that mask on.'

'Bugger the mask.'

'No, Dad. Put it on. Otherwise I'll go.'

George coughed again, with a weak, rasping sound.

'There!'

Nick came over and eased the mask back over his father's nose and mouth.

'Mother was in earlier but you were sleeping. She sends her love.'

George nodded. He tried to see the time but his wristwatch had been removed.

'It's nine-thirty,' said Nick.

George rested his eyes on him, admiring his handsome face, his dark, thick hair, his lively movements. 'This,' he thought, 'is what it's like to feel old.'

Nick said, 'You've had other visitors. Dimitri from downstairs. He brought flowers from Evantheia.'

George glanced at them. A pot of creamy-blossomed gardenias. He wished he could smell their gorgeous scent.

Nick took a note from the bedside table.

'There's also this from a man I don't know. *G.Z. from C.S.*'

George put out his hand for the note and fumbled it open.

'Zafiris,' it said, 'I did not wish to wake you so I leave this note with your son. The Mercedes men left EAP in haste having torched the building – their speciality, it seems. They started the fire in the woodyard and it quickly spread: cars, petrol, firewood – an inferno. E and P were trapped inside, no chance of rescue. This is regrettable, but the workings of

Nemesis are rarely delicate. We picked up the Mercedes men but not Ventouris, who has eluded us. I will visit you again tomorrow. Remember to keep your mask on or you will die. We do not want that. Constantine Sotiriou.'

George let the note drop on the bed.

'Good news?' asked Nick.

George nodded. He pushed the note towards his son, who scanned it quickly and reacted in disbelief, 'If that's good news, what's bad news like? That's horrific.'

George lifted the mask. 'In my business it's good news,' he said.

Nick looked appalled. 'I wish you'd take up safer work. Go back to the bank! Sit in an office! This is crazy stuff. Sick, sad, horrible psychos, burning people alive. You don't need to work around people like that! I worry about you. So does mother.'

'You're right,' said George. 'Totally right. Just a few more evil bastards to chase down, then I'm done.'

He dropped the mask back onto his nose and closed his eyes. The news was good, even if nothing could bring Mario back. Now he must concentrate on staying alive, clearing the poison from his blood, soothing his lacerated throat and lungs. It gave him joy to see his son, a joy which was physical, sustaining, flooding his body like the warmth of spring. What more could he ask?

He set his mind on that, swept aside other thoughts, and breathed deeply on the cool, clean, healing air.